OCT 1 8

His
Unlikely
Lover

THE UNWAN

D0701364

Also by Natasha Anders

The Unwanted Wife

A Husband's Regret

His
Unlikely
Lover

THE UNWANTED SERIES

NATASHA
ANDERS

Montlake
Romance

Published by Montlake Romance, Seattle

www.apub.com

ISBN-13: 9781477823859
ISBN-10: 1477823859

Cover design by Laura Klynstra

Library of Congress Control Number: 2014901286

Printed in the United States of America

To Ma Ruby. Thank you for getting me my very first library card and opening up my eyes to so many other worlds.

CHAPTER ONE

Roberta Richmond was a fool. At least that's what she told herself. Because only a fool would stand idly by while the man she loved romanced another woman in front of her very eyes. But it wasn't the first time she had done so, and it probably wouldn't be the last. Yes, indeed, Roberta Richmond was a colossal fool.

Time for you to move on, Bobbi, she told herself, grimacing when the aforementioned man placed his hands on his latest conquest's naked back—how low was the back of that dress anyway? One could almost see the top of her butt crack—and steered her toward the dance floor. It was unacceptable really; he had brought *Bobbi* to this party. So why was it okay for him to hit on other women?

Because he's your friend, her inner voice shrieked at her.

"Oh shut up," she said out loud, and a couple of the people standing nearby directed startled glances over at her. "Not you," she clarified. They moved away anyway, making her feel like even more of a social pariah.

Great.

Gabriel Braddock, her longtime best friend—the object of both her teen and adult fantasies—was whispering something into that woman's ear, and she laughed in response. Beautiful, vibrant, tall, and *built*—she epitomized femininity, something Bobbi sorely lacked.

"You look rather lost over here, Bobbi." The hostess of the party, her good friend Theresa De Lucci, had moved over to join Bobbi in her Lonely Loser's Corner. Theresa held up a flute of champagne, onto which Bobbi gratefully latched.

"Great party," Bobbi told her after taking a thirsty sip of the fizzy drink, and Theresa smiled.

"I could almost believe you meant that, if not for that glower on your face," her friend teased, taking a sip of her own drink.

"I'm sorry, it's just . . ." She sighed. Her eyes drifted miserably over to Gabe again. "Who's the babe?"

"That's one of Sandro's sisters, Rosalie," Theresa informed her, and Bobbi caught a flash of sympathy in the other woman's eyes before lowering her gaze back to her champagne. "She flew in from Milan yesterday. She's just ten months older than Sandro, so they're very close. Unfortunately none of his other family members could make it."

"Well, that explains the astonishing good looks then." Bobbi laughed bitterly.

"Bobbi." Her friend paused before taking a deep breath and continuing. "I'm going to give you the same advice that Lisa gave me when I was having problems in my marriage—you're either going to have to do something about the way you feel or you're going to have to move on."

"It's that obvious?" Her horrified eyes latched onto Theresa's, and she was relieved when the other woman shook her head.

"To me, yes. I can recognize unrequited love when I see it." Her friend reached out and gave her a one-armed hug. "And I'm here if you need to talk to someone."

"Thanks." Bobbi's eyes drifted back to the couple on the dance floor.

"If it's any consolation, Sandro would probably go ballistic if Gabe messed with his sister. He can be a bit protective—especially over Rosalie.

"Stop looking like it's the end of the world and try to enjoy yourself, okay? You're making me feel like an awful hostess." Theresa's gentle teasing made her smile.

"Oh heaven forbid." Bobbi raised a hand in mock horror. "This is a great party and you know it." It was Theresa's husband's birthday party. It was supposed to be a surprise party, and while Sandro had acted surprised, Bobbi knew—thanks to Gabe—that the Italian had been far from startled. Theresa was terrible at subterfuge and hadn't been able to hide her plans from her husband. According to Gabe, Sandro had known something was up for weeks, but in an effort not to disappoint Theresa, he had gone all out with the shocked reaction.

"He wasn't at all surprised," Theresa confided in Bobbi, a sweet smile tugging at the corners of her lips. Startled that the woman's thoughts had so accurately mirrored hers, Bobbi directed a questioning glance her way.

"Sandro," Theresa clarified. "He wasn't surprised. I could see through that act a mile away—but it'll gut him to know that I know that he knew about the party. So I'll just keep on pretending to believe he was surprised." Theresa paused for a second, absorbing her words before laughing. "God, that all sounded like the setup to a terrible joke."

"Your explanation did get rather complicated," Bobbi agreed.

"Love often is complicated," Theresa quipped, and Bobbi sighed as she took a sip of champagne and directed her troubled eyes back to Gabe.

"Isn't it just?"

∼

Gabriel Braddock reluctantly relinquished his hold on his gorgeous dance partner and let her go with a lingering kiss to the back of her hand. She was totally off-limits, of course, as his good friend's sister. There wasn't a chance in hell he'd indulge himself with this exotic beauty. It would create too many complications in his structured life. She wasn't his type anyway. He preferred blondes—but this was one brunette for whom he would gladly have made an exception. He glanced over at Sandro . . . *yep,* the guy was staring daggers at him— so that meant Rosalie was still very much forbidden fruit. Too bad. She was charming. He always enjoyed her company and was naturally attracted to her. Still, he had managed to keep their brief interactions over the years limited to harmless flirtations.

He shoved his hands into his trouser pockets—uncaring that it ruined the cut of the garment, which was uncharacteristic for him. He liked neatness. He liked to keep his jaw smoothly shaven, his hair conservatively cut and precisely parted, and his clothes immaculately pressed and tailored to perfection. He preferred to keep things as orderly and controlled as possible. Anything else and he started to feel frayed around the edges.

He glanced around the room and spotted a familiar rumpled figure—the one bit of chaos in his otherwise well-ordered life—and made his way over to where she stood. Their friendship surprised most people who didn't know them. They were complete opposites— Bobbi's untidiness against his neatness and her free spirit versus his buttoned-down conservativeness—and their friendship sometimes baffled him too. He'd known her for most of his life and was used to having her around—no, more than that, he *enjoyed* having her around. Gabe didn't confide in many people, but Bobbi was someone he trusted with most of his secrets. She listened to him and was his one constant. His mother and brother were preoccupied with their own lives; his father was a completely hopeless case. His other friends were mates, good for a laugh and a drink at the pub but not for sharing his deep and darkest secrets. When he worried about his brother, Chase, he knew that Bobbi would be there to listen patiently and offer words of comfort and advice. She understood him, and he appreciated that about her. He would be the first to acknowledge that he tended to take her for granted, but he couldn't quite imagine his life without her.

He watched as she tossed back the remaining contents of a champagne flute before substituting the empty glass for a full one from a passing waiter's tray. She was as dressed up as it was possible for Bobbi to get, wearing a shapeless navy-blue slip dress, one he had seen her in a million times before. It was her go-to party dress. It kind of skimmed her slender body, falling from thick straps on her shoulders, which seemed to have been designed to hide bra straps, to somewhere between her knees and her calves.

The dress was accompanied by clunky ankle boots that added absolutely no height to her five foot nothing frame, and the entire ensemble was topped off with some ugly plastic tribal jewelry—chunky bracelets that looked horribly out of place on her delicate wrists, a pendant that appeared to weigh heavily on her neck, and truly awful hoop earrings that seemed to tug painfully at her earlobes.

Bobbi was a tiny waif of a girl, so her ghastly outfit seemed to be wearing *her*. The top of her head barely came up to his chest. She had slender arms and legs, a flat chest, and no curves to speak of at all. He supposed she was okay-looking as such things went, with luminous, thickly lashed amber eyes that shone like dark gold in the sunlight, a snub nose that was crooked as a result of a childhood fall, and a perfect cupid's bow of a mouth, which—in addition to her eyelashes—was one of the few feminine things about her. She had beautiful skin though, clear and golden, and her short, silky, straight black hair molded the elegant shape of her head.

"Hey, Runt," he said by way of greeting, knowing that it aggravated her to be addressed as such. "You having a good time?"

"No," she groused. "You're supposed to dance with me."

"I am?" He was?

"You brought me here," she pointed out, enunciating her words carefully, the way inebriated people tended to do when they were trying to convince others of their sobriety. "You're my date. You should dance with me."

"I'm your *date*, am I?"

"Stop talking to me like I'm a child." Her words threw him. He *did* tend to speak to her in the indulgent, paternal tone her dad or older brothers used on her. It was easy for all of them to lose sight of the fact that she was a woman of twenty-six with her own business.

"I'm sorry." Her pretty eyes reflected her surprise at his apology. She shrugged awkwardly, grabbing yet another glass from a passing waiter and downing it in almost one gulp. She swayed and he reached out to steady her, placing his hands on her slight shoulders.

"Whoa, Bobbi . . . how many of those have you had?"

"How many of whats?" she asked with a frown, and he grinned at her butchering of the language before elaborating.

"Of those glasses of champagne?"

"They're called flutes . . . like a flute . . . like music. You know?"

"I get it," he said, keeping his tone somber to match the earnestness in her voice. "So how many have you had?"

"What?"

"Never mind." He decided not to push it when it was clear that she couldn't quite muddle her way through the conversation. "Entirely too many, as far as I can tell. Come on, let's find a quiet spot to sit you down."

"I'm not tired. I want to dance."

"You can barely stand," he pointed out patiently. It wasn't like her to get drunk. She was a lightweight when it came to alcohol and tended to restrict her alcoholic intake to no more than two glasses when she was in company.

"I can stand." She looked offended by his words and wriggled her shoulders out from beneath his hands to prove it to him. She swayed only a little without his support. "Come on, let's dance." She pushed past him and walked confidently toward the dance floor. When she got there and turned around to find him still standing where she had left him, she spread her hands in a *what gives* gesture.

He groaned to himself before making his way to her side. It would be best just to dance with her and get it over with. Arguing with her in her current state would cause a scene. He was being jostled by the crowd and felt a bit harried when he eventually reached her. She smiled up at him before latching her arms around his waist, resting her head on his chest, and snuggling up against him like a contented cat. Floored, he stood with his arms outspread—not quite sure what to do with them—staring down at the top of her silky head.

He hesitantly closed his arms around her slight frame while trying to maneuver away from her and force some distance between their bodies, but she'd latched on so tightly they wouldn't have been able to squeeze a sheet of paper between them. He sighed and moved his hands down to either side of her waist and was surprised to discover that it was curvier than he'd anticipated. There was a definite, defined, nipped-in waist that curved out into gently flared hips. His hands spanned the entire length of her waist, with his thumbs brushing the underside of the slight swell of her breasts and his pinkie fingers resting on the flare of her hips. Before this very moment he had thought—when he'd given any consideration to the matter at all—that Bobbi was straight up and down. He never would have guessed at this perfectly proportioned, petite, hourglass figure.

Curious, he allowed his hands to explore further, moving one to her back and spreading his fingers so that it covered her entire narrow expanse. He angled his hand until the tips of his fingers just brushed at the swell of her butt and then was immediately besieged with guilt, as he comprehended that he was *actually* trying to cop a feel off *Bobbi*! What the hell was wrong with him?

He tried to move away again, but she moved closer, and he tilted his head to see her face. She was *nuzzling* at his chest, her breath hot against the naked flesh just above his unbuttoned shirt. Strange, he didn't quite remember unbuttoning that third button or the second for that matter! He had only loosened his tie and unbuttoned his collar.

"Hey, hold up there, sweetheart." He could feel her fingers busily working on the fourth button. "What the hell are you doing, Bobbi?"

"Dancing." Her lips brushed against his flesh as she spoke, sending hot darts of pleasure racing from the point of contact all the way down to parts he'd best not be thinking about right now.

"Okay. Enough, Bobbi. I don't know what you think you're doing, but it's gone far enough." He moved his arms back up to her shoulders and moved her away from him, using gentle force.

She kept her face angled down, and he used a thumb and forefinger to slant her chin up and meet her eyes. She possessed enough of her faculties to look embarrassed; a flush stained her delicate cheekbones and made her look somewhat feverish.

"What's up, Runt?" She winced at the nickname, and he immediately regretted using it. Not the best timing—not when something was clearly eating at her.

"I'm such a fool." Her voice was so low that he had to bend his head a few inches to catch the words.

"No, you're not. Why would you say that? Did somebody say something to upset you?"

She raised a slender, slightly calloused hand to his cheek and stroked the flesh softly. He found the combination of soft and hard on his skin disturbing and unthinkingly dragged his face away from her gentle touch, leaving her small hand hovering in midair. Her eyes immediately filled with pain, and he felt like a complete ass for putting that look on her face. He didn't know what was going on with her tonight, but he had no doubt that the amount of alcohol she had consumed would have her regretting her actions in the morning.

She dropped her hand down to her side, and he reached up to cradle her delicate face between both of his hands.

"What's wrong, sweetheart?" he murmured, and watched with a perplexed frown as her eyes filled with tears. Bobbi hardly ever cried; in fact he could count on one hand the number of times he had seen her cry over the last twenty years. He didn't know how to respond to this. He watched as a single tear slid down her smooth cheek, until it collided with one of his thumbs and formed a tiny pool beneath the digit.

"I'm a fool," she repeated, her tone numb.

"Bobbi, I . . ." Every thought fled from his mind when she went up onto her toes and firmly planted her soft, sweet lips on his mouth, catching him in midsentence. The next breath he inhaled was hers. It filled his lungs and he held it in for one long, possessive moment until he had no choice but to relinquish it back to her.

Oh my God! It was the only coherent thought he had as he found himself taking control of the kiss that she had initiated, sweeping his tongue into the sweet, hot depths of her mouth, relishing the taste of her, the smell, the feel . . . God, she felt good—a small, perfect armful that he couldn't seem to get close enough to. He moved one hand down to the small of her back, anchoring her to him, bending her backward in an attempt to get even closer.

Oh my God!

Every delectable inch of her was plastered to him from chest to thighs, and he wanted her even closer. Some distant part of his mind was making faintly alarmed noises, but most of his higher brain functions had short-circuited the moment her soft lips had touched his. Sure they'd exchanged kisses before, perfunctory pecks that were *nothing* like this. Where the hell had *this* come from?

She tasted like champagne—sweet and tart—and her kiss effervesced through his system, sending his nerve endings tingling with ebullient messages that were hard to ignore.

He lifted his mouth from her intoxicating lips for a second, needing air, but all he inhaled was Bobbi . . . the heady scent of vanilla and freesias. Why had he never known how good she smelled before now? he wondered absently before angling his mouth to take hers again.

She murmured his name, and despite the music and noise swirling around them, the fractured sound registered just as he reclaimed her lips, and it was as effective as being doused in ice water. He jerked his head back and shook it to clear his befuddled brain.

What the hell am I doing?

He stepped away from her a second after that thought rang through his mind, putting some desperately needed distance between his aroused body and hers. He was still too close to her for his liking—her every gasping breath threatening to bring her chest within touching distance of his ribcage—but the crowd made it difficult to move farther away from her.

She had her face tilted up toward his, her heavy-lidded eyes were liquid with longing, her every breath emerged on a hitched sob, and her skin had a flushed, dewy look that immediately betrayed her arousal. It was all he could do to prevent himself from reaching for her again. She was drunk, he reminded himself. He was the one who had to maintain control; he couldn't take advantage of her. It was unthinkable—this was *Bobbi*! That thought immediately dampened his arousal and brought his body firmly back under his control.

He clung to that: Bobbi. It put things into jarring perspective. He didn't know what the hell had just happened, but it had to have been a temporary aberration.

This was Bobbi.

He pushed memories of her as a small girl with a gap-toothed grin and pigtails into his brain, and then as an awkward preadolescent, a gawky teenager, and lastly a permanently disheveled young woman in overalls, with grease smeared on her face, and he immediately felt . . . *less*. Just less.

He forced one of his hands to reach for her elbow and ignored the residual tingling in his fingertips as he latched onto her silky skin. He dragged her to the side of the dance floor and looked around until he found an empty chair in a relatively quiet spot. He led her to it and urged her to sit down. She still looked a bit dazed and thankfully sat down without protest. He sank onto his haunches in front of her.

"Wait here," he ordered, and she blinked up at him, looking totally out of it. "Bobbi, do you hear me? Do not move from this spot! I'll be right back."

She nodded. He got up and headed for a refreshment table on the opposite side of the room, intending to get her some water. He glanced back and nearly stumbled when she brought one of her hands to her mouth and traced the outline of her lips.

Could she still taste him? He *could* still taste her.

He felt like his structured, well-organized world was on an express train to hell, and he needed to find the emergency brake immediately or his life would descend into absolute chaos.

Bobbi! He reminded himself sternly before turning and continuing his progress to the refreshment table.

～

Gabe had kissed her!

Okay, she was just sober enough to remember that she had kissed him first, but he had kissed her back! He had definitely kissed her back. That hadn't been her imagination. Had it? She could still feel the pressure of his warm, smooth lips on hers, the scrape of his just emerging stubble against her cheek. And she could taste the whiskey-tinged flavor of his tongue in her mouth.

But why had he left her here?

She accepted another glass—*flute*—of champagne from a handsome waiter and contemplated that question. He had left absolute ages ago. She stood up and swayed before moving in the direction she was sure he had gone. Maybe he was with that woman again. Rosalie. Was he kissing *her* now?

She stumbled and bumped into someone.

"Roberta?" She didn't need to see the owner of that dark, accented voice to know to whom it belonged. She grinned up at him.

"Aaah, the birthday boy!"

"Are you okay?" Alessandro De Lucci asked in concern, and she squinted up at him. He was a handsome man, but his two noses made him look kind of freakish.

"You should have that seen to." She waved her gl— flute at him and he frowned.

"What? You're not making sense, *piccola*."

"That second nose . . . where did it come from?"

"Aaah. Too much champagne for you, I think." He grinned, snatching her half-full gla— flu— *whatever*, and latching an arm around her waist when the unexpected move unbalanced her. "Okay, I've got you, *piccola mia*. Let's find my wife and get you put to bed." Theresa and Sandro had offered rooms to some of their guests who lived farther away, hoping to eliminate any incidences of drunk driving.

"Okay. I *am* rather sleepy," she told him.

"I'm sure you are," he agreed.

"You're much nicer than you used to be," she informed him drowsily, and he chuckled.

"So I've been told."

~

Bobbi was gone! Gabe swore softly and frantically looked around for her in the throng of people surrounding him. He hadn't been gone more than a couple of minutes. Where the hell had she disappeared to?

"Shit," he whispered beneath his breath and pushed his way through the chatting, laughing groups of people. He spotted Max Kinsley, an old university friend standing at the far side of the room. Bobbi may have wandered over to chat with him . . . or *dance* with him. Would she have kissed him too? The question hit him like a fist to the solar plexus and expelled the breath from his lungs as he visualized Max with Bobbi in his arms, with his mouth on hers and his chest plastered to hers.

Hell no!

He told himself that the rage he felt at the vision that formed in his mind's eye was the same protective instinct Sandro felt toward his sister . . . that had to be it.

"Where's Bobbi?" He demanded to know when he eventually managed to reach Max's side. The other man looked surprised by his question.

"No idea. *You're* her minder, bro. Not me." Seeing the truth on his friend's face, Gabe's eyes roamed the crowded room again. He couldn't help picturing her flitting from one guy to the next, bestowing her dances and kisses freely on every one of them like some horny, drunken little fairy. She could get herself into some serious trouble if she ran into the wrong guy.

"Lose something?" a deep voice murmured from behind him, and he whirled around to see Sandro smirking at him.

"I assume you know where Bobbi is?" he asked. The other man took a lazy sip of whiskey before replying.

"Theresa just escorted Roberta to her room. She's feeling the effects of too much champagne." Gabe grimaced at that information; she could go from tipsy to violently ill in pretty short order. He should have known it would only be a matter of time before she got sick.

"I'll take care of her and send your wife back down to you," he offered, and Sandro nodded.

"That would be appreciated."

~

They had put her in the room next to his, Gabe remembered. What had seemed perfectly acceptable just a few short hours ago now seemed . . . inappropriate.

He rapped on the door before opening it after the briefest of hesitations. Theresa De Lucci, looking stunning in her evening wear—probably by one high-end designer or the other, he wasn't sure which, he never really paid attention to women's wear unless he was in the process of removing it—was stroking a damp cloth over Bobbi's face. She looked up in surprise when Gabe walked in.

"How is she?" he asked, shrugging out of his tux jacket and draping it carefully over the back of a chair so as not to wrinkle it.

"Somewhat under the weather," Theresa said with a slight smile. "I think she got most of it out of her system though."

"She doesn't handle alcohol very well," he stated unnecessarily.

"I noticed." Her smile widened.

"She's usually better at managing her alcohol intake. I don't know what came over her tonight." Theresa said nothing in response to that and merely continued to stroke Bobbi's face gently.

"I'm sorry about this. Why don't you head back to the party? I'll take care of her."

Theresa slanted her head questioningly. "Are you sure about that? I don't mind staying with her."

"Sandro's already looking restless without you."

She laughed with an indulgent shake of her head. "He has no patience with parties that serve no function other than an excuse for people to gather in a festive social setting."

"All business all the time, huh?" Gabe rejoined, and she rolled her eyes.

"I've been attempting to change that, and he does try, but he tends to get short-tempered if I'm not around to make sure he maintains his civility."

"You'd better get down there before he tosses everybody out then." He ushered her out, and after one last look back at Bobbi, she left the room.

Gabe shut the door behind her. He stood there for a while with his hands braced on the door and his head bent as he steeled himself to turn around and walk back to that bed.

"Gut up, Braddock," he whispered, thumping his forehead against the wood before pushing himself away from the door and turning back toward the large bed.

She was so small that she barely made a dent beneath the covers. He removed his diamond and gold cufflinks, slipping them into one of his trouser pockets, and folded his sleeves meticulously up to his elbows. He sat down on the chair so recently vacated by Theresa and forced himself to look down into her unconscious face.

It was just Bobbi. He nearly laughed his relief out loud. He didn't know what he had expected, but this short-haired, golden-skinned, sleeping urchin stirred no desire in him—no crazy, ill-advised lust. Nothing close to it. He felt fondness, affection, even love. Every insipid emotion associated with platonic friendship one could hope for. No desire. None at all.

He shook his head, unable to keep the grin from his face.

"Thank Christ for that," he whispered. He could only conclude that he'd been more affected by his dance with the stunning Rosalie De Lucci than he'd known. It was past time for him to form a new relationship. His last one had ended months ago and he'd been celibate ever since. The lack of sex seemed to be manifesting itself in seriously weird and unanticipated ways.

He linked his fingers and rested them on his torso before dropping his head back on the cushioned chair. He mentally inventoried all the single women he knew, with the intention of calling one or two of them up soon for some sexy times, and fell asleep in the middle of his strategizing.

CHAPTER TWO

Something—some small, rodent-type creature—had died *in her mouth*. Why else would the latter taste so putrid and feel so furry? And some cruel prankster had glued her eyelids together, because she couldn't seem to open her eyes.

She groaned and the small sound set a tsunami of pain into motion in her head. Even with her eyes closed it felt like the room was spinning, and the vertiginous sensation made her feel sick to her stomach. She was almost certain she was going to vomit. She gritted her teeth and breathed through her nose, trying to quell the nausea.

Was she ill?

"Bobbi?" Even though the word was whispered, it sounded like a gunshot in the silence and she winced.

"Gabe?" she whimpered, managing to unstick her eyelids at last and peer at him. The room was dim, with only one wall lamp spilling the barest amount of light across half of his face. "I'm sick."

"Have a sip of this water," he instructed, and his neutral tone set her mind at ease. He slid a hand beneath her neck and gently helped her sit up. She tensed, and shut her eyes again, trying to keep her breathing deep and steady.

"You need to puke?" he asked gruffly. She shook her head and clamped a hand over her mouth.

"Give me a second," she groaned from behind her hand. "I'm okay."

"Come on, drink the water." He held a glass up and she took it in both of her trembling hands. He closed his own hand over hers to keep the glass steady and guided it to her lips. She took a sip, then another, and then realized that she had a raging thirst and gulped the rest down eagerly.

"Good girl," he praised, still in that quiet whisper. He refilled the glass from the carafe on the pedestal and this time handed her a couple of aspirin to go with it.

"I drank too much champagne, didn't I?" she asked as she remembered, and he nodded, his face expressionless. She downed the aspirin and handed the glass back to him. He placed it on the pedestal with that precise economy of movement that she always found so inordinately fascinating about him. How could such a large man keep his every movement so neat and controlled?

"I'm sorry. You should go back to the party. I think I'm okay now."

"The party's mostly over," he said. "There are a few stragglers still lingering, but it's only a matter of time before Sandro loses his patience with them." She smiled weakly at that and sank back against the headboard, shutting her eyes for a second.

A sinking feeling of dread was starting to form in the pit of her stomach. Something wasn't right. She had done something at the party and the exact details remained infuriatingly elusive and couldn't seem to take any coherent shape in her mind.

"Try to get some sleep," he instructed.

"I just woke up."

"That wasn't sleep," he corrected. "You had passed out."

"Charming." She snorted.

"Indeed."

"I'm sorry I spoiled your evening," she whispered.

"You didn't."

"I did. I . . ." And that's when she remembered. Her eyes flew open to meet his enigmatic stare and her hand fluttered helplessly to her lips. His eyes seemed to darken as they watched her fingers trace the outline of her mouth, but it could merely have been a trick of the light. His face still held very little expression.

"Oh my God." How much had she revealed? Had she said anything? She tried to remember everything that had preceded the kiss, but it was all frustratingly hazy. "I'm sorry. I was . . . drunk." She had forced herself on him. The very idea of how she must have behaved was horrifying.

"I know. Forget about it." There was something *off* about the cadence of his voice and it worried her. Had she irreparably ruined their friendship? Would they ever get past this? Had she *told* him she loved him? She had all but violated him and had even fooled herself into believing that he had returned her kiss.

She buried her face in her hands, absolutely mortified—after years of self-restraint and hiding the nature of her feelings from him for the good of their friendship—she had probably destroyed that same friendship on some drunken whim.

"I'm so sorry."

"Stop apologizing, Bobbi, there was no harm done."

No harm done? She peeked at him from between a gap in her fingers—not quite sure how she felt about that. Relieved? Or even more humiliated because her kiss had had so little impact on him?

There was still no expression on his face. Gabe had never been one to wear his emotions on his sleeve. He was the most self-restrained man she knew, but she could usually read him better than this—one couldn't be a friend to someone for nearly twenty years without learning his moods, but he was a complete mystery to her at this moment and it confused her.

She needed to get away from him for a few minutes, needed to gather her thoughts and compose herself. She pushed the bed covers down to her hips and swung her legs over the edge of the bed. She sat there for a couple of seconds, swallowing down the nausea when her movements caused the room to swirl sickeningly around her.

"What are you doing?" he asked, and in her disorientated state it almost sounded like there was a slight edge of panic in his voice.

"Bathroom." She kept her response succinct, not really feeling capable of saying anything more than that. He used his feet to push the chair farther away from the bed, giving her room to maneuver.

"Thanks." She glanced down at him and caught a flash of something dark in his eyes. She paused—not certain of that look—but then his face went back to that maddeningly neutral expression. She sighed quietly and wobbled to the en suite, shutting the door firmly.

Gabe groaned softly and ran his hands roughly over his face and into his hair—he sat there for a brief moment, hands clenched in his hair before inhaling deeply in an attempt to calm himself. He had been doing pretty well, had had the situation under control. She was his friend, they had grown up together—there was absolutely nothing but friendship and deep affection between them. That was the way it had always been, the way it *would* always be.

So why the hell did the sight of her in that tiny white tank top and those skimpy blue boy shorts send his blood pressure sky-rocketing? He'd seen her in similar clothing before, seen her in less really—but he'd never fully appreciated the pert perfection of her small breasts and had certainly never wanted to cup the firm, ripe curve of her butt before.

And even worse, the inescapable realization that she was wearing absolutely nothing beneath all that innocent cotton had him fighting a losing battle to keep his inevitable hard-on at bay.

One kiss . . . one damned kiss and he was behaving like a teenager with his first crush. He needed to regain his perspective here. He needed to put these unsettling and erotic thoughts aside.

With that in mind, he pushed out of the chair and walked over to the bathroom door, listening for a few seconds to ensure she wasn't sick again. He knocked quietly.

"Bobbi?"

"I'm fine," she called back. "I just need . . ." The rest of her words were said too quietly for him to catch.

"If you're sure you okay, I'm heading off to bed, okay?" He waited, but she didn't respond. "I'll be in the next room. I'll leave the adjoining door open. If you need anything, just let me know." God, he hoped she wouldn't need anything. It would be bad enough getting any sleep with that damned door open between their rooms.

"Okay," he heard her say, the word soft and uncertain.

"Good night."

"'Night." Her response was faint.

He stood there for another few seconds before shaking his head and striding toward her bedroom door, collecting his jacket along the way. He was in his own room a few moments later and went straight to the adjoining door, knocking once before opening it. Her room was still empty and he heard the sound of running water coming from the en suite.

He shed his shirt and jacket hurriedly and took less care putting them away than usual. He wanted to be in bed with the lights out when she returned. He didn't want to see her or speak to her again tonight. Everything would be back to normal in the bright light of day. It had to be . . .

He had stripped down to his trousers by the time she stepped back into her room, and the shadow her small figure cast on her bedroom wall startled him into pausing while unbuttoning his fly. His hands dropped to hang loosely at his sides. He was facing the adjoining door; his intention had been to keep an eye on her room in case she needed him, but her abrupt reappearance had caught him off guard.

She froze when she saw him and her eyes dropped to his naked chest. He swallowed audibly as her eyes tracked over his body . . . *God*, he could feel her gaze brushing across his skin like a brand.

"*Don't*." The word jerked from him involuntarily.

"I can't *not* . . . ," she said hoarsely, taking a small step toward him and then another and another still. He was helpless to stop her and watched her approach until she stood right in front of him. A mere handsbreadth away from him, so close he could feel her heat being absorbed into his naked skin.

"Bobbi." He tried to instill some sense of warning in his voice, but her name on his lips sounded like a plea. His hands clenched into fists as he fought his desire to touch her.

"You're gorgeous," she whispered in a reverent voice. He watched fascinatedly as she lifted a hand, and in that moment felt absolutely powerless to stop her from touching him. His breath sawed from his lungs in an uneven whoosh as the silky pads of her fingertips traced delicately from the outer edge of his left clavicle straight across to the other end of his right clavicle. Her fingers drifted down to his shoulder before scorching their way over his chest, skimming over his flat nipple in the process. He shuddered and the sound that was torn from his throat was halfway between a long groan and a sigh. The noise startled her into jerking her hand away and she peered up at him uncertainly. He almost howled in disappointment, aching to have her hand back on his skin, but not daring to touch *her* for fear that he'd be unable to stop until he had her naked and writhing beneath him.

Her luminous amber eyes searched his sherry-colored ones for an infinite amount of time while he tried to regulate his uneven breathing. He had no idea what she saw because she seemed to nod to herself before returning to the task at hand. Her fingertips began their agonizing exploration again and his knees nearly buckled in response as her hands fluttered to the center of his chest, exploring the texture of the fine hairs sprinkled there before following the trail down . . . past the taut ripples of his abdomen, tracing the faint circle of hair around his belly button before resuming the path even further down . . .

"*No.*" Unfortunately, reason reasserted itself when he discerned exactly where she was headed. He caught her hand just before it reached the fly of his trousers. He was so damned hard he was straining against his zipper and eagerly seeking her delicate touch.

"Gabe." This time she was the one pleading.

"Go to bed, *Runt*, before we do something . . . ill-advised." He used the nickname deliberately, wanting to shock them both out of this erotic haze and it worked—too well. He watched her flinch and pale and steeled himself against the pain he had caused her with his deliberate callousness. She yanked her hand from his grasp and reeled away from him.

She turned and fled, slamming the adjoining door shut and leaving a turned-on, frustrated, and confused Gabe standing in the middle of his room with one hand absently rubbing at the dull ache in the center of his chest.

He felt like a man who had just lost his best friend.

~

After a restless night, Bobbi felt ill-equipped to face Gabe the following morning. She had been up for hours and had listened to the house come alive outside her door. It was the first week of January, so the guests who had opted to stay the night awoke to a bright, beautiful summer morning. The plan was to have a buffet breakfast and a poolside *braai* for lunch, and as she listened to her friends' cheerful chatter when they walked by her closed bedroom door all she wanted to do was curl under the nearest rock and die.

She still didn't know what on earth had possessed her to touch him the way she had. Her only excuse was that there had been just enough alcohol left in her system to lower her inhibitions and give in to the overwhelming temptation to caress him. That was most certainly the flimsy explanation she would offer when she summoned up the guts to talk to him about it.

Bobbi knew that Gabe had vacated his room at seven thirty; she had listened to the quiet rustling coming from the other side of the wall as he had showered and dressed. The tension that had taken up residence in her neck and shoulders had only fled after she'd heard his bedroom door open and then close again. She had held her breath for what seemed like an eternity when his quiet footsteps had halted for a brief moment outside her door before moving on.

She had tried to formulate a plan of action—an emergency blueprint on how to get through this day and the ones to follow. It wouldn't be easy—but she stood to lose too much if she messed up these next crucial days. She had to weigh the cost of her friendship with Gabe against the fresh anguish she felt every time he treated her with such casual, impersonal affection. Years of the same had taken its toll and after last night, she knew that she couldn't do this anymore. She couldn't stand on the sidelines and watch as every leggy blonde who crossed his path snagged his attention while she never warranted a second glance.

And really, why would he look at her? She was good old Bobbi, his surrogate sister, the girl who had tagged along behind him and his friends when he was a boy. The girl who had made a pest of herself and who would never outgrow the condescending nickname Gabe and her brothers had bestowed upon her.

It was after ten before she summoned up the courage to leave her room and make her way down to the pool. Only the De Luccis' most intimate group of friends remained: the Palmers—Rick, Lisa, Bryce, Bronwyn, and their toddlers—and Max Kinsley, Rosalie De Lucci, Gabe, and Bobbi. Everybody was already gathered beside the pool, either lounging in the sun or splashing about in the water.

Theresa, who was feeding her fourteen-month-old daughter at the patio table, was the first to spot her.

"Bobbi," she called with a warm smile. "Good morning. How are you feeling?" Bobbi cringed when Theresa's voice drew everybody else's attention and a multitude of good-natured salutations came her way. She managed a sickly grin and waved back in everybody's general direction—almost preternaturally aware of Gabe, who was sitting on one of the loungers wearing nothing but board shorts and a pair of sunglasses. His superb body was bronzed and toned, with not a spare bit of flesh anywhere to be seen; he was lean and fit and perfectly proportioned. A quick glance his way confirmed that he was studying her but she couldn't tell what he was thinking, not with those mirrored sunglasses hiding his striking eyes from her. He had a proud nose, just slightly too long but it went beautifully with his bluntly defined cheekbones, which in turn slotted into his narrow, craggy face magnificently. All of that, combined with his thin bow-shaped upper lip and the full sensuous curve of his lower lip, made for an unconventionally handsome man. His dark brown hair, glinting with the faintest hints of auburn beneath the morning sun, was always conservatively cut and brushed and lent him a sophisticated air that went well with his reserved personality.

He was her complete opposite in every way, and she knew that he would never belong to her. They were friends who came from similar backgrounds but occupied totally different worlds. As she joined Theresa and Lily at the patio table, she knew that it was time to let the fantasy of any kind of romantic involvement with Gabriel Braddock go—and it broke her heart.

"Are you okay?" Theresa whispered, and knowing that Theresa was asking about more than her physical condition, Bobbi shook her head. She reached for Lily's chubby little hand and lifted it to her mouth for a kiss, disguising the flash of tears in her eyes.

"Oh Bobbi . . . ," Theresa murmured, trying to hide the distress on her face. "I'm so sorry."

Lisa ambled over to the table and grinned at them, but the smile faded immediately when she discerned something was wrong.

"What's up?" she asked in concern, as she sat down next to Bobbi.

"We can talk about it later. Tomorrow maybe, at our girls' night?" Theresa said, the mere suggestion telling Bobbi that the other woman was aware of how close to the proverbial edge Bobbi was. They usually had their girls' nights on a Saturday but rescheduled to Sunday because of the party. Lisa nodded but remained by Bobbi's side, seeming to sense how much her friend needed the emotional bolstering. She started chatting about the party and her wry observations about some of the guests soon had Theresa in stitches and even coaxed a smile or two from Bobbi.

She tried not to notice that Rosalie De Lucci was in the lounger next to Gabe's, tried to ignore the way he'd occasionally lean over to say something to the bikini-clad woman, and tried not to cringe when he laughed at something the woman had said. But all the not noticing was taking an emotional toll on her and she excused herself with a bright, completely fake smile about an hour later—saying she needed another nap before lunch. It was obvious that neither Theresa nor her cousin believed her, but they let her go.

～

Gabe surreptitiously watched Bobbi leave. She hadn't so much as glanced at him this morning, while it had been all he could do not to openly study her. She had been wearing the tiniest black bikini he'd ever seen. Nothing fancy, just a simple string bikini that sent his blood pressure soaring and made him infinitely grateful that his board shorts were baggy. It clung to her perfect body in all the right places, and he had found himself fantasizing about untying the bows at her shoulders to reveal those sweet, pert breasts to his gaze.

God, so much for hoping things would be back to normal this morning.

She had spent an hour talking to Theresa and Lisa as if everything was perfect in her world, while he felt like his own life had just taken the turn into crazy town. It bothered him that she hadn't touched the buffet laid out in the chafing dishes on the other side of the pool. She needed to eat and stay hydrated. She hadn't even had a glass of juice.

His conflicting desires to take care of her or throw her on the nearest flat surface and bury himself in her were confusing to say the least, and he felt like he had lost his mind somewhere between last night and this morning. He slowly became aware of Rosalie De Lucci leaning toward him and recognized that the high note, which had entered her melodic voice, signified a question. He had been so absorbed by his thoughts that he hadn't heard a word of what she'd been saying.

"Pardon me?" he prompted, focusing his attention back on the lovely woman lounging beside him.

"I asked if you were okay? You seemed preoccupied."

"I'm fine . . ." He nodded, glad that the sunglasses hid the lie in his eyes. He was so far from fine it was ridiculous. He wasn't sure if he should talk to Bobbi about what had happened the night before or if he should leave it alone. This situation didn't lend itself to any of the usual precedents. Any other woman and he would have known how to deal with the situation—acknowledge the attraction and do something about it. Despite knowing Bobbi better than most other people, he didn't know her as a sexual being and it terrified him that he was suddenly so acutely aware of everything that made her female and desirable.

Sandro and Rick had headed toward the grill and were getting the fire started for the *braai*. Bryce and Max drifted over to the fire, as men tended to do at barbecues the world over, and a lively conversation about cricket started up before Sandro deftly diverted the conversation to *his* favorite sport and the men began to argue about the day's forthcoming Italian Premier League football matches. Gabe made his excuses to Rosalie, who had flipped over onto her stomach and seemed to be snoozing beneath the warm sun, and pushed himself off the lounger to join the men—thinking that the distraction would be exactly what he needed. But after standing there for a few minutes, watching Sandro stoke the fire while Rick, his deaf brother, Bryce, and Max were engaged in a half-spoken, half-signed conversation about exactly how hot the coals should be before the meat went on the grill, Gabe found himself wandering away from the intense huddle of nouveau cavemen and toward the table where the women—who had been joined by Bronwyn—were sitting. They all looked up at the same time at his approach, making him wonder uncomfortably if they'd been talking about him. He briefly considered the notion that Bobbi may have confided in them about the night before but dismissed it almost immediately. Bobbi wasn't the type of female who had girly chats with other women about man-related problems.

"Hey." He nodded casually and moved to sit down in one of the free chairs. The strained silence that greeted him made him reconsider his former opinion—they'd *definitely* been talking about him and he could feel a flush stain his cheekbones.

"Gabe," Bronwyn greeted with a regal nod.

"Great party last night, Theresa." He canted his beer bottle toward the pretty redhead and she smiled her thanks. The usually gregarious group remained unusually quiet and Gabe forged ahead uncomfortably. "Do you think . . . uh, Bobbi will be down again? For lunch, I mean. Has she indicated that she'll be down for lunch?"

"She's not feeling up to company after last night," Theresa said in a gentle voice that seemed to be brimming with accusation and Gabe tensed, expecting censure. "You know . . . after drinking too much? The noise level out here was too much for her to deal with."

He slowly and silently exhaled the breath he'd been holding. His own guilty conscience was making his imagination run riot . . . or maybe not? Theresa couldn't seem to meet his eyes and that pissed him off. He hadn't done anything to warrant being treated like a damned sex offender.

"I'll go up and check on her," he mumbled, happy for a reason to leave the strained company and the excuse to go up and see Bobbi. He leapt to his feet, spilling some of his beer in the process, and rushed inside, not needing to look back to know that the women were watching his ignoble retreat.

CHAPTER THREE

The sharp knock on her door left no doubt in Bobbi's mind as to whom was on the other side of the wooden barrier. She sucked in a deep, calming breath before walking over to open the door.

The first thing she noticed was that he had thankfully put on a pristine white T-shirt before coming to her door and had removed the sunglasses. It didn't stop him from still looking incredible though, especially since his skin had bronzed a shade darker in the morning sun and contrasted attractively with the crisp whiteness of his shirt. She forced that thought from her mind and smiled up at him with just the right amount of friendliness and apology.

"Gabe," she exclaimed, sounding absolutely *thrilled* to see him. "I was just coming down to have a chat with you." She turned her back and walked back into her room, glancing over her shoulder to be sure he followed her inside. He was very careful to leave the door slightly ajar, probably terrified that she'd attack him again. She successfully hid her grimace by heading for the comfortably overstuffed pair of chairs that were situated beside a huge picture window overlooking the Atlantic Ocean and sank down into one, curling her legs and dragging her feet up under her butt, trying to keep her posture as relaxed and nonconfrontational as possible. He warily sat down in the second chair, which was angled to face hers.

Unlike Bobbi he seemed tense, both feet were braced on the floor, giving him the appearance of someone who would bolt at the slightest provocation, and his hands were precisely placed on the armrests of the chairs with his fingers curled around the edges. He couldn't seem to meet her eyes, which just about broke her heart.

"I'm sorry about last night." She tried for casual but the words were soft, filled with regret, and the tiniest bit wistful. His throat worked as he swallowed.

"Yeah? Which part?" That threw her somewhat. She hadn't expected him to ask for specifics.

"All of it. Getting drunk, kissing you . . . *touching* you." She watched as his fingers clenched the armrests and brought her regard back up to his face. He had his eyes averted and was staring unsee-ingly out at the horizon, where the shimmering cobalt-blue ocean blended seamlessly with the azure blue of the sky.

"Why did you do it?" He asked, his voice gruff, and she blinked. This wasn't the way she had pictured this conversation going at all. Gabe was supposed to gratefully latch on to the excuse to maintain the status quo of their friendship. He wasn't supposed to ask specu-lative and penetrating questions.

"What?" She stalled for time, hoping to give him the chance to withdraw the question when he figured out that he was just drawing out the uncomfortable situation longer than was necessary.

"I asked why you did it?" He repeated, leaning forward to bring his sharp gaze onto her face and watching her every reaction with a maddeningly impersonal expression.

"Why did I get drunk?" She deliberately misunderstood, hoping again that he would grab onto *this* avenue of escape. There was a long pause while he continued to study her with those eyes that missed nothing. She kept her friendly smile pasted to her face but was gradually aware with each passing second how very fake it must look to this man who knew her so well.

"You know what I meant, Bobbi, but if you want me to spell it out—*why* did you kiss me and w*hy* did you touch me?" He leaned forward even more, bringing his elbows to his thighs and clasping his hands loosely together in the empty space between his knees.

"I was drunk." It was all she could do not to stammer. She kept her eyes up and kept that damned fake smile plastered on her face.

"You said I was your date," he reminded her, and she froze for the briefest of seconds before forcing a laugh out of her tight throat. She managed another one and then another until the sound that emerged *almost* resembled her natural laughter.

"Oh my God, Gabe . . . you had me going. So serious . . . *Why did you kiss me? Why did you touch me?*" She did a terrible impression of his voice, deepening her own to try and mimic his. "But the date thing? You *know* how drunk I was when I said that! Why else would I have said it? I thought you were angry with me or something, but you're having me on aren't you? Don't scare me like that!"

His eyes had narrowed on her laughing face, but he leaned back in his chair and allowed a small smile to play about his lips. He seemed content to let her latch on to what she considered to be an "out."

"I'm not angry with you, sweetheart," he said softly. "I was worried about you. I still am . . . you haven't eaten much today."

This was the Gabriel Braddock she had fallen in love with, the one who treated her with a gruff tenderness when he was alone with her, who cared about her well being and always seemed to want what was best for her. When she was growing up, she had loved him like her own brother. In fact, in some ways, she loved him more than any of her brothers.

Billy, Edward, and Clyde had never listened to her aching desires to be like the taller and prettier girls at school. They hadn't been the ones to comfort her at fifteen, when she had lamented her lack of feminine curves. None of them had been interested in her disastrous crush on Timothy Carfield, the handsome captain of the rugby team. Gabe was the only one who had been there for her during those painful teenage years, before she had adjusted to the changes in her own body and admitted to herself that she would never be like those girls in school, that she had no *desire* to be like any of them. He had listened, he had advised and had always known exactly how to cheer her up whenever her adolescent fantasies of fitting in had ended in disaster. So often she had trudged home from school and straight to the Braddock house to tell Gabe about whatever humiliation she'd had to endure that day. Depending on the scope of the catastrophe, he would produce ice cream, take her to the movies or drive her down to the closest junkyard—his least favorite place in the world—where she could happily scrounge around for car parts. And so often, he had simply hugged her and told her that everything would be okay.

Bobbi had no pride where this man was concerned. She was desperate to keep him in her life and if it meant slowly bleeding to death from every tiny, slashing wound that his romantic indifference inflicted on her, then so be it.

Still the last day and a half had exhausted her and she just wanted to get home and lick her latest wounds in private.

"I don't really want to stay for lunch. I just want to get home and sleep," she told him, and he frowned at her sudden mood shift.

"You haven't eaten yet," he reminded.

"I'm not hungry. I feel too sick to eat, and I'd really prefer to go home. If you're hungry we could stop for some fast food or something." It was a thirty-minute drive from the affluent coastal suburb of Clifton, Cape Town, where Sandro and Theresa lived to Bobbi's and Gabe's homes in Constantia, which was a suburb located in the heart of the Cape Winelands. On a clear day like today, in his sleek Lamborghini, Gabe could do it in less time than that.

"If you're sure?" he asked with marked reluctance.

"I'm sorry. I've totally ruined this weekend for you, haven't I?" She felt awful about that. She would have to take a minibreak from Gabe after this weekend, focus on her business, and maybe spend more time with her female friends.

"You haven't ruined it," he said with a slight smile. "Not at all."

Gabe watched the relief flood into her expressive amber eyes and the tension seep from her shoulders. She had tried to be so casual and unaffected but had failed miserably. He knew her too well to be fooled by the lighthearted act she'd just put on for him. Something fundamental had shifted in their relationship, and while she was desperately scrambling to take them back to where they had been before The Kiss, Gabe perversely wanted her to acknowledge that she had kissed him and touched him because she had wanted him. Not because she had been drunk and exercising flawed judgement. He knew that he was being an idiot. He should have grabbed onto the lifeline she had thrown him and their friendship with both hands, but it just *grated* to see her sitting there trying so desperately to look relaxed.

On the positive side, she looked like herself again. She was wearing an old pair of denim shorts that had been hacked off at mid-thigh and her favorite Pink Floyd T-shirt, which was faded and torn in places. Her hair, which he had never paid particular attention to before, was a silky mess that was long in the front—with her side-parted fringe sliding over her left eye—and short in the back, just brushing at the nape of her neck. The glossy black stuff sleekly conformed to the pretty shape of her head, and while it hadn't been styled in ages, it still gave her an appealing gamine quality, which when combined with her pretty, thickly lashed amber eyes, flawless golden skin, and irregular features, made him want either to ruffle her hair in affection or kiss her senseless. And therein lay the negative side of the situation: she looked like Bobbi again, his familiar and lovable best friend, his unkempt Runt, but damned if he didn't still *want* her. It wasn't an easy thought to adjust to, and it made him feel vaguely uncomfortable—like it was somehow *wrong* to want a girl he had known for most of his life.

He cleared his throat and tested a perfectly bland smile on her— it seemed to work because she relaxed even further.

"Why don't you get your stuff packed and meet me downstairs in ten minutes?" he suggested. "We can say our good-byes and be on the road."

"Sounds good."

They left twenty minutes later, and Bobbi curled up in the luxurious black and red leather bucket seat of Gabe's gorgeous Lamborghini Aventador. On any other day she would be crooning over the car's features and begging Gabe to let her drive it, but right now she wanted to avoid all conversation with him. He put on some music, seeming content to let her pretend to doze in the passenger seat. It was classical music of course—Gabe had sophisticated tastes, evidenced by the clothes he wore and the classy women he dated. Bobbi had never really known how she had managed to remain so firmly entrenched in his life despite their differences. She'd always assumed that she was a remnant of his youth that he enjoyed clinging to. After all he still remained friends with her brother, Billy, and most of their other childhood mates.

She flipped over in her seat to face the window and opened her eyes to focus miserably out at the passing scenery. Gabe handled the car competently of course. He did everything competently—Bobbi didn't. She was a mess, the only thing she had done properly was open her auto shop and even that fledgling venture was floundering.

The car was slowing down and she frowned, they were only halfway to Constantia. She sat up in time to see Gabe turn in to the parking lot of a popular franchise restaurant.

"I'm starving," he said by way of explanation. "And you could do with some food too."

"I'm not hungry," she repeated, pushing her hair out of her eyes and absently noting that she needed a haircut, the fall of hair that kept flopping into her eye was becoming an irritant.

"I don't care. You're eating."

"Oh my God, you're such a bossy bastard," she griped; it wasn't the first time she had made the complaint, and he grinned and replied the way he routinely did.

"It's my best character trait." She rolled her eyes, relieved to have fallen back into their familiar banter.

They got out of the car, which had drawn a crowd of admiring boys and men. There were a few women too, and they cast speculative looks at Gabe's tall, handsome frame, but none of them seemed to notice her of course. That was always the case—she often found herself overlooked when she was standing beside him. She would be relegated to nothing more than an insignificant bystander beside someone so charismatic, and yet, Gabe *never* overlooked her. He'd go off and flirt with the women and laugh with the men, but he always made his way back to her to side to check if she needed anything. More often than not, he hurried to find her in order to share an amusing anecdote or a juicy bit of gossip about someone in the crowd.

Gabe ignored the people milling around the car and took hold of Bobbi's elbow in order to safely lead her through them. She ignored the familiar jolt of sensation she always felt when his bare skin touched hers, but for some reason *he* broke stride after that initial touch and frowned down at his hand where it gripped her elbow. It was a barely noticeable moment, but Bobbi found herself obsessively wondering about it throughout the lengthy seating and meal selection process. Had he felt that current too? Before now it had been wholly one-sided, with only Bobbi feeling that frisson, but after Gabe's hesitation, she wondered if just maybe he had felt it too.

She looked up into his familiar features and was disheartened to note that he didn't look the slightest bit disconcerted and sighed quietly at that ember of hope in her chest that just wouldn't die.

One of his elbows was on the table and his chin was resting in the palm of his hand as he stared unnervingly at her. His free hand was toying with his fork.

"When was the last time you heard from Chase?" She felt the need to break the lengthening silence between them.

"A couple of days ago. On Skype. He seemed . . ." He sighed and shrugged, his concern for his twin brother obvious. Chase was an award-winning photojournalist and regularly traveled to war zones around the globe. He was currently covering a civil war in the Middle East and a number of journalists had already been kidnapped and murdered in the area. Bobbi knew that Gabe had been urging his brother to come home and leave this one be, but Chase was a stubborn man. "He seemed tired. Distracted."

"I'm sure that he's fine," Bobbi comforted. "He knows how to take care of himself. He knows what precautions to take."

"Hmmm . . ." Gabe sounded unconvinced, but he forced a smile. Bobbi wasn't fooled by it and dropped her hand over his larger one on the table.

"You know what your problem is?" She asked with a slight grin, and he raised an eyebrow at her.

"Do tell?" he invited.

"You're so bossy and arrogant that not being able to keep everybody you care about well and safe just chafes at your ego." She kept her tone light and it worked, coaxing a smile from him.

"Yeah, well, if everybody just followed my advice, their lives would be so uncomplicated," he teased.

"Because you always know best, right?"

He gave her a smug, condescending nod.

"Naturally."

"Well, you're going to have to let everybody lead their own lives and instead focus on your own because you're surrounded by stubborn people who hate being dictated to," she reminded him, glancing up when the waitress brought their drinks. Realizing that she was still holding his hand, she released her hold abruptly and grabbed her Coke—grateful when the cold condensation on the outside of the glass neutralized the annoying tingle in the palm of her hand. She drank thirstily, abruptly grateful for the fizzy, cold drink as it hit the back of her parched throat. She was more dehydrated than she knew. She hated that she was proving Gabe right once again and tried to disguise her thirst from him by reluctantly wrenching her lips away from the straw.

When she glanced up at him, he was grinning and she was happy to note that the deep-seated concern he had over his brother's welfare seemed to have been pushed to the back of his mind for now. Proving him right in this instance was well worth it.

"Thirsty?" he asked casually, and she tossed a napkin at him.

"Okay, I'm thirsty, and once my lunch gets here I'll probably realize that I'm famished too so you're right once again. Try not to gloat too hard, you might break your ego bone or something!" He laughed outright at that and she was happy to have coaxed the sound from him when he had been so depressed just moments before. She tried not to think about how pathetic she was: living for the sound of his laughter and proud of her measly ability to tease him into a good mood. She really needed to stop living her every moment for this man—with her only solid accomplishments in life being how often she had made him smile or laugh.

She watched in exasperated affection as he neatly arranged the condiments on the table to his liking: salt, pepper, tomato sauce, chutney, mayonnaise, and mustard—always neatly lined up from left to right like good little soldiers. It was something he always did and they were all used to it.

"You want to come over tonight? For popcorn and movies?" he asked unexpectedly, moments after their food arrived. Bobbi, who had indeed discovered that she was ravenous, paused in the act of lifting her burger from its plate and watched as it messily dripped sauce and melted cheese over her hands. She put it back down without taking a bite and reached for a napkin to wipe the juice from her hands. Gabe had taken a huge bite out of his steak sandwich and was chewing slowly as he contemplated her from across the table.

"I'm rather tired," Bobbi said after a long pause. She picked up a knife and sliced her burger into four neat sections, which was more in keeping with the way Gabe ate and quite uncharacteristic for her. Bobbi never minded getting her hands dirty, be it with food, soil, or grease. But for some reason right at that moment, with him watching her—she felt self-conscious about getting bacon grease, sauce, and cheese all over her face and hands.

"I didn't mean as soon as we got home," he clarified. "I thought you might want to get some sleep first, come around later."

"I don't know if it's a good idea," she said, and he pinned her with an accusatory glare.

"Why not?"

"Gabe . . ."

"Bobbi, either we're okay after what happened last night, or we're not. Which is it?"

"Are we okay?" she asked in a small and uncertain voice, and he sighed softly, carefully putting his sandwich down.

"I'm not sure," he admitted. "I want us to be. But . . ."

"But?" she prompted, and he sighed again before gesturing toward her plate.

"We're going to talk about this at some point, Bobbi . . . but right now I need you to finish that burger. You have to eat something, and if we get into this now, we'll talk and you won't eat." Frustrated, Bobbi glared down at the quartered burger on her plate and lifted one of the portions to take a nibble. He went back to his own sandwich and an awkward silence reigned between them until the last morsel had been consumed.

He paid for their meal and escorted her back to the car, which still had its fair share of teen admirers taking showboating cell phone photos around it. The boys looked both disappointed and awed when Gabe and Bobbi climbed into the car. One of them asked how fast the car went, and Gabe wound down the window to answer him patiently. The questions came thick and fast after that, and after answering a couple more, Gabe excused himself and started up the car, gunning the engine impressively for his admiring audience before pulling away at a disappointingly respectable speed. Bobbi rolled her eyes when she noted a few crestfallen young faces in the rearview mirror and mustered up a bit of empathy for them despite her lack of energy.

They were back on the road in seconds and there was more silence until Gabe switched the radio back on. They didn't speak again until the car slid to a stop in front of her front door. He switched off the engine and turned in his seat to face her, one arm curled over the steering wheel and the other across the top of his seat.

"So, sevenish?" he asked, and she played with the seat belt clasp, keeping her eyes down. "Bobbi? Don't do this. Come on, look at me." The plaintive note in his voice compelled her to obey and she reluctantly lifted her eyes to meet his. He smiled warmly at her when she looked at him.

"Are you coming over?" he asked again and she nodded, feeling like an idiot for being unable to stick to her resolution to take a break but unable to deny him.

"What movie?" she asked.

"Let's go for a classic, what about *Aliens*?" he suggested, naming one of her favorites, and she sighed before nodding. "Great! I'll see you then. You're fixing the popcorn."

"We'll toss a coin for the honor," she responded casually, taking her cues from him.

"Nope. I called it already," he said smugly, and she punched his shoulder affectionately.

"Stop changing the rules," she protested, lining up to take another shot at his shoulder, but he caught her fist in his, preventing her from making contact. It was something he had done countless times and he usually released her hand immediately, but this time his head was bent and his eyes were fixed on the sight of her small fist held captive in his. He turned their hands over and used his other to unfurl her fingers one by one—taking the time to stroke each one as he uncurled it—until he held her open hand palm up. He traced the lines on her pink palm slowly and thoroughly, not missing a single one. His gentle touch made her skin burn, and Bobbi was vaguely aware of the fact that her breath was coming in ragged gasps.

"Gabe?" Her voice was embarrassingly shaky but it seemed to snap him out of whatever daze he was in; his head jerked up and his eyes met hers in alarm. There was a dull red streak running across his cheekbones and his eyes still looked unfocused.

"What the hell is going on here?" His voice was low and rough and shaking almost as much as hers had been. He looked genuinely unsettled, but he still hadn't released her hand and his thumb was absently stroking back and forth across the callused pads beneath her fingers. He held on for a moment longer before dropping her hand rather abruptly and turning to face front again. Bobbi looked at his profile, aching to reach out and stroke that clenched jaw and smooth out the tense lines that bracketed his mouth. She curbed the impulse and instead held her hands tightly clutched in her lap.

"I'll see you later," he said curtly. Hurt by the dismissal, Bobbi turned to open the door. She was in the process of shutting it behind her when his words halted her movements. "Bobbi . . ."

She turned back expectantly but he seemed at a loss and she watched his throat work as he swallowed down whatever words *might* have emerged.

"Later," she said, putting him out of his misery. She walked away without looking back.

As usual the house was as silent as a tomb when Gabe got home. His mother, Lucy Templeton-Braddock Colbert, the sole heiress to one of the most profitable vineyards in the country, had moved out nearly ten years ago after her marriage to Francis Colbert—wealthy entrepreneur and all-round good guy. The same couldn't be said for the loser who had fathered Gabe and Chase and who had run off to "find" himself in Southeast Asia when the twins were eight years old. As far as Gabe knew, Leighton Braddock was still blowing his seemingly endless trust fund while emulating Leo Di Caprio's character from *The Beach* somewhere in Thailand. Gabe felt nothing but a distant bitterness on the rare occasions that he actually thought of the man whom he had worshipped as a boy.

Gabe had been mildly shocked when his mother and Francis had produced a baby girl less than nine months after their marriage. He and Chase doted on their ten-year-old half sister, Kim, but saw her very rarely. Gabe was too busy with GNT—Global Network Television—a subsidiary of Bobbi's father's multimedia conglomerate, Richcorp, and Chase was usually off working in some far-flung place.

Gabe headed straight for the den, poured himself a scotch, and downed it in a single gulp. He shuddered as the liquor burned its way down his gullet. He couldn't think straight and the alcohol hadn't helped at all, instead he found himself recalling how small and delicate Bobbi's hand had felt in his and how erotic he had found the contrast between the calluses just below her fingers and the softness of her palm. Naturally that thought was immediately followed by how that same hand had felt trailing across his naked flesh the night before and . . . yeah, he was hard as a rock again. He glared down at his crotch irritated, confused, and aroused all at the same time.

He didn't even know why he had insisted she come round for movies later. Part of him wanted them to get back into their usual routine and another part of him, the one he was staring at right now, was hoping that they would be anything but normal tonight. That part of him was completely okay with more kissing, caressing, and tasting. Yes, a little more and then some of what they'd shared last night, thank you very much.

He dug into his back pocket for his mobile phone—thinking of cancelling—but the thing started vibrating even as he reached for it. Hoping it was Bobbi wanting to cry off and thus saving *him* from doing it, he didn't bother to glance at the caller ID before connecting and lifting it to his ear.

"Yes?" His eager greeting was met with a long, crackling silence. It was a bad line and he immediately knew who it was. His stomach sank as he imagined the worst. "Chase?" There was more static before he heard his brother's faint voice at the other end of the line.

"Yeah, it's me."

"Are you okay?" Gabe asked, envisioning bombs and snipers and IEDs. His hand tightened around the phone when he heard nothing but crackling.

"I'm on my way home," Chase said after a moment. "Can you . . . can you pick me up from the airport on Tuesday? Not sure about the time . . . flying into Joburg. Getting the first available domestic flight from there. I'll let you know when I know."

"What's going on?" Chase sounded *off* and it concerned Gabe. "Has something happened?"

"I've got to go," Chase dodged his question. "Don't tell Mum."

"Wait, Chase . . ." The line was disconnected before he could say anything else and Gabe nearly tossed his phone in frustration. He immediately reached for the television remote and tuned into CNN. If anything out of the ordinary had happened, they would definitely have something about it. He skipped between the BBC and CNN, but there was nothing close to what his imagination had been conjuring up.

He was still urgently surfing news networks hours later when Bobbi walked into the den. It wasn't unusual for her to let herself in. The light in the room had changed, dimmed somewhat, and Bobbi's slight silhouette hovering in the doorway startled him.

"Bobbi? Shit . . ." He'd forgotten to cancel.

"Yeah, that's what every girl wants to hear when she walks into a room," she responded wryly before ambling in clutching a covered plate and wearing indecently short denim cut-offs that immediately sent his blood pressure soaring, combined with another of her ubiquitous tanks and a pair of trainers. Like the tiny black bikini that morning, what she was wearing wasn't anything he hadn't seen her in previously but he had never truly appreciated the golden glow of all that revealed skin before now. Every naked inch seemed to invite his touch, and he had to curl his hands into fists to prevent them from responding to that tempting invitation.

"Faye sent dinner; she's convinced you'll starve if she doesn't feed you." She held up the plate with a grin, referring to the Richmonds' housekeeper. When Gabe did nothing but look at her from where he was seated in front of the huge TV, the smile slid from her face and was replaced with a concerned frown.

"What's wrong?"

"Chase called," he replied. Bobbi quickly placed the plate on the coffee table and sat down next to him.

"Is he all right?"

"I don't know," Gabe shrugged. "He says he's coming home."

"But that's good, right?"

"Something's wrong . . . he didn't sound like himself."

"Gabe." She took his hand and he looked over at her. "He's fine. You spoke with him. Focus on that. You'll find out soon enough if something's wrong. It's better not to allow your imagination to run riot."

He laughed softly.

"When did you get so wise, Roberta Richmond?" She winced at his use of her full name and he remembered that she had once likened it to a "superhero's lame girlfriend's name." He hadn't ever given it any thought before but he kind of liked the simple grace of the name.

"I've always been wise, you guys have just never appreciated my wisdom," she scoffed. He smiled automatically and—while he was still worried about his brother—at that moment he was even more concerned with the way her shorts had ridden all the way up her smooth, taut thighs and he was pretty damned sure she wasn't wearing a bra under that tank top. His eyes fell to her pert breasts and his breath hitched when her nipples tightened against the thin material.

Yep, no bra. She folded her arms over her chest, looking somewhat uncomfortable.

"Cold?" he asked. His throat had gone dry and had hoarsened his voice so that the word was barely a grunt.

"No," she denied from between gritted teeth, keeping her arms tightly folded over her chest.

"You looked somewhat cold to me," he pointed out.

"You were *staring* at me," she hissed.

"And my staring made you respond like that?" She didn't reply and he watched as gooseflesh broke out all over her body—with so much of her skin revealed it was hard to miss.

"I should go," she said.

"I don't want you to go," he stated. She chewed on her lower lip, a habit that she'd had for years but had never before made him want to suck on that lip and lick the sting away until now.

"Then what *do* you want?" She asked, her voice laced with frustration.

You. He looked at her mutely for a moment, the word hovering on his tongue.

"I want to watch a movie and eat popcorn and forget this entire day happened," he said instead.

"Then let's do that," Bobbi said, and he could hear the relief mingled with . . . *disappointment?* In her voice.

Well, damn. Could it be that Bobbi Richmond wanted him too? Well wasn't *that* just frikken fantastic? Knowing that she may want him in return was going to make it so much harder for him to resist her. That was just one more complication he didn't need. He needed to fix this fast.

CHAPTER FOUR

Bobbi found herself outside her auto repair shop bright and early that Sunday morning. The men and Bobbi took turns taking weekends off and this was to have been hers, but she had too much invested in the business to stay away from it for a full weekend, so she usually headed in for a couple of hours on most of her days off anyway. Besides, after the confusing events of the past forty-eight hours, starting with that ill-advised drunken kiss on Friday night, she welcomed the distraction work would offer. Her employees were all at work; the shop was usually open seven days a week with the guys working shifts during the week. Weekends were their busiest times because most people couldn't find the time to bring their cars in for minor repairs during the week.

In an effort to keep her mind away from Gabe, she had been thinking about the vintage Chevy Corvette that her team was supposed to start overhauling on Monday. It was one of her biggest accounts and her client was an old friend who had allowed her to twist his arm into renovating the old car that had been rusting beneath a drop cloth in his garage. She was excited by the opportunity. Her business was still fairly new—just over a year old—and if they did this well she could make a name for herself in the very exclusive vintage car restoration market. At the moment engine repairs, bodywork, and other small jobs were keeping the business afloat, but this beauty of a car could be the break that she was looking for.

"Hey, boss, didn't expect to see you in today," Sean, the youngest of her three mechanics, called when saw her.

"You know that I can't stay away from this place," she joked, and he laughed, before ducking his head back under the bonnet of a badly dented sedan. Bobbi headed directly to the car that she had so many hopes and dreams invested in.

"Wow, you are *gorgeous*," Bobbi whispered reverently, when she came to a halt in front of the faded beauty that graced her auto repair shop floor. "Hello darling, I'm going to make you even more beautiful. I'm going to give you a makeover. Would you like that?" She ran her hands worshipfully over the sleek lines of the battered 1970 Chevy Corvette LT-1. Craig Farrow, her head mechanic, grinned when she leaned over the car's bonnet, spread her arms wide, and lay her cheek against the cold metal. She hugged the car as if it was a living, breathing entity and really to Bobbi it *was*. Cars spoke to her —they clearly communicated their pain, their suffering, their wants, and their needs. She lay there for a long while before sighing deeply and standing upright to look down at the car regretfully.

"I can't promise that it won't hurt," she said solemnly. "But it'll all be worth it in the end."

Another long sigh before she glanced over at Craig, Sean, and Pieter, her other mechanic. While Sean was cheerful, Pieter, who was only slight older, was skinny as the proverbial rake and surly and uncommunicative. He did brilliant work though and seemed content to let everybody around him do the talking. They were all standing off to the side watching her commune with the car. Craig and Sean—who had stopped what he'd been doing for the moment—looked amused while Pieter merely looked bored.

"Dya wanna start today, boss?" Craig asked. All business now, Bobbi outlined her plan of action and her timeline for the car's "makeover." A lot of the parts had to be imported and the cost for it was coming straight out of her pocket, since she had all but begged her friend for the opportunity to work on this baby. Jason Claiborne hadn't been willing to foot the expense of overhauling the vintage car and had been quite prepared to leave her to rust, but he was unwilling to sell what had once been his father's pride and joy. Bobbi had convinced him that she could restore the car to its former glory, agreeing to charge him for only the bodywork and half of the cost of the mechanical repairs if he agreed to drive the car regularly and talk her business up if anyone asked about the car. That meant she would have to pay for the replacement parts and they didn't come cheap. The project was an ambitious one for a young, struggling business like hers and she sometimes woke up in a cold sweat knowing that she was putting all her eggs into one very rickety basket.

She hoped to keep the money trickling in with the more minor jobs but her business didn't have much of a reputation in the area yet. Added to that, she was a woman and most people didn't trust a female near their cars. She had discovered that women were worse than men when it came to rampant sexism; her small clientele consisted mostly of men. The only women who supported her were her so-called "Mommy Club" friends and they weren't in the area enough to use her services regularly. She'd had women drive into her shop and take one look at her before hastily claiming to have made a mistake and driving right back out again. And more than a few men had had the same reaction. It was disheartening to say the least.

She sucked in a breath and focused on the task at hand. She had a lot riding on the grand old lady parked in front of her but she was determined to succeed. She had dreamed of owning her own shop since her early teens, when her father had allowed her to help him "tinker" on his cars. The man hadn't been the most attentive father, content to let his children run wild for the most part while he focused on his business and the only moments Bobbi had felt close to him when she was a child was when he allowed her to help him work on one of his precious cars. It was his hobby, something he did to unwind, and he had always welcomed Bobbi with her questions and her eagerness to help.

He hadn't quite known what to do with a girl child and had been quite happy when she hadn't shown an interest in more feminine pursuits, at least allowing them to have *some* common ground. He didn't know that Bobbi had deliberately forsaken more "girlie" pastimes so that she could have her father's approval and could have something in common with her brothers. She had been desperate to fit into her testosterone-laden family and so dresses and make-up had been sacrificed in favor of jeans, football, and grease.

Out of that need for approval had come this genuine love for auto mechanics. Her brothers had all gone to university after high school and had gone on to become a lawyer, architect, and doctor, respectively. Bobbi hadn't wanted to be anything other than a mechanic and she had worked at an auto shop all through high school. She had halfheartedly pursued an aimless BA degree in English Literature before eventually dropping out to get an automotive certification instead. She had studied and worked hard and had apprenticed at three different auto repair shops. Years later a combination of savings, a small business loan, and some money her mother—who had died of a pulmonary embolism when Bobbi was just five—had left in trust for her had afforded her the opportunity to open her own shop in town at the relatively young age of twenty-five. Her father had been willing to finance the whole shop but she had wanted to do this by herself. Nobody could ever accuse her of being a pampered, spoiled brat whose wealthy daddy bankrolled her life. It was bad enough that she still lived at home. It was her only viable option at the moment, with every spare cent going into the business.

Starting an auto repair shop wasn't cheap and if not for Gabe's emotional support and encouragement back when the idea was just a nascent seed floundering beneath mounds of crushing self-doubt, Bobbi would probably not even have tried to get it off the ground. Gabe had always made her feel like what she wanted was equally as important as her brothers' lofty ambitions. The costs of her state-of-the-art equipment, building rental, and employee payrolls were immense and Bobbi would swallow her pride and live at home if it meant saving money on rent and food. She'd had a lot more privacy since her brothers had all moved out anyway and usually only saw her father at mealtimes. The man was a workaholic and was always closeted away in his office running the multimillion dollar family business that none of his children had wanted to take over. Instead, Gabe was the one who was being groomed to succeed him as Richcorp's chairman.

Gabe had been Mike Richmond's first, last, and only choice as successor once it had become clear that none of his children were interested in learning anything about his huge multimedia conglomerate, which owned five local newspapers around the country, three national radio stations, four glossy multilingual magazines, and a premium cable television that serviced most of the country and a large portion of the continent as well. Gabe had been the one who had asked the intelligent questions on career day when Mike Richmond had graced his classroom—which he shared with his twin, Chase, and her brother Billy—with his formidable presence. Gabe had been the one to dog the older man's footsteps and beg for a summer job when he was fifteen. While Chase and Billy had flirted with girls and been typical adolescents, Gabe had worked his butt off in the stuffy mailroom of the Cape Town branch of the company. He had eventually obtained his MBA—all the while working his way up through the ranks until he had reached his current status as the CEO of GNT, Richcorp's most prolific subsidiary. Now he was poised to take over the whole kit and caboodle.

"Hey." As if she had unconsciously summoned Gabe with her thoughts, his glossy, expensive shoes suddenly materialized at her feet. Startled, she lost focus and raised her head, hitting it on the underside of the car with a bang. *Damn it!*

She swore roundly and he chuckled in response to her colorful curses. He went down on his haunches and she felt his hands wrap around her ankles. Before she could question him, he dragged her out from under the car. The creeper that she was lying on eased his task significantly. He didn't budge as he pulled her closer and she had no choice but to part and bend her knees so that they were splayed on either side of his thighs. He halted her progress before the creeper—which was long enough only to support her from shoulder to backside—could whack him on the ankles.

Disgruntled, she sat up but then immediately realized that the move hadn't been well thought out on her part. It brought her chest within a hairs' breath of his much broader one and she could feel the heat poring off him. He also smelled delicious—hints of green forest mixed with his own earthy scent—while she was self-consciously aware of the fact that she reeked of Eau de Grease. Still she was so hyperaware of his proximity that her breath shortened into ragged gasps, and her nipples tightened into hard ingots of excruciating sensation. She was grateful for the fact that she wore her loose gray overalls since they hid the embarrassing development from his all-encompassing scrutiny. After the night before she would rather not have it known that it was a pretty typical reaction to his presence.

Once could be written off as a fluke. Twice and he'd be onto her longest-kept secret in no time.

She licked her lips nervously and his eyes dropped down to her mouth to track the movement. His rapt gaze traveled over her face and his eyes widened for a fraction of a second before he raised his hand to cup one of her cheeks. He leaned in and Bobbi swallowed painfully. Oh dear God, he was going to kiss her . . .

Of course he was going to kiss her!

It was inevitable. He had confused her so much over the past couple of days but perhaps he was ready to acknowledge he was attracted to her as well? Her lips parted, her eyes slid shut, and his thumb brushed over her cheekbone before his hand abruptly left her face. She was startled into opening her eyes just in time to see him raise his thumb into her line of vision.

"Grease," he said, wrinkling his nose. She gasped and humiliated color flooded into her cheeks as she caught the mixture of laughter and distaste in his eyes.

She was mortified that she had once again allowed herself to entertain the notion that Gabe could possibly be attracted to her. Her inability to separate reality from her crazy fantasies was one of the reasons she simply *had* to keep him at a physical distance. That meant no more ill-advised movie nights. She would start being firmer and saying no to him more often. It was mortifying how very little backbone she had when it came to this man. Bobbi reached for a rag that she kept tucked into her pocket and scrubbed self-consciously at her face.

"I'm surprised to see you here." Her voice was muffled as she continued to wipe her face. "I mean, aren't you afraid of getting grime on your lovely suit? Grease is impossible to get out, you know." She eyed the expensive tailor-made three-piece iron-gray suit disdainfully, desperate to get back into familiar territory with him. She didn't ask him what he was doing in a suit on a Sunday afternoon; Gabe was a real workaholic and since he'd taken Saturday off it was inevitable that he'd go to the office on Sunday.

Knowing him, he'd probably swum a few laps this morning, headed out to the office afterward, had a few high-powered business meetings—achieving more in a few hours than most people achieved in a full day at work. Just a typical morning for the industrious Gabriel Braddock, and now he was here with nary a hair out of place and enough time left in his day to torment her.

He merely grinned in response to her words before leaping nimbly to his feet. She felt a profound sense of loss when he moved away and ducked her head to disguise her reaction. When she looked up again only after carefully cultivating a blank expression, it was to see him holding out a hand to her. She hesitated before reluctantly taking the outstretched hand. His long, elegant fingers curled around her grubby paw and the muscles in his thighs tensed as he leaned back to tug her up.

He overestimated her weight—using a smidgen too much strength—and Bobbi lost her balance. For a few awkward seconds she found herself plastered against his hard body before—after a seemingly interminable amount of time had passed—he grabbed her upper arms and shifted her away.

Dazed, she peered up at him for a moment while she tried to force herself to forget about the burning imprint of his chest against her cheek, his torso against her breasts, and most startling of all—the firm masculine bulge between his thighs against her stomach. For a brief moment, she allowed herself to speculate about that substantial bulge. She had easily felt it through the fabric of their clothing, even though he wasn't aroused and it made her—*very* inappropriately— wonder about the size of him when he was erect. She remembered

Friday night, in his room, when she had touched him. He had seemed . . . affected then, but she hadn't considered *how* affected he might have been until now. Had be been turned on? Hard? The thought sent her face up in flames.

She lifted the rag and pretended to rub off the grease on her face again in an effort to disguise her inexplicable blush.

"Hey," his hand reached out to halt hers. "You got it all. You'll scour the skin off your face if you keep that up."

"What are you doing here, anyway?" she asked him sullenly, determined to regain her equilibrium.

"Taking you to lunch," he informed authoritatively, elbowing his jacket aside to shove his hands into his trouser pockets. Naturally her eyes fell to where the expensive fabric strained across his muscled thighs and crotch. She cleared her throat nervously and averted her eyes.

Jesus! Pull yourself together, Richmond, she lectured herself sternly. This was beyond ridiculous. She could get past this; she'd done it before and she'd undoubtedly have to do it again—even though it was becoming increasingly and devastatingly painful for her to deal with Gabe's affectionate disinterest.

"I'm busy today . . . and I had a big breakfast," she lied, and he rolled his eyes at her.

"A slice of toast isn't anybody's idea of a big breakfast," he said.

"Faye?" she asked with a resigned sigh. Faye tended to jump at every opportunity to get Bobbi to eat more. The woman often said that Bobbi's skinny frame served as a very poor testimonial to Faye's cooking skills.

"Um-hmm," Gabe confirmed with a sexy hum that immediately had her stupid nipples standing to attention again. God, this was ridiculous . . . why did she have to be so *aware* of him?

"It doesn't matter, I snacked throughout the morning."

Gabe raised a questioning brow at Sean and Craig. The other men had their lunch bags in hand and were obviously getting ready to take a break.

"If you call a half-eaten apple a snack," Craig said with a jovial shrug, ignoring Bobbi's glare before he and the other two men waved and traipsed off to enjoy their lunch in the park opposite her shop.

"I guess that settles it," he said with a charming grin that set her teeth on edge and made her want to slap him and kiss him at the same time. It was the latter impulse that made her snap at him defensively.

"It settles *nothing*! You're not my keeper, Gabe, and if I choose to have a working lunch it's nothing to you." Okay, she sounded like a total bitch and immediately felt awful about it—especially when she saw the flash of confusion in his eyes.

"You're angry with me," he observed. "Why?"

"No. I'm not." She sighed. It wasn't his fault that he couldn't see her as anything other than a surrogate sister, while she wanted so much more than just friendship from him. "I'm sorry, Gabe, I'm just tired. Let me get cleaned up and we can grab something to eat."

Gabe watched as Bobbi prowled off to the tiny glass cubicle that served as her office. He didn't know how to deal with her or talk to her anymore.

He'd thought that coming to her shop and seeing her in her element, with grease on her face and hands, would help him get over whatever was going on with him. But when he had dragged her out from beneath that car and she had spread her legs around his thighs, his thoughts had been so X-rated that if anybody had been able to read his mind at that moment, he would have been arrested for obscenity right on the spot. He had quite frantically searched for a way to get himself back under control and had found it in the speck of grease on her cheek. He had imagined her at any of the social events that he was regularly required to go to as the CEO of GNT, and Bobbi was hardly the type of female he'd want gracing his arm. But then he had tugged her up, she had fallen against him, and all rational thought had fled his mind again.

He watched, a reluctant smile tugging at the corners of his lips, as she headed over to a sink in her office and rinsed her hands and face before sticking her entire head under the faucet to wet her short black hair. There was really no artifice about her. What you saw was what you got with Bobbi. She reached for a towel and draped it over her head before tugging at the zipper of her overalls and dragging it down. Gabe found himself riveted and took an inadvertent step closer to the office as she revealed a seemingly endless expanse of pale, naked skin to his eyes. What the hell was she wearing under that damned thing? The heavy material eventually parted enough to reveal a tight blue tank top and she dragged her arms out of the sleeves in quick, practiced movements. The top half of her overalls was now bunched at her waist with the sleeves dangling down the backs of her legs.

Twin rivulets of water streamed from her wet hair and followed the path of her delicate clavicles down over the slight swell of her breasts to merge into a single stream just before disappearing into the shallow crevice of her cleavage and dampening the light cotton of her tank. His eyes widened as he watched her nipples bead in response to the cold trickle of water. She obviously wasn't wearing a bra, *again*! And again that knowledge made his mouth go completely dry. For God's sake, didn't the damned woman own a bra?

Her hands went to her hips as she pushed the material of her overalls further down, her slight shimmy as she wriggled her way out of it, making her pert breasts bounce slightly. At last, the overalls dropped to the floor, and his eyes trekked down from her chest over the flat expanse of her stomach to her silky, naked legs as she stepped clear of the discarded pile of cloth. She was wearing another pair of tiny cut-off denim shorts that made her slender legs look impossibly long, which was crazy for a woman whose height barely scraped in past five foot. She turned and bent at the waist to pick up the discarded overalls and Gabe swallowed painfully as he watched the denim go taut over the curve of her butt. The material rode up just enough to give him a tantalizing glimpse of the pouty curve where thigh met arse.

"*Christ Almighty!*" he swore shakily. He was—for the umpteenth time that weekend—fully and painfully erect and had been since the moment she had pushed the damned overalls down over her slim shoulders. Shaken, he turned away from the cubicle and tried to compose himself. This was beyond ridiculous . . . He pushed a trembling hand through his hair and inhaled deeply as he tried to get himself under control again.

This for damned sure couldn't be healthy. Surely a man couldn't will away this many erections in such a short time without suffering severe physical and mental repercussions? He was just managing to get it under control when he felt her hand curling around his bicep. He nearly leapt out of his skin at the contact.

"I'm ready," she said with a slight smile, and he blinked, confused.

Ready for what? No way in hell was she ready for what he wanted to do to her. She wasn't ready for him to lift her onto the bonnet of that damned car she'd been under just minutes ago. She wasn't ready for him to cover her tight body with his own and shove her thighs apart. And she sure as hell wasn't ready for him to drag those tempting shorts down her thighs before thrusting his full length into her.

He peered down into her expectant face and found his eyes dropping down to her smiling mouth. Her lower lip had a generous curve to it that made it look as ripe and juicy as a peach . . . and damn it, remembering that it tasted as good as it looked wasn't helping one bit.

"Gabe?"

"Hmmm?" Another small taste wouldn't do any harm would it? He leaned toward her and her hand tightened around his bicep to give him a slight shake.

"Gabe!" He shook his head and the haze of lust that had obliterated his reason for the past few moments reluctantly dissipated.

"Are you okay?"

Was he? Who the hell knew anymore? He was riveted by her pretty mouth: bow-shaped and bee-stung, it would look more at home on a '40s bombshell movie star than the skinny tomboy standing in front of him. He barely stifled a groan as he suddenly pictured those lips wrapped around his length and . . .

"I'm fine," he gruffly assured the still-concerned Bobbi. "Sorry about that. I was thinking about a problem at the office."

"Okay . . ." She sounded unconvinced but didn't push it. "You ready to go?" He nodded and led her toward his car parked out front.

"Guys, keep an eye on the place, okay?" she yelled at the three men who were sitting at a picnic table in the park opposite the road. None of them bothered to look up when they heard her voice and the only acknowledgment she got was a lazy thumbs-up from Sean.

She headed to the driver's side of the car and watched Gabe expectantly from across the gleaming red roof. He stifled a grin and merely raised an eyebrow at her. She seemed to recognize the *no way in hell* look he was giving her, and her shoulders slumped a bit.

"When are you going to let me drive this baby?" she asked, her hand lovingly trailing over the sleek curve of the Lamborghini's bonnet. Gabe tried, *very hard*, not to remember that same hand running over his body with equal reverence. He mostly succeeded and tried to focus on her question.

"I don't know. I think that the answer to your question lies in a place called *Never* Land, which is located just east of when hell freezes over and to the north of when pigs sprout wings."

She didn't respond to that and lowered herself into the comfortable black and red leather passenger seat with a blissful sigh. She took a moment to enjoy the new car smell and turned her cheek to nuzzle the luxurious leather headrest. The last time she had traveled in the car, she had been too hung over to pay the respectful homage she seemed to reserve for this automobile in particular. She made up for that now. Her hands traced every feature on the control panel between the seats and her fingers caressed their way across the dashboard until she was leaning over to stroke the smooth leather of the steering wheel. Gabe had made his way around the front of the car and was now staring at the sensual movements of her hands in fascination. Aware of the fact that his crotch—which was showing embarrassing signs of life again—was in her direct line of sight, he crouched with one arm resting on the roof of the car and the other on the head rest of the driver's seat.

"Are you quite done groping my car?" he asked, cringing when the words emerged in a growl rather than in the casual tone he was aiming for. She sighed and settled back into her seat. While she fumbled with her seat belt, he lowered himself behind the wheel.

God, he *loved* this car. It had been his reward to himself after stepping up as CEO of GNT. He wasn't one for the usual trappings of wealth—he lived in the house he'd grown up in and rarely traveled unless it was for work. But he had a weakness for sleek, expensive, classy cars and sleek, expensive, classy women, and he frequently indulged himself. He collected sports cars and dated women that

Chase loved to call brainy, beautiful, boring babes. Which was somewhat unfair. Sure his ex-girlfriends all tended to be a bit on the . . . dry side, but they weren't *that* bad, just a bit serious. Okay, so the last one—a pathologist—had talked about blood a *lot*. So much so that Bobbi had taken to calling her Vampira behind her back. The name had stuck and all his friends had started doing the same—Gabe had broken it off after nearly slipping up and calling her Vampira while they were on a date. He hadn't known until that moment that he had started thinking of her by that unfortunate nickname as well.

"You're so selfish with your toys, Gabe," Bobbi accused with a pout, and he shrugged as he turned on the car, grinning in satisfaction at the low, throaty purr coming from the engine.

"Manny's for lunch?" he asked, pulling away from the sidewalk as he spoke.

"Only place I'm dressed for," she pointed out, and his eyes involuntarily dropped to her bare thighs again. He cleared his throat before refocusing his attention on the road. An uncomfortable silence followed and Gabe hunted for a way to fill it.

"So how do you plan to save that old heap of Jason's?" he blurted out.

"She's not an old heap," Bobbi protested. "She's just a bit faded and I'm going to restore her to her former glory. She'll look amazing afterward and she'll handle like a dream."

"How's business?" he asked, hating how he seemed to be reaching for conversational topics with her—usually conversation flowed naturally between them, but suddenly he couldn't think of a single thing to say that didn't feature the words *screw you senseless* somewhere in the mix. She didn't seem to notice his discomfort, leaning forward to investigate the speedometer instead.

"Passable." She shrugged, tapping at the glass pane. "Is this thing broken or are you *really* going that slowly? In a frikkin *Lamborghini?*"

"In case it's escaped your notice, we're on a busy main road," he pointed out. She said something less than complimentary beneath her breath. For some reason her disdain grated and he was stricken by the unfathomable urge to gun the engine and disregard the rules of the road. He had never felt this uncharacteristic need to impress her before.

"I'll take you out on an open, quiet road sometime and let her loose," he offered, and her pretty eyes lit up as they met his for a few brief seconds before he had to focus on the road again.

"Seriously? Will you let me drive?"

"No."

"I'm a good driver."

"You're a *reckless* driver." He could feel the waves of fury emanating from her after his words but she said nothing in response. She said nothing at all even when he parked in front of Manny's a couple of minutes later, and that's when he realized that she was actually giving him The Silent Treatment. He hid a grin. She could never keep it up for longer than five minutes—so it didn't bother him at all that she chose to seethe in silence. She *was* a reckless driver. She loved speed way too much, and while she handled cars competently enough, being in a car with her in the driver's seat was enough to give anyone gray hairs.

They walked into Manny's together, and Gabe curbed the ridiculous impulse to rush forward and get the door for her.

"Hey, Bobbi," a chorus of male voices called as she walked in.

"Come over here and settle a bet will you?" It sounded like Jason, but Gabe couldn't be sure, there were too many bodies between them and the voice.

Gabe watched with a frown as she wove her way through the tables that were scattered haphazardly around the pub's floor to make her way to the bar where a random group of their friends were gathered. The men were all laughing and talking loudly and the tall, bulky frames soon enveloped Bobbi's slight figure as she disappeared from his line of sight completely. Irritated, he stepped forward, determined to reclaim his lunch date. He could hear her quiet voice above the deeper voices of the men, and they all paused for a beat before an eruption of whoops and groans went up in response to whatever she'd said or done. Money exchanged hands and curious now, Gabe stepped into the throng. Bobbi was grinning impishly.

"Gabe," Jason eventually noticed him and slapped him on the back enthusiastically. "Good to see you, man! I just wanted Bobbi to do that thing with the dart. My old university buddies are visiting and wouldn't believe it until they saw it."

"What thing?" he asked, hoping it wasn't the same "thing" he had warned Bobbi against doing years before.

"You know," Jason prompted with a laugh. "When she balances the sharp end of a dart on the bridge of her nose?"

Damn it! The crazy woman could put an eye out with that stunt. He found her defiant eyes through the crowd of still laughing men and she angled her stubborn jaw upward, obviously daring him to say something about it. He bit back the words of censure, not wanting to be too predictable and knowing that while she was braced for them they would have little to no impact on her.

"You ready for lunch yet?" he asked pointedly and saw the flicker of surprise on her face before she nodded. He made a sweeping gesture with his arm as he sarcastically ushered her toward one of the empty tables in the middle of the room. She kept her head down as she passed him and when he turned to nod his farewell to Jason he noticed that all of the other man's friends had their stares firmly fixed on Bobbi's derriere and naked thighs. He barely refrained from shoving the guy closest to him, the one who was actually tilting his damned head for a better view and instead took immense satisfaction in placing his own bulk between Bobbi's departing figure and the leering gazes of the gathered men.

She was already sitting down when he reached the table and took the seat opposite hers, fighting back an irrational surge of anger and frustration when he saw the slight indent and red mark on the bridge of her cute nose. The minute mark marred her pale, smooth skin and seeing it there aggravated him beyond measure. She was watching him warily, but he refrained from commenting and merely called over a waitress and then waited for a long irritating moment while Bobbi perused the familiar menu for ages before placing her order of calamari and chips. He didn't bother to glance at the menu and instead ordered his usual fare.

Bobbi snorted when she heard his order and he inclined his head in question.

"What?"

"They *do* have other stuff here, Gabe," she elaborated—her voice lightly frosted with scorn. "But you always order the ribs, chips, and salad."

"I know they have other stuff here," he countered, his tone measured as he arranged the condiments to his liking. "And I've tried them all but I like the ribs the most. I don't see why I should order anything else when I know that this is what I like best."

"Some variety wouldn't kill you, you know?" She groused as she very deliberately rearranged the bottles that he had painstakingly placed in order of preference. "It's okay to order the steak instead of the ribs. It's perfectly fine to get a buzz cut or grow your hair down past your collar." Her eyes went up to his conservatively cut and parted hair, and it took every ounce of his willpower to refrain from self-consciously raking his fingers through said hair. Instead he focused on putting the bottles back into order, ignoring her snort of amusement.

"And while we're at it, it's all right to date a dumb brunette once in a while instead of a brainy blonde. I swear to God, that bloodless parade of boring blondes you date has sucked every ounce of life and fun out of you."

"I suppose I should be more like you?" he murmured scathingly, raking his eyes over her scruffy figure scornfully. It nearly killed him not to linger over her silky smooth legs and pert breasts but he had a point to prove. "More careless and carefree? You live your life without any structure or order, Bobbi. Sure you've managed to open that shop but you have no real business plan and you have everything vested in that damned car of Jason's. What will you do if, or more likely *when*, that plan fails? It would behoove you to be less carefree and more responsible. You now have employees—people who, unfathomably enough, depend on you for their livelihood. Maybe it's time to stop being such a child. Stop balancing darts on your nose, racing motorcycles at the track, and dressing like a two-bit little . . ." He stopped himself before he completed the sentence but her wide eyes told him that she knew exactly what he'd been about to say. He swallowed past the lump in his throat and tried to apologize but the words wouldn't come.

They sat in silence until the waitress brought their food, avoiding eye contact at all costs, and Gabe felt like a complete bastard for the unspoken word that now hovered between them.

"What's wrong with the way I dress?" She suddenly broke the loaded silence—her voice small and uncertain.

"Nothing."

"But you said . . ."

"Look I was being an idiot." He kept his eyes firmly on his plate.

"You wouldn't have mentioned it if you didn't think there was something wrong with my clothing."

"There's nothing wrong with your clothing," he snapped.

"Don't lie to me!" she snapped right back at him.

"Jesus." This time he *did* rake a frustrated hand through his hair. "Look, those shorts are just too . . . *short* okay? And um . . ." He waved his fork at her chest area, trying not to look and then totally looking. God, she had pretty breasts . . . *Focus, Gabe!* "Wear a damned bra, for God's sake! You keep flashing those nipples at me and I won't be responsible for my actions." And then, as if the mere word had conjured them into being, there they were again, tightening against the soft material of her tank top, unfurling like perfect little rosebuds right beneath his very eyes. And this time he couldn't help but focus directly on them; he couldn't drag his eyes away from them. He lost his train of thought and felt sweat beading on his brow and above his lip, felt it pooling beneath his arms and in the center of his chest.

Want! Need! Now!

CHAPTER FIVE

The three words blindsided him and rang like a bell in his mind. His throat went dry with the astonishing realization that this wasn't some bizarre, fleeting aberration. That he really *wanted* her and would continue wanting her until he had done something about it.

Under him, over him, in front of him—he wanted her any way he could have her . . . He wanted her more than he wanted his next breath and it was insane! He dragged his apologetic eyes up to her embarrassed golden regard. How the hell did you tell your friend that you wanted to sleep with her? But that that's *all* you wanted from her. He was honest enough to admit that he desperately wanted to have sex with her—why now, after all these years? He had no clue but that was what he wanted. What he *didn't* want was anything more than that. He loved her but she wasn't a woman he could ever envision spending his life with. They were too different. The woman of his dreams was tall, graceful, refined, and had an immaculate sense of style and design. Bobbi was the complete opposite of that woman.

But how could he propose no-strings sex to this woman who meant so much to him and expect to still retain a friendship after the affair ended? Bobbi would expect more from him and he could very well wind up breaking her heart. That thought was perfectly unbearable.

∾

Bobbi folded her arms tightly across her chest and lowered her eyes to her plate, she knew that her cheeks were blazing with color but she couldn't do much about that at the moment. She wished that the floor would just open up and swallow her—she was so embarrassed. Thankfully he wasn't staring at her traitorous breasts anymore; instead he was focused intently on his plate, with his jaw clenched and his hands curled into fists on the table. He was concentrating so fiercely on that plate that she half expected it to start levitating.

"I'm sorry . . ." The words were so quiet they were practically swallowed up by the buzzing conversations of the crowd around them, and if not for the fact that he had raised his blazing eyes to meet hers, Bobbi would have dismissed it as imagination. "That was completely out of line."

"Which part? Your comment about the way I dressed or your reference to my . . ." She nodded down at her breasts which were still shielded by her crossed arms. She watched as his eyes drifted back down to her chest and lingered for a long moment before jerking back up to her face.

He cleared his throat uncomfortably.

"I made it personal—I shouldn't have brought your . . . your body into it," he admitted.

"It was already personal when you criticized the way I dressed," she pointed out.

"Bobbi, we're surrounded by men, not all of whom know you . . . and those shorts would tempt a saint." She was riveted by the dull red that stained his cheekbones and narrowed her eyes as an intriguing possibility occurred to her.

"Do they tempt *you*?" Right—she needed a filter between her brain and her mouth—because she couldn't keep saying every single thing that popped into her head. Yet . . . the red stain on his cheekbones darkened and spread inexorably.

"*No!* Of course not . . ." She kept her eyes trained on his face, fascinated to note that he couldn't quite meet her eyes and for the first time *ever* felt in control and powerful around this man who so unsettled her at times. She deliberately dropped her arms and braced them on either side of her plate, before leaning toward him. She was rewarded by the brief, panicked glance he directed down at her cleavage before dragging his eyes back up to her face—and even then he couldn't seem to look higher than her mouth. Deciding to test him even further, she flicked out her tongue to moisten her lower lip and noted the convulsive movement of his throat as he swallowed while his eyes tracked the slow, deliberate movement of her tongue with ferocious concentration.

"I'm not changing the way I dress after all these years, Gabe," she told him—and his eyes snapped back into focus as they met hers. "It's never bothered you before, so what's different now?"

"It doesn't bother me." Two blatant lies in as many minutes. Bobbi was starting to enjoy herself.

"Then why mention it?" she pushed.

"Just forget I said anything." He picked up his knife and fork with hands that were trembling ever so slightly. She didn't respond and kept staring at him until he put the cutlery down again. "You don't understand men, Bobbi . . . they're easily aroused and . . ." Her rich laughter cut him off and the sound halted his awkward lecture mid-sentence.

"Gabe, I'm not naïve. I don't need you to explain the birds and the bees to me. Trust me, you're years too late with that particular lecture."

"What do you mean by that, exactly?" His voice had taken on a dangerous edge and she merely smiled at him.

"That's nothing you need to concern yourself over," she said dismissively, with a flick of her hand. She picked up her own utensils and dug into her meal with relish, suddenly feeling inordinately cheerful. "Eat your lunch, it's getting cold." He bristled at the dismissal and even though he tried to broach the subject again, she ignored him and raved about the Corvette instead, telling him what she had planned for the car.

"I know you think I'm being foolish by investing so much into this," she said after running out of steam since Gabe had contributed nothing more to the conversation than grunts and nods, making her sharply aware of the other criticisms that he had leveled at her business sense earlier before he had distracted her by bringing her lack of dress sense into the conversation.

"I would be less concerned if you had a long-term plan for the business," he admitted. "But I didn't mean to make it sound like I had no confidence in your ability to make a success out of the shop, Bobbi." Unfortunately, that was *exactly* how it sounded and Bobbi was still hurt by his lack of faith in her. Gabe had always made her feel like he had the utmost belief in her ability to achieve everything she set her mind to. That's why the doubt, the outright cynicism, she had heard from him earlier had cut so deeply. Now, she shrugged and—as she always did when he inadvertently hurt her—brushed it aside in order to make *him* feel better.

"It's okay." *It's not okay.* Her subconscious was riled. "I know you're just concerned." *I don't need your concern! I need your support. I want you to have faith in me and in what I can do.*

She didn't voice what she was really feeling—as was always the case when it came to Gabe. She remained mute . . . for the sake of their friendship.

~

Relieved to have things back on an even keel, Gabe smiled at her. He hadn't even glanced at her breasts in over ten minutes and he'd barely *thought* about them in well over a minute. Thankfully she'd left her uncomfortable line of questioning behind and they were back in familiar territory. His unfair—if not unfounded—zinger about her plans for Jason's car had been forgiven. Things were practically back to normal . . . until Jason ambled over to their table with a tall, smiling guy in tow.

"Hey guys, mind if we join you?" He didn't wait for an affirmative and dragged a couple of chairs over and waved the guy into one before plonking down into the other.

"Gabe, Bobbi, this is Kyle Foster—an old friend of mine." The man reached over and shook Gabe's hand firmly before angling his chair toward Bobbi's and taking her hand in a gentler grasp and bringing it to his lips.

"Charmed." He grinned and Bobbi laughed—clearly enjoying the guy's smarmy attentions.

"So Bobbi, huh? That's an unusual name." He kept his voice low and intimate and it grated on Gabe's last nerve.

"Well, it's Roberta, actually. Roberta Richmond." Gabe couldn't believe he'd just heard that. She *never* told anybody her full name. For her to simply volunteer it was highly unusual.

"So Gabe, I wanted to ask for your advice on a couple of investments I'm interested in making," Jason was saying, trying to gain his attention but Gabe could barely focus on his friend, far too interested in the low-voiced conversation between Bobbi and Foster.

"Hey, mate," Jason waved a hand in front of Gabe's eyes, demanding his attention, and Gabe blinked over at him.

"What?" he snapped, his voice low and frustrated. Jason leaned in toward him.

71

"Work with me here, bro." He kept his voice low enough for only Gabe to hear. "Kyle wanted to meet Bobbi. Guy's smitten—so give him a chance to chat her up. He's a decent bloke."

He was setting Bobbi up with this jerk? Gabe practically choked on a sip of beer and had to do everything in his power not to glare at Jason. He focused his attention back on Bobbi and Foster and was alarmed to note that the guy was whispering in her ear and she was listening to whatever he was saying with a delighted smile on her face. That smile was goddamned *radiant* and it set his teeth completely on edge. Gabe couldn't remember the last time she had smiled at him like that. In fact, he couldn't recall her *ever* smiling at him like that.

"Bobbi," he growled. "Time to go."

Jason swore, keeping his voice low so that only Gabe could hear him. "Come on, Gabe . . . they're hitting it off."

"I don't mind driving her back to her shop," Foster volunteered. Gabe was about to tell him what to do with that unwelcome offer when Bobbi agreed to the guy's suggestion. He was completely outvoted when Jason enthusiastically agreed that it was a *brilliant* idea.

"Bobbi?" He kept his voice reasonable and his eyes level but she barely glanced at him.

"I'm fine, Gabe, I'm sure Kyle will make sure that I get back safely." Her casual dismissal stung like hell, and Gabe felt irrationally betrayed by it. He dug his wallet out of his jacket pocket and left enough cash on the table to cover both of their meals. He strode away without a backward glance, ignoring the chorus of cheerful "see you's" that followed him out the door.

When he got to his car, he braced his hands on the roof of the car and dragged in a deep breath. He glanced through the pub's windows and saw Bobbi laughing at something Foster had just said and barely refrained from kicking at his tire.

Okay, so he was attracted to her but he couldn't possibly be *jealous*, could he? Bobbi hooking up with some other guy might be just what he needed to get over this ridiculous desire he felt for her.

He shook his head, ran a hand through his hair, and climbed into his car. He was just overtired and horny. He needed rest and a woman in his life. Rest he could take care of immediately, and he had always had a few prospects in the female companionship department. He just wished he could drum up a bit of enthusiasm at the thought of spending time with some other woman when it was *Bobbi* that he couldn't stop fantasizing about.

~

Bobbi genuinely liked Kyle Foster; he was witty and charming and she found herself enjoying his company on the drive back to her shop. When he drew the car to a stop, she invited him in to have a look around.

"I'd love that," he enthused, climbing out and hurrying around to the passenger side to open the car door for her. It was a charming gesture that very few men had ever performed for the tomboyish Bobbi, and she was completely flattered by it.

"Wow, this is amazing, Roberta." He sounded suitably impressed as he walked around the shop, running a light hand over the tools before pausing in front of the Corvette where Craig was currently using the overhead hoist to remove the engine. The older man managed a distracted greeting before focusing his attention back on the car.

"Thank you," she murmured. Kyle turned to her with a warm smile on his attractive face.

"So . . . I was wondering if you'd like to go out sometime? Lunch or dinner, maybe?" She was on the verge of making up some lame excuse when she stopped herself. *Why not?* Gabe would never return her feelings and she couldn't keep turning down perfectly nice guys in the hopes that he would someday come to the unlikely realization that she was the one for him. But then she thought about his *bizarre* reaction to the way she was dressed earlier and found herself indulging in a bout of entirely self-indulgent *what if's* . . .

"Roberta?" Kyle's quiet voice jerked her from her favorite fantasy of Gabe sweeping her up into his arms and she shook herself. It would do her good to go out with a man as something other than just a buddy—but with the way she felt about Gabe, it hardly seemed right to string along a perfectly lovely man like Kyle.

"I'd like that . . . very much actually," she said uncertainly. His smile widened and his eyes crinkled appealingly at the corners. He wasn't as gorgeous as Gabe but then few men were, and Bobbi resolved then and there to stop comparing every man she met to Gabe—it wasn't fair. Kyle was tall, he had shaggy dirty-blond hair, and kind gray eyes and the masculine craggy features of an outdoorsman. He was a landscape architect and all the time he spent outside had darkened his skin attractively. He also seemed to like her—shorts, tank top, unstyled hair and all—and that soothed her ego after her lunchtime conversation with Gabe.

"I sense a 'but' in there somewhere," he observed, watching her carefully.

"*But* . . ." But what exactly? But she was in love with her best friend? But she was longing for a guy who was oblivious to her charms? Every thought that popped into her mind seemed stupid and irrational. She was a fool. She wasn't blind to that truth but she still couldn't help . . . *hoping*. She sighed quietly. "But I'm kind of in a really weird place right now."

He seemed to think that over before nodded thoughtfully.

"I won't pressure you but I'd like to know if you'd be open to the idea of drinks some time in the future once you manage to find your way out of that weird place?"

"Yes," she said with a relieved smile. "Definitely."

"Here's my card." His hand brushed against hers when he handed the slip of paper over and Bobbi was disappointed when she felt nothing close to what she felt when Gabe's skin accidentally touched hers. She really was a lost cause.

"Thank you," she said, running her fingers over the raised lettering on the no-frills business card. She really didn't know what else to say to him and he seemed to sense it and ended his visit soon after that.

"I really hope to see you again soon," he said as she walked him to his car and smiled somewhat uncomfortably. Bobbi had been out of the dating game for more than a year, choosing to focus on her business instead, and even before that she had only dated sporadically because most of the guys she knew were the buddies she had grown up with. The few men who had shown a romantic interest in her had always been on the losing end of an inevitable comparison with Gabe.

So she stood in the parking lot and watched another perfectly fine man drive out of her life and felt like an idiot for yet again closing herself off to other possibilities. It was a cycle she couldn't seem to break.

"Look at you," Craig teased softly after Bobbi had changed back into her overalls and joined them on the floor again. "Leaving with one guy and coming back with another."

"Gabe's not a 'guy' he's just . . . *Gabe*," she muttered, keeping here eyes down and Craig snorted.

"Sure he is." That sarcastic rejoinder had her head snapping up to meet his regard in alarm.

"What do you mean by that?" she asked, her face hot with embarrassment. Craig darted a quick glance around the room to ensure that Sean and Pieter weren't listening to their conversation, but both of the other guys were focused on their own tasks.

"You know what I mean," the older man said seriously. "You like him. I have two teenaged daughters and you're about as transparent as they are when it comes to affairs of the heart." How humiliating to be compared to adolescent girls.

"Fantastic," she said beneath her breath. "This is getting ridiculous."

"Didn't mean to embarrass you, boss. I just liked that you came back with the other guy. Time for you to stop mooning over that Gabe with his fancy suits and shiny shoes. This new guy looks like he knows how to get his hands dirty."

"He's not the new guy," she corrected, wondering miserably why she was still talking about this with him. Craig was the last person on earth she would ever consult on matters of the heart. For his anniversary last year he had forgotten to make reservations at the fancy Italian restaurant his wife had been hinting at for weeks before the big day and had made it up to her by microwaving a pizza and serving it with boxed wine. Needless to say he had slept on the couch that night—a fact that he had lamented over for days afterward. He still couldn't understand his wife's "unreasonable" reaction when he had gone all out to serve it with paper napkins and a couple of scented candles. He'd even used paper plates so that she wouldn't have to worry about washing up.

"Anyway there's no old or current guy either, so let's just drop this ridiculous subject and get back to work." He shrugged and did as he was told. Bobbi watched him leave and was tempted to call Kyle and take him up on that drinks date.

~

Gabe was *restless* . . .

There was no other word to describe the way he felt. He couldn't settle down. The house just seemed empty and huge. It was the first time he'd ever felt that way about his home. While he co-owned the house with Chase, his brother also owned an apartment in Camps Bay and often stayed there when he was in the country. Of course, he had a housecleaning staff, but none of them lived on the premises.

Gabe hadn't shared the house with anybody in years and he was usually content with the peace and quiet. Tonight though, his excess energy was driving him crazy. He had contacted a couple of the women in his so-called "black" book (it was in fact just a folder on his phone) but in the end hadn't been able to summon up the energy or inclination to arrange a date with any of them. He had ended the calls with vague promises to contact them again "sometime" and now found that he was unable to concentrate on anything.

He glanced at the clock—it was just after eight—and decided to head out to Manny's for a couple of drinks. A few of games of darts, entertaining company, harmless flirting . . . just what the doctor ordered.

So he was more than a little confused when he found himself ringing the Richmond doorbell less than fifteen minutes later. There was no answer at first so he depressed the button again and listened to the deep *bingbong* echo through the house. He was about to ring it for a third time when the door was jerked open by a frazzled looking Mike Richmond. The tall man glared at Gabe over the rims of his glasses for a few moments before stepping aside and allowing him in. He didn't say anything, merely led the way to the den. The room reeked of cigar smoke—it was the only room where he was allowed to indulge in his habit—and there was a movie paused on the big screen smart TV.

Eyeing the older man once more, he saw that Mike was wearing a handsome smoking jacket—a prank gift from Bobbi—and a pair of comfortable slacks. He appeared to be having a relaxing evening in his man cave. Mike Richmond rarely relaxed, so Gabe felt a bit guilty for disturbing him.

"Something wrong, Gabriel?" the older man asked, refilling a Waterford crystal whiskey glass and lifting the matching decanter questioningly. Gabe nodded and unbuttoned the top two buttons of his shirt. He usually changed into less-restrictive clothing after coming from the office but he was still wearing his crisp shirt and suit trousers—at least he'd lost the tie and jacket somewhere along the way.

He took the filled whiskey glass from Mike, unbuttoning his cuff at the same time and rolling the sleeve up to his elbow before switching the glass to the other hand and doing the same with the opposite cuff. Mike had dropped down into his easy chair again and was watching him with those astute amber eyes that rarely missed much. Gabe avoided his scrutiny and sat down opposite him, taking a sip of the Glenlivet and leaning back on the leather recliner with a slight sigh.

"Well?" Mike prompted after a long silence, taking a puff from his cigar.

"Can I have one of those?" Gabe asked, and Mike waved the blunt cigar at the table between their chairs to the mahogany humidor residing there.

"Help yourself . . ."

Gabe grunted a thanks and took his time picking one of the expensive Cubans. When he found one to his liking, he rolled it appreciatively between his thumb and index finger and took a deep whiff before reaching for the cutter and snipping off the end.

"What are you watching?" Gabe asked around the cigar that he now had clenched between his teeth. He rarely lit the cigars and he wasn't sure if he'd indulge tonight either.

"*Die Hard*," the older man answered.

"Aah. One of the good ones." Gabe grinned.

"You're not going to tell me what you're doing here?"

"It'll keep," Gabe responded, picking up the remote control that was resting beside the humidor. "I'd rather watch John McClane kick butt."

~

It was another half an hour filled with witty one-liners and loud explosions before either of them spoke again.

"Bobbi not in?" Gabe asked casually, blowing on the end of the cigar that he'd lit ten minutes earlier. "She loves this movie."

"I haven't seen her but Faye told me that she's gone out with some friends. About damned time, you ask me," Mike muttered, keeping his eyes on the screen.

"What do you mean?"

"I mean the girl seems to forget she's female half of the time. It will do her a world of good to spend time with other women. And your buddy—De Lucci's—wife is a damned fine lady."

"So she's not out with that guy?"

The older man's gaze sharpened.

"What guy?"

"She met him at the pub this afternoon and left with him. I thought she might have gone out with him . . ." And the thought had made him feel close to murderous. Mike continued to inspect him with those shrewd eyes. "Uh . . . anyway, do you know what time she'll be home?"

Mike shrugged, shifting that uncomfortable stare to the television screen and wincing as he watched Bruce Willis drag his bare feet through broken glass.

"Who knows? These things can go on for hours."

"Is it safe for her to be out that late?" That pulled Mike's attention from the on-screen action.

"It's none of my business how late she stays out. I'm well aware that she'd be living on her own by now if not for the fact that she opened her shop. I can't tell her what to do."

"You're not concerned?"

"She won't drink and drive, she won't take risks—she's perfectly fine."

"Anything could happen . . ."

"What's this really about, Gabriel?" he asked astutely, and Gabe backed off immediately. How could he answer a question he didn't know the answer to?

"Nothing, I was just a bit concerned. You're a wealthy man, Mike. Have you even considered that Bobbi could be at risk because of that?"

"Of course I have. When my children were small I had security details on them, you know that. Now that they're adults, my sons take care of their own security and Bobbi is well aware of the dangers. You know my daughter . . . stubborn to her core, that girl. So I compromised—I provide security at her shop but her personal life is just that. No big, bulky men trailing after her wherever she goes. Now do you mind? I'd like to enjoy my movie without this constant chatter."

Gabe shut up but he was starting to feel restless again. How could Mike be so damned sanguine about Bobbi's safety and security? It wasn't anything Gabe had even considered until just now and he was suddenly petrified that Bobbi would be kidnapped at any moment. He had lost interest in the movie but kept his eyes pinned to the screen even while his mind raced. Why had he never considered the risks to Bobbi before now?

It was making him edgy.

He chewed the end of his cigar and glared at the screen without really seeing the action. As soon as he realized the credits were rolling, he glanced at his watch. Just after ten, too early for her to come home yet.

"What do you want to watch next?" he asked Mike, and the older man's brows leapt to his hairline. "One of the sequels?"

"Since you were barely paying attention to the last movie, I doubt a second one could hold your interest. Do you want to tell me what the hell is going on in that head of yours now, Gabriel? Something at work?"

"Nothing's going on . . . I'm fine. I just thought I'd come over and hang out for a bit."

"Hang out?" Mike Richmond choked back a laugh. "With me? I'm sure you have friends closer to your own age to *hang out* with."

"Well, I thought Bobbi would be around," he lied. "If you don't want to watch a movie, why don't we play a game of billiards?"

"Gabriel, I'm a boring old fogie and I'm headed to bed. Stick around and watch another movie if you really feel inclined to—help yourself to anything in the kitchen. Faye's staying with her daughter tonight, so you'll have the place to yourself."

"But . . ."

"But nothing. Set the alarm on your way out," The older man pushed himself to his feet and ambled to the door. "Good night."

"'Night."

Gabe sighed as the door swung shut behind the man and got up to flip absently through the selection of disks beside the Blu-Ray player. Deciding to stick to another modern "classic," he inserted

Con Air into the machine and halfheartedly sat back to watch. Ten minutes into the movie he picked up his phone.

~

Bobbi glanced down at her vibrating phone and did a double take when she saw who was calling. She *ignored* the call before refocusing her attention on Bronwyn, who was sitting in the center of their circle, and then blushing furiously when she caught sight of the object in the woman's hands.

"Oh my God, that thing's a monster!" Alice squealed.

"It's got *nothing* on Bryce." Bronwyn waved the *thing* in her hand dismissively.

"Or Sandro," Theresa added loyally.

"Please, Rick could give that thing a serious run for its money." Lisa giggled.

"Hmmm . . . now that I look at it from this angle it's definitely smaller than Pierre," Alice said with a barely suppressed smile. "Why are we doing this again? None of us really *need* these things."

"Does anybody ever really need one that big?" Bobbi asked, appalled. Bronwyn was hosting a sex-toy party, and all the goodies were samples from a well-known adult shop in the area. The other four women all swiveled their heads in Bobbi's direction, varying degrees of pity on their faces.

"And that answers your question, Alice. God, Bobbi, we need to find you a boyfriend!" Lisa groaned.

"We-ell, I kind of met a guy today," she informed them smugly, and they all squealed, the gargantuan vibrator instantly forgotten. Bobbi really enjoyed these girly sessions with her friends. She had never really had much feminine influence in her life before meeting Theresa a couple of years before. All of her friends growing up had been male, and while Gabe's mother and Faye had done their utmost to steer her in a more feminine direction, Bobbi had been so determined to fit in with her all-male family that the two women had given up halfway through Bobbi's teens. It was only after meeting Theresa and the rest of the women that Bobbi had realized how very much she had missed out on in foregoing female friends for so many years.

"And you're only telling us this *now*?" Bronwyn groused.

"It didn't come up before now," she shrugged, deliberately casual. She winced when her words caused even more squealing. One of the things she would never get used to was how high-pitched other women could be. She really couldn't fathom why they screamed so much.

"Tell us everything," Lisa demanded, and everybody else nodded encouragingly.

"There's nothing much to tell . . . I was . . ." Her phone buzzed again and she glanced at the display. Gabe, *again* . . . what was his problem?

"Is that him now?" Theresa asked, her voice—like her personality—gentler and less demanding than the other women.

"No. It's Gabe," she said with grimace, *ignoring* the call again.

"Is that wise?" Theresa asked again. "What if it's an emergency or something?"

Bobbi sighed, conceding Theresa's point.

"Well if he calls back she'll answer it, just in case," Alice said reasonably. "So tell us about this guy in the meantime?"

"There's nothing much to tell." Bobbi smiled. "Jason introduced us and he asked me out."

"What's his name?" Alice wanted to know.

"Is he good looking?" Lisa interjected.

"What does he do?" That was from Bronwyn.

"Is he nice?" Trust Theresa to ask that question.

"His name's Kyle, he's good-looking; tall and blond . . . wonderful gray eyes."

"Just my type," Bron sighed. Her husband, Bryce, was tall and blond.

"Mine too," Lisa agreed; she was married to Bryce's equally blond brother.

"Let her finish," Alice prompted.

"He's a landscape architect." They all swooned at that.

"Outdoorsy," Alice sighed blissfully. "I love them outdoorsy."

"He does rock climbing to relax," Bobbi continued, ignoring the interruption.

"Well, Rick would probably *love* him," Lisa grumbled. Her husband was an adrenaline junkie who enjoyed any and all kinds of extreme sports. He had toned it a down a bit since the birth of their son the year before though.

"He's very nice," Bobbi concluded.

"But . . . ?" the ever-observant Theresa prompted. She might be quiet and sweet but she rarely missed anything.

"No buts . . . he's nice, interesting, handsome, intelligent. I like him." Now the rest of them were eying her skeptically as well.

"I'm with Theresa," Bronwyn said. "There's a but in there somewhere."

Her phone buzzed again and she shut her eyes for a brief second before lifting it to her ear.

"Gabe?" Her voice was more abrupt than she'd intended it to be.

"Hey," his deep voice sounded uncertain. "Are you okay?"

"I'm fine . . . why?"

"It's nothing . . ." There was a long pause. What was going on with him?

"Gabe, is everything okay? Is my dad okay? Billy?"

"No. Everything's fine. It's rather late, Bobbi."

"I know. Which is why I don't understand why you're calling me."

"When do you think you'll be home?"

"What?" She actually drew the phone away from her ear to peer at it incredulously for a moment. "*Why?*"

"Your dad is worried."

"He is? How do you know that?"

"I spoke with him earlier." His voice sounded weird.

"Well then, I'll call him and tell him not to worry," she said, and there was another long silence before he spoke again.

"Don't. He's asleep."

"What? Gabe, you're not making any sense. Are you drunk?"

"No . . . I mean I had a few drinks but nothing . . ." He sighed, the sound an exasperated huff, and broke off in midsentence. "Look, I just wanted to know when you'd be home."

"That's none of your business," she told him.

"Where are you? I could escort you home," he suggested.

"For God's sake, Gabe, you're being ridiculous. I'm hanging up now." She disconnected the call before he had a chance to respond and switched the phone off.

"And that," Theresa said, pointing at the phone, "would be the *but* we were discussing earlier."

"Oh he's a butt alright," Bobbi seethed, and Lisa grinned.

"Do you want to talk about what happened the other night?" Theresa asked and the rest of them nodded encouragingly.

"I was drunk and I kissed Gabe," she said, and more than one pair of eyes widened; only Theresa looked unsurprised.

"What did he do?" Alice asked.

"He kissed me back at first and then he stopped. And later that night, he was in his room with his shirt off and I . . . touched him," she confessed, trying to keep her embarrassment at bay but failing.

"Touched him? How? Where?" Bronwyn questioned.

"His chest, he has a gorgeous chest." There was a chorus of agreeing hums from the other women. "I touched him and he let me, before stopping me."

"And what was this phone call about?" Lisa asked, nodding toward the phone in Bobbi's hand.

Bobbi sighed and told them everything else that had happened over the weekend since The Kiss and leading up to the bizarre phone call. By the time she had finished they were all staring at her in disbelief.

"Firstly, Kyle Foster sounds adorable and if it weren't for the fact that you're head over heels in love with your idiotic friend, I would totally encourage you to tap that," Lisa said. "And secondly, Gabe really *is* a butt but he sounds like a totally confused butt." The other women laughed but Lisa ignored them, keeping her focus on Bobbi's flushed face.

"Personally, I think he wants you and he has no idea how to deal with that," Theresa stated.

"I agree," Bronwyn said.

"Me too," Alice concurred and Lisa indicated her agreement with a thumbs up.

"I'm not his type," Bobbi said, shaking her head.

"I wasn't Sandro's type," Theresa pointed out.

"Pierre preferred tall, skinny, flawless models," the short, slightly plump, and scarred Alice said.

"Rick liked to date adrenaline junkies. A nerdy, bookshop owner was a far cry from his usual girlfriends," Lisa added.

"Tastes change and what men—or women—think they want, isn't necessarily the type of person they end up with," Bronwyn said.

Sage words that made perfect sense of course, but none of them had had a years-long friendship to lose with the men in question.

Bobbi shook her head and pointed to the abandoned vibrator that lay off to the side.

"What else can that thing do?"

"It can't cuddle you afterward, that's for sure," Alice said with a frown.

"Or whisper Italian endearments in your ear." This from Theresa who had a dreamy gleam in her eyes.

"Oh my God, you guys are the worst! I give up." Bronwyn tossed the thing to the side just as her husband, Bryce, walked into the room. It landed at his feet and he looked down at it blankly. A flush crept up his face to the tips of his ears. His sharp ice-blue eyes flew up to meet his wife's, and she had both hands over her mouth either to stifle a laugh or a scream, Bobbi couldn't be sure which.

He said something in sign language that made Bronwyn go bright red, and the other women who could all understand sign language as well, laughed. Bobbi, who wasn't as adept as they were, felt lost.

Bryce's stern face melted into a grin, which made him go from scary to gorgeous in a split second.

"After Massive Marvin, nothing you ladies do can surprise me anymore," he said in his carefully modulated voice, referring to a stripper they had all fawned over the previous year on another girls' night. Bronwyn groaned and covered her eyes, causing Bryce's grin to widen. "Anyway, I just came to check when you were wrapping it up? I've been getting frantic texts."

"Sandro?" Theresa asked with an eye roll, once Bryce's eyes were on her and the man shook his head.

"Surprisingly not. Gabe." Every eye in the room focused on Bobbi, who felt her blood pressure rising.

"That . . ." Words failed her and she shook her head.

"Well it *is* getting late and we all have work in the morning," Theresa pointed out. "And you have a long drive ahead of you, Bobbi."

"And since none of you are going to buy any of this stuff, we may as well end now," Bronwyn said.

"Hold on, I didn't say I wouldn't buy a pair of the . . ." Lisa glared up at Bryce, who was reading her lips avidly. "Do you *mind?*"

He laughed and left the room with a wave. The group disbanded soon afterward and Bobbi was left to seethe on the drive home. The roads were fairly empty, which cut ten minutes off her drive. She nearly bypassed her own driveway to head over to Gabe's but common sense prevailed; she would confront him in the morning. She'd had just about enough of him this weekend.

CHAPTER SIX

She let herself into the house, annoyed to find that the alarm was off. She sighed at her father's carelessness. There were security guards all over the premises, and the property was surrounded by a large electrical fence, but he had to do his bit too. As she headed for the stairs, she heard the explosive noise of an action movie coming from the den and changed course, meaning to give her father a piece of her mind for his negligence.

"The alarm won't just set its . . ." Her voice trailed off when Gabe's tall figure rose from one of the large leather recliners.

"You're back," he stated unnecessarily. She didn't respond, and a quick glance around the room confirmed that her father wasn't present.

"Where's my dad?" she asked.

"He's asleep."

"Then why are you here?"

"I was waiting for you to come home. I was concerned about you."

"You have no right to be *concerned* about me." She tossed her bag onto one of the chairs and folded her arms across her chest, trying to appear in control despite the fact that her stomach was swarming with butterflies.

"So what did you and that Kyle guy talk about this afternoon?" he asked, choosing to ignore her last statement, as he took a step toward her. She maintained her position, refusing to step back even though the distance between them now seemed too close for comfort.

"Not that it's any of your business, but he asked me out." Her voice was starting to sound shaky; he took another step toward her and Bobbi started to feel like prey.

"You're not going out with him," he murmured confidently, his third step bringing him to within an inch of her. She kept her gaze trained on his chest, refusing to meet his eyes, hating that he knew her so well.

"What makes you so sure of that?" She tried to sound strong but instead her voice emerged on an uncertain whisper, and he used his forefinger to angle her chin until she met his eyes.

"Because you want *me*."

With just four words one of her deepest, darkest secrets was out in the open. It lay exposed and writhing like a wounded animal between them and Bobbi was absolutely helpless to deny it. She knew that the truth was there to see, on her face and in her eyes. He could hear it in her ragged breathing and feel it in her racing pulse when he reached down to cup her fragile neck in the palm of his hands. He used his thumbs to stroke the underside of her jaw, sending shudders of pure sensation through her already trembling body.

"Gabe . . . ," she whispered, wetting her lips as her eyes fell to his mouth. She watched that mouth stretch into a beautiful smile and then form the most miraculous four words in the world.

"I want you too."

"Oh." The sound was a gasp of wonder and disbelief. How was this possible?

"I haven't been able to stop thinking about that kiss," he went on to say. "Or how your hands felt on me. How in the hell have I not noticed your gorgeous body before?"

"Stop," she whispered, and his eyes darkened in confusion.

"What?"

"Stop talking . . . ," she clarified, before going on tiptoes and plastering her mouth to his. His breath was half gasp and half groan as he leaned into the kiss and took control of it. His hands left her neck and buried themselves in her hair, tugging her head back so that he could deepen the kiss. She parted her lips and his tongue swept in, bringing with it a tidal wave of sensation. She savored every taste, every smell, every sensation . . . She didn't know how her hands had gotten under his shirt but they were on his hard chest, exploring the contours, the firmness, the dusting of hair, then around his waist up his strong back until her fingers were digging into his wide shoulders.

She was vaguely aware of him shifting her until her back was braced against the wall. He lifted his head, his eyes glazed, his cheeks flushed, and his mouth swollen.

"Okay?" he asked, and she nodded. He barely seemed to register the movement before his lips were on her neck, licking and sucking their way down to her collarbone and nuzzling aside the strap of her tank top.

"These damned tops of yours drive me crazy," he said thickly, bringing a hand up to assist with the task. Bobbi watched in a daze as he pushed the strap down her shoulder, around her bent elbow and then picked up her wrist to slip it completely off. He repeated the process with the other strap, until just the slight slope of her breasts held the garment up. He paused to inspect his handiwork for a brief moment before manacling both of her wrists in one of his hands and pinning them to the wall above her head.

"Forget what I said this afternoon." His eyes ate her up, lingering hungrily on her breasts. "Never wear a bra."

He brought his free hand up between their bodies and lightly traced the outer edge of one breast with his fingers. Bobbi's breath caught and held as she watched that large hand, fascinated by the stark contrast between his dark flesh and the whiteness of her top. One long finger brushed across the sensitive skin above the cotton and Bobbi's knees weakened.

"Please," she whimpered, but he was concentrating so fiercely on the task at hand that he barely seemed to hear her. After *forever* his hand ever so softly closed over one of her breasts, and he squeezed gently, testing the weight and learning the shape of it. The barrier of cotton between his skin and hers added an element of erotic frustration that drove Bobbi wild. She pushed herself into his hand but he released his hold almost immediately. His hands switched tasks and the other breast received the same tormenting treatment.

"Gabe . . . more," she begged, and this time he listened, and his thumb flicked her excruciatingly sensitive peak—the friction of thumb and fabric against the engorged tip made her arch against him, and he hissed when she pushed up against his straining erection.

"God," he groaned, releasing her wrists and sweeping her toward the recliner that he had been occupying when she'd first entered the room. He sat down and arranged her on top of him until she sat straddling his lap, her wet core very firmly wedged against his hardness—the denim of her shorts and the fabric of his suit doing nothing to disguise either's arousal.

He dragged the tank down to her waist and then just stared at her naked breasts for a long while.

"Jesus, they're perfect," he said reverently, bringing his hands up to cup and explore, tease and torment. He plumped one up and brought it to his lips, laving the tortured crest gently with his hot tongue before sucking it roughly into his mouth. The combination of tender and tough felt amazing, and when he repeated the process with her other breast, she was helpless to prevent the inevitable from happening. She had wanted him for so long that she was primed for an explosion, having his mouth on her breasts while she instinctively rode the ridge of his erection was more than enough to send her spinning into the biggest orgasm of her life.

~

She was coming! The knowledge nearly propelled Gabe down the same blissful path but he somehow managed to keep himself under control. *Barely*.

She was so damned hot. Her body tensed, her breath hitched, and the already sexy back and forth movement of her hips became a deep, slow grind as she pushed herself against him, taking her pleasure like a woman who knew exactly what she wanted and how to get it. He tried to prolong it, sucking the hard bead of her nipple into his mouth and flicking it with his tongue to maximize her pleasure, while his free hand played with her other breast, stroking the swollen tip with his thumb.

She came quietly—with a held breath, a series of soft moans, and then a long exhalation. She wasn't a screamer, his Bobbi, and damned if he didn't find that a huge turn-on too. He gave her nipple one last, regretful kiss before grudgingly releasing the firm globe of her breast. She slumped against him with her face buried in his neck.

He could feel her wet heat against his aching penis and it was all he could do to prevent himself from thrusting against her to achieve his own satisfaction. He wrapped his arms around her waist, allowing his hands to drape over her firm, curvy bum and held her trembling body against his.

He wanted her more than his next breath, but he wasn't going to allow this to go any further until they'd established a few ground rules. If push came to shove, their friendship was too important to mess up, and if she felt that it wouldn't be able to survive a temporary affair then this "interlude" would have to be the extent of it. He figured that it should be relatively easy to return to normal with Bobbi, whom he already cared for deeply, after they'd gotten this craziness out of their systems. He just needed to know that she would be on board with the mutually beneficial arrangement he had in mind for them.

After a few painfully long moments, her breathing finally regulated and her limp, sated body started to grow tense as awareness returned to her. She brought her hands between their bodies and pushed against his chest until he loosened his grip around her waist enough for her to slide into a sitting position on his lap. He bit back a groan at the movement, still unbearably turned on and she grimaced apologetically.

"Sorry," she murmured, tucking the damp hair of her fringe behind an ear.

"It's okay," he said.

"Doesn't feel okay." She deliberately slid herself up and then down against the hard column that she was straddling. "Feels rather uncomfortable to me."

"*Stop* that." His fingers dug into her flesh when she did another sinuous up and down shimmy. Where the hell did this seductive minx come from? He would never have taken Bobbi for such an accomplished tease.

"But I want to take care of it." She pouted, and he couldn't resist kissing that pout away. He kept the kiss short and sweet, not wanting to get carried away again and this time when she leaned back, he took the opportunity to—quite regretfully—drag her top back up over her pert breasts.

"Later," he promised. "But we have to talk, Bobbi." Her eyes reflected concern as she leaned back to study his face.

"Yes," she agreed. "We do."

"Like I said before, I want you . . . *very* much. It's weird having these . . . *feelings* for you but the attraction is so overpowering that getting you naked is pretty much all I've been able to think about over the last two days. But there are other factors to consider here, sweetheart."

∽

Bobbi understood that this was easier for her because she'd felt this way about him for years but for him it was brand new. He probably felt as weird as she had that first time she had looked at Gabe and saw someone other than just a good friend. She would never forget that moment, on her birthday six years before. Gabe had been out of town on business. He had rushed to get back before midnight and had come straight to the Richmond house to present her with his gift—a charm bracelet filled with tiny screwdrivers, cars, wrenches, nuts, and bolts. The trinkets must have taken him months to collect and it had been absolutely perfect. Wholly impractical since she couldn't wear it to work but perfect nonetheless.

She had looked up at the man standing in her doorway, so uncharacteristically disheveled, with messy hair, skewed tie, and wrinkled clothing, and had fallen hopelessly in love with him. From one breath to the next he had transitioned from platonic friend and trusted confidante to the single most important person in her life, and she had wanted him with a fierceness that still shocked her to this day.

They would have to take things slowly. The transition from being friends into a couple would be strange for them as well as their family and friends, who would be blindsided by the match and possibly uncomfortable with it too.

"We'll sort it out," she assured him, linking her hands with his and squeezing encouragingly. She smiled and kissed him, happy that she was free to do so. He tasted faintly of whiskey and cigars. Delicious.

He returned the kiss, running his tongue over her lips and then sucking her lower lip gently into his mouth.

"Hmmm," he groaned, the sound a masculine rumble that she felt against her chest. He dragged his mouth away from hers with obvious reluctance. "I've been wanting to suck on that juicy lip for a while now." He ran a rough thumb over her lip and she caught it in her mouth, nipping wickedly at the pad.

"Come on, Bobbi," he growled. "Time enough for this later. We need to talk."

"Fine." She rolled her eyes. He clearly needed to get this out of his system. "I'm all ears."

"This is awkward because this isn't a scenario I ever imagined," he said. "The women I . . . the ones before, they knew the score. But you and I, that's complicated."

"What's complicated about it?" she asked, a sinking sensation forming in the pit of her stomach. There was nothing complicated about this, they were attracted to each other and now that they had both acknowledged that attraction they were free to be together. Simple.

"We're friends, good friends, when this ends—when we eventually get this *thing* between us out of our systems—what happens to our friendship? If there's any danger of losing you, Bobbi, it just wouldn't be worth it for a few encounters of meaningless sex."

Meaningless sex? That's all he wanted?

Bobbi almost laughed but she managed to bite back the impulse, knowing that the sound that emerged from her throat would be filled with disappointment.

Of *course* that's what he wanted! She was such a dolt.

Be careful what you wish for. That was how the saying went and it had never been truer than at this very moment. Bobbi had always wished for him to want her as much as she wanted him, to look at her with desire in his eyes and that wish had been more than granted. There was so much heat in his regard that she felt scorched by it and his zipper was fighting a losing battle against the hard physical proof of his lust. She had what she had hungered for day after day for years but she wanted more than that.

All those years of wishing for him to want her, it had never occurred to her to ask that he love her too. Why would she wish for something she already had? Gabe loved her, he always had—but he wasn't *in* love with her.

"So what do you suggest?" she asked, her voice sounding hollow even to her own ears, but he didn't seem to notice.

"I was thinking we could come to an understanding. We keep this affair and our friendship separate . . ."

What? She didn't understand what that meant. "I don't understand."

"It would be better if nobody else knew about it. If we kept it between us," he said, keeping his face averted. She was thankful for that because she didn't want him to see the pain in her eyes. "That way it would be easier for us to go back to being friends afterward. No unpleasant and intrusive questions from family and friends, you know?" She nodded absently in response to the question, feeling a piece of her heart wither and die with every word he spoke.

How stupid of her to think that he would want a proper relationship with someone like her and that she could show the world how she felt about him. How foolish of her to fantasize about actually staking a claim on him and keeping all those annoying blondes at bay by right of possession.

Her fantasies were completely laughable in light of that fact that *Gabe* wanted to hide the attraction he felt for her in a dark and moldy place where it would be unable to flourish. Instead it would shrivel and eventually die and they would walk away and carry on as if it had never existed.

Their family and friends would remain completely oblivious while Gabe slept with her in secret as if what he felt for her was something to be ashamed.

≈

Gabe watched Bobbi closely but her expression revealed nothing—it was as if a porcelain mask had slid over her face—her features perfectly frozen. He was desperate for her to accept this agreement. He didn't know what he would do if she refused—she simply couldn't refuse.

"We could have everything, Bobbi," he insisted. "The sex *and* our friendship. Nothing has to change; we just have to keep it under wraps. It's the only way to keep things *normal*. Once other people get involved, they'll start placing their own expectations on us. That wouldn't be fair on either of us. This is our business not theirs. It's the only way I can think of to protect you." And he really wanted to protect her. He didn't want her friends forcing their opinions on her, didn't want her brothers or his to make her feel like she was doing something wrong by being with him, and, yes, he was protecting himself too. God knew, her brothers, her father, and his mother—everybody would be horrified. They would insist he "do the right thing" and when he refused it could cause a rift between their families. He was on very shaky ground here and needed to tread carefully.

"So how would it work?" she asked, and he exhaled shakily, relieved that she had broken her silence. "Will we have some kind of secret password or handshake when we want to sleep together?"

He laughed uncertainly, not sure of her mood. Her words had been sarcastic but her eyes looked . . . sad. He swallowed past the lump that had formed in his throat. He didn't want to hurt her, he was suggesting this arrangement so that he could avoid hurting her—full disclosure was essential, that way she wouldn't form any unreasonable expectations.

"You'd come round to my place as you normally would and we'll see where the mood takes us."

"So we won't have to set up some kind of schedule then? Sex tonight, darts at the pub tomorrow . . . that kind of thing? I mean, I've never had a friend with benefits before, I don't know how it works."

"This is new to me too, Bobbi." He wasn't deaf to the cynicism in her voice but was unsure how to respond to it.

She pushed herself up and off him, rearranging her clothing to the best of her ability. He felt the loss keenly and leaned forward to brace his elbows on his knees—staring at her intently, not sure what to expect next. Her face still had a dewy, post-orgasmic glow to it and her lips were swollen from his earlier attentions. She was so damned sexy—he wanted her back on his lap, wanted to feel her tightness close around him as he pushed himself into her, but he needed her to agree to his terms before he could have her and waiting for her answer was excruciating.

"Well how does it usually work with your blondes?" she asked pointedly, sitting down on the chair opposite his—the one her father had occupied earlier.

He usually took his other female companions out to dinner, dancing . . . some kind of event. Followed by a night of sex at their homes—which insured a quick and easy getaway afterward. Bobbi wouldn't be getting the fancy dinners; he acknowledged guiltily but then appeased himself with the reminder that it wasn't her scene anyway.

"Our arrangement will be different," he muttered.

"Oh yes, of course . . ." She snapped her fingers as if just remembering. "We won't be seen together."

"Bobbi," he chastised miserably, hating her unpredictable mood. She clearly wasn't receptive to his idea. "What do *you* want then?"

The question shut her up and she peered at him mutely before shrugging.

"Fine, let's do this." She held her right hand over her chest and the left hand up as if she was about to swear an oath. "I, Roberta Rebecca Richmond, hereby do solemnly swear to expect nothing more than sex from one Gabriel Andrew Braddock. I promise to not disclose details of our affair to any third parties, promise to not behave inappropriately toward him in public places and, once our affair has run its course, I promise to never speak of it again and to go back to being Gabriel Andrew Braddock's bestest buddy. So help me God."

"Bobbi, you're making it seem . . ."

"Cold?" she finished, her voice so icy it nearly froze him on the spot and he nodded. "Cynical? Clinical? Maybe because that's what it is."

"Then tell me what *you* want." He repeated his previous demand, not bothering to keep the exasperation out of his voice.

"Nothing more or less than you're willing to offer." She shrugged before sending him a seductive look that—despite his tension—immediately grabbed his attention.

She got up and walked to the door, and his eyes remained riveted on the deliberate swing of her tight behind. She threw him a look over her shoulder and combined it with a sultry smile.

"Come on, Gabe . . . I'll walk you home."

❧

Bobbi didn't know what the hell she was doing. This was going to end in heartbreak and she knew it . . . but she didn't want to go through her entire life without being with him. She couldn't force him to love her the way she loved him so she would take whatever meager substitute he was offering her, and when it ended she would try damned hard to keep her end of the bargain and go back to being his friend. She felt weak and stupid and while her brain screamed at her not to be foolish, her heart urged her to accept his sordid little arrangement and be grateful for it.

In the end her heart had won the fierce battle and so here she was, holding his hand in hers as she dragged him across the lawn toward the fence between their homes. There was a security gate between the two properties that their parents had had installed when the Braddock and Richmond children had still been small—it had been put there to stop the kids from creating shortcuts by climbing the trees that bordered their yards and jumping over the high fences, especially after Chase broke his arm. Once Bobbi had led Gabe through the gate and was safely out of view of her house and numerous security guards, Gabe stopped moving. Bobbi glanced back impatiently but all she could see in the darkness were the whites of his eyes before he tugged on her hand and dragged her into his arms.

She was enveloped in his scent, by his warmth, and then before she could brace herself, completely devoured by his hungry mouth. She moaned and gave herself over to him. There was no finesse to the kiss, it was a meeting of lips, tongue, and teeth, and it made Bobbi feel wanton, wild, and starved for more.

"God, sweetheart, you drive me crazy." His voice sounded feral in the dark as he forced the words out between gasps. "Come on."

This time he led the way as he tugged her to his house, up the porch steps, and into the foyer. His hands were all over her body as he led her into one of the rooms closest to the front entrance. A quick glance around confirmed that they were in his study and she had no time for any other observation before he sat her down on a large sofa and knelt between her legs.

"Gabe, I think . . ."

He held a finger up to her lips.

"Ssh, sweetheart, no more talk," he begged gently. "There's something I've been meaning to do all evening." Bobbi grabbed his finger between her lips and sucked the tip hungrily, watching his face tighten as he moaned shakily. It was amazing how such a simple gesture was able to render a strong man like Gabe as weak as a kitten.

"Oh?" she asked huskily, after running her tongue up and down the length of his index finger before releasing his hand to fall limply to his side. "What could that be?"

"You're killing me, Bobbi." He laughed unsteadily. His trembling hands went to the hem of her top and dragged it up and off before she even had time to blink, and then he sat back on his heels and just studied the skin that lay bared to his gaze. She fought the urge to cover her breasts, battling her instinctive shyness and kept her arms down, enjoying the appreciative look in his eyes as they studied the slight curves of her body.

"I love these." She drew in a sharp breath as he bent over to plant a reverent kiss on one pointed tip and then the other. "They're absolutely perfect . . ."

"Small," she lamented, and he glared up at her.

"*Perfect*," he maintained before he lavished each tip with even more attention until she fell back onto the sofa and writhed beneath him, lost in the sensation of his mouth and hands tormenting the overly sensitive peaks. After what seemed like hours, he raised his head to study the wet, rosy crests in satisfaction.

"My turn." Bobbi could barely get the two words out but he understood her well enough and his head jerked up, while his eyes narrowed in anticipation. She sat up and tugged his shirttails from his trousers before burrowing her questing hands beneath the expensive fabric to find the velvety warmth beneath. She unbuttoned his shirt leisurely, kissing each wedge of skin as it was revealed, marveling at how hard, muscled flesh could be so satiny to the touch. When she'd unfastened the last button, she parted the two sides and scrutinized his muscular chest in purely feminine appreciation.

He was gorgeous: all bronzed flesh, hard muscles, and downy cinnamon hair. Her slightly work-roughened hands entangled themselves in the sprinkling of hair on his chest before making their fluttering way to his flat male nipples. When she found the rigid nubs, she thumbed them experimentally and smiled in delight when Gabe sucked in a harsh breath.

"You like that?" she asked huskily, glancing up to meet his burning eyes. No answer was required . . . he seemed to have relished it! "Great, then you're probably going to *love* this!" She dipped her head and drew one of the stiff crests deeply into her mouth. Gabe made a strangled sound and jerked violently before grabbing her head between his hands and trying to drag her away from her task. Bobbi ignored him and continued to lick and suck seductively, relishing the musky taste of him.

She shifted her attention to the other peak and nipped at it sharply, before licking away the sting. Gabe's breath was coming in harsh pants and when he once again tried to drag her away, she complied and latched onto his mouth almost aggressively, relishing this new role of seductress. Gabe's helpless groan was muffled against her mouth and he allowed her to take the initiative, his tongue playing court to hers.

Eventually he began to dominate their love play, as she bowed to his experience. His fingers initially fumbled with the button fly of her shorts before he found a rhythm and seductively undid one after the other. He tugged at the waist once he had them all unfastened and Bobbi raised her hips allowing him to wrestle off the tight scrap of material. After he had tossed the shorts aside he leaned back to admire what he'd revealed. He shook his head in wonder as his scrutinizing look traveled down her slender torso to her concave stomach, her tiny waist, and the delicate flare of her hips.

"Dear God, Bobbi, you're . . . ravishing." He breathed.

Damn him, she adored him. She wished she didn't but it was hard not to when he was staring at her with such reverence in his eyes.

Gabe smiled at the sight of the plain white cotton bikini panties she was wearing. Bobbi probably had nothing that could be labeled lingerie in her underwear drawer. His Bobbi was a cotton-panties girl through and through. Lingerie was not for the practical mechanic, but he figured she would look pretty damned sexy in silk and lace too and vowed there and then to buy her some lingerie. It would definitely drive him wild to see her in overalls and fantasize about what sexy confections she might be wearing beneath them!

The very thought now had him so revved up that it was difficult not to rip the aforementioned panties off and bury himself so completely within her that he would be lost forever. He was irresistibly drawn back to her breasts, bending to tug one of her raspberry pink tips into his mouth. She gasped and arched back, offering herself up to him. He maneuvered her until she was lying down on the sofa and he was on top of her with his hips cradled between the welcoming warmth of her thighs. Not once during the move had he lifted his head from her tormented breast and she was groaning and pleading with him to let up on his exquisite torture. He eventually did, but only to create havoc with the other, neglected nipple.

Despite her pleas for him to stop tormenting her, Bobbi was contradictorily arching her back and thrusting her chest closer to his mouth. He laughed triumphantly and claimed her lips for yet another hungry kiss. The kiss was torrid enough to leave her limp and breathless, and she watched languidly as he got up to divest himself of his already unbuttoned shirt, then his shoes, and lastly his trousers and socks. Soon he wore only his black briefs, which did absolutely nothing to conceal his fierce erection from her. Her hungry eyes were riveted to the straining bulge between his thickly muscled thighs, and she was trembling uncontrollably when he settled back down between her spread legs. He smiled down at her before, without a word, lifting one of her legs and resting the slender ankle on his broad shoulder.

"Gabe . . . what are you doing?" she asked in confusion, but he merely smiled down at her, before kissing her inner ankle. His warm, large hands circled the ankle, then traveled slowly down the length of her leg purposely allowing the back of his hand to lightly brush against the warm wetness between her legs, his knuckles grazing the moist material of her panties, before his hand stroked its way sensuously back up to her ankle. He then repeated the whole agonizing process with her other leg, this time allowing his hand to linger longer at her sensitive core.

He grinned down at her and he *should* have looked ridiculous with his face framed by her feet but instead he looked absolutely wicked and oh-so-sexy. He winked mischievously before hooking his thumbs in the sides of her panties and sliding them up over her hips with tormenting slowness. Bobbi was arching her hips impatiently and he bent to kiss her lips gently.

"Patience, my sweet," he whispered against her mouth. "This is going to be so *good*. More than merely *good* . . . It's going to be exquisite." He'd completely removed her panties by now and had tossed them over his shoulder, uncaring of where they landed. He scrutinized her naked flesh raptly. A gentle hand found its way to her abdomen and down . . . to where the softest sprinkling of curls lay in wait of his touch. His long, blunt fingers entangled in the grasping curls and then moved down even farther, to where there were no curls and only a warm moistness that ached for his touch.

Bobbi cried out when his fingers found her sensitive clit and she went unbearably tense when he stroked her there. *God*, it was divine. She sobbed and tried to dislodge the tormenting touch.

"No, Gabe. It's too much . . . , " she pleaded, but he ignored her and that same finger slipped deftly inside of her.

"Oh Christ." Gabe was groaning too now and his chest was heaving uncontrollably as he fought to breathe. "You're so *hot* and tight, sweetheart."

Bobbi's hands were doing some exploring of their own; she was learning his hard curves and angles and kissing every inch of flesh accessible to her. She pushed impatiently at his briefs—needing to have him completely naked and open to her touch. Understanding what she wanted, he pushed the briefs down his hips and kicked them off.

Bobbi's eyes widened in awed disbelief at the sight of him. The last time she had seen Gabe in the buff had been on a skinny-dipping adventure when he was ten and she five and he had certainly *grown* a lot since then. The childhood memory reminded her of exactly whom it was she found herself naked with and she flushed unexpectedly, going crimson with sudden embarrassment. She may have wanted him for years but this was still *Gabe* and she was seeing him naked. What *should* have felt awkward felt comfortable and right and the embarrassment was fleeting.

Her eyes were focused on his erect penis and she shook her head in amazement. Yes, this was Gabe, and God, he was *gorgeous*.

"Oh *Gabe*," she breathed in awe, and he grinned, understanding and appreciating her tone.

"Oh *Bobbi*," he mimicked in the exact same tone of voice. His hand fumbled around on the floor beside the sofa before finding his discarded trousers and removing a condom from one of the pockets.

"You're ready, right?" he asked, his voice tight with barely restrained urgency, and she smiled.

"You have no idea how ready I am," she assured him, and he grinned in relief, before tearing the packet with his teeth. He efficiently donned the condom, the back of his hand brushing against her as he did so, and she bit back another cry at her almost unbearable sensitivity down there.

Without any hesitation at all, Gabe kissed her deeply and entered her with one long, sure thrust. Bobbi stiffened but when there was no further discomfort, she relaxed and began to follow his lead.

After that initial fast and economical thrust, Gabe began to move almost leisurely. He was hunched over her slender form and moaned whenever she lifted her hips to meet his gentle strokes. His tongue parodied the lazy movements of his body and Bobbi found herself rocking slowly to the edge of an insidiously looming pit. Her fingers dug into his back and both of them were soon sobbing each other's names. Their pace quickened abruptly and they soon began to fly out of control. They were melded together in more ways than the most basic, their chests were glued together, their lips were locked, and their arms and legs were inextricably entangled.

"Gabe," Bobbi whispered his name on a note of pleasure so intense, it almost resembled pain. It took her breath away and she shuddered quietly around him as she was catapulted headfirst into a frighteningly deep black abyss, where she felt herself free-falling to an end that she could not see. Gabe's thrusts were so fast now, one could barely finish before the other started, his face was contorted and dripping with sweat.

"Bobbi . . . ," he grunted. "*God!*" He came with one final, massive thrust. He went completely boneless in her arms and was waiting to catch her when she floated to the bottom of the abyss.

He withdrew his still throbbing penis from her with a wince, while she sucked in a shocked gasp at his abrupt departure from her body. He immediately dispensed with their protection and gathered her into his arms.

CHAPTER SEVEN

They were silent for a very long time afterward. The sweat dried and cooled on their bodies, and Bobbi began to shiver despite the warmth of the evening. Gabe tightened his arms around her and turned her so that she was sandwiched between the back of the huge, lavishly upholstered sofa and his hard body. She immediately felt safe and warm and buried her face against his chest with a contented sigh.

She dozed off but woke with a start when Gabe adjusted his position carefully.

"Sorry," he whispered. "My arm fell asleep."

"Oh." She felt inexplicably shy now as she tried to sit up. He reluctantly released her and allowed her to disentangle herself from his arms and legs. She kept her eyes averted as she got up and began hunting for her clothes.

"You okay?" he asked, his voice rough. He also got up and ran a hand through his hair, dishevelling it thoroughly in the process. He looked way too appealing and Bobbi found that she couldn't look at him for too long without wanting to run back into his arms again.

"Fine . . ." She found her shorts but couldn't find her panties or her top. Wanting only to get herself covered as quickly as possible, she tugged on the shorts and grimaced at the uncomfortable sensation of rough denim against her overly sensitive flesh. She found his shirt instead of her top and, deciding that it would do, dragged it on and buttoned it up only high enough to cover her breasts, leaving a deep V of exposed flesh from neck to cleavage. She didn't know how sexy she looked with her messy hair and the masculine shirt that was so long on her it completely hid the shorts from view.

"Are you hungry?" he asked stiltedly, and she shook her head. God this felt so uncomfortable suddenly. How did one behave after something like that? What did one say to your secret lover slash best friend after you'd had amazing sex for the first time? Bobbi was at a complete loss.

"No. I have an early start tomorrow morning," she said, searching for her shoes and finding them beneath his discarded trousers. She slipped on the trainers without socks and blasted him with a bright, insincere smile. "I have to go."

"You don't have to leave yet," he protested. "Have a snack . . . or something."

"I'm not hungry and I'm rather tired."

"Do you regret what happened?" he asked, a surprising amount of uncertainty in his voice. She sighed and made direct eye contact for the first time since getting dressed.

"No. I don't," she said truthfully. "I just don't know what happens next. Do you?"

"Not really," he confessed. "But we could find out together." She smiled at him before closing the distance between them until she stood directly in front of him. She cupped his jaw with her hands and tugged his head down, going up on her toes to meet him halfway. The kiss she gave him was sweet and filled with aching promise, but she moved away before he could deepen it. His eyes remained shut for a heartbeat longer before he sighed and looked at her regretfully.

"That felt like a good-bye kiss."

"Hmm, a good-*night* kiss," she confirmed. "I have to go."

"You don't," he denied. "You could stay the night."

"Gabe, that's not how we keep this thing between us secret," she said with an incredulous laugh. "The first person who spots me making my way home in the morning would know exactly what we'd been doing all night."

His eyes were filled with mute frustration, and she watched the muscles in his tight jaw bunch as he bit back whatever he'd been about to say in response to her words.

"I'll see you soon," she assured before turning away and heading for the door. She just needed to keep it together long enough to get out of this house. She refused to allow him to see how much he had hurt her, and if she stayed much longer he would surely notice her eyes shining with the tears that she absolutely refused to shed. She wasn't a crier. Crying never solved anything. He let her leave without any further resistance, and Bobbi fled. Only when she was halfway across her own yard did she succumb to an extreme bout of trembling as the shock finally crept in.

~

Gabe felt like punching something. This felt so . . . *wrong*. It shouldn't have been so difficult to let her leave. But he'd had the best sex of his life tonight and he wasn't done with her yet. Not by a long shot.

And yet . . . afterward, the distance between them had left him feeling sick to his stomach. He wanted to have sex with her again, but he could do without the extra dose of scorching guilt that came after he came, so to speak. He felt like he was cheating on someone and he didn't understand why.

He hadn't been thinking clearly when he had suggested that she stay the night, but from the moment the words had emerged he'd wanted it desperately. He had wanted to make love with her again, fall asleep next to her, and wake up with her in his arms. It had been all he could think of and when she had—quite justifiably—shot him down, the blow had been pretty damned devastating.

Sleeping with her would complicate things. It was better to keep the sex impersonal but even as he nodded in response to the thought, he felt that hollow sensation in the pit of his stomach again.

But this was still new to them—they'd get used to the arrangement, more comfortable with it. They just needed time to adjust that was all. The words provided scant comfort but they were all he had.

~

Work the next day wasn't quite the distraction Gabe had hoped it would be. He glared at his computer screen without really seeing the information on display.

"Mr. Braddock." His executive assistant's face popped up on the screen, providing a welcome diversion. "I have Mr. Richmond on the line for you."

Gabe scowled; just what he needed. How the hell was he supposed to look the man in the eye after all the raunchy things he had done with his daughter the previous night?

"Put him through. Voice only." He lifted the telephone's handset to his ear.

"Mike, good morning." He tried to keep his tone light but sounded stilted to his own ears.

"Morning, Gabe. Glad you decided to go the old-fashioned route with this call. I hate those face-to-face calls, you know? Having my every expression analyzed can be a bit disconcerting," the older man greeted jovially.

"You just don't want people to see the gleam in your eyes when you go in for the kill," Gabe scoffed, and the other man laughed appreciatively.

"I wanted to know if everything was still on course for next month."

Gabe rolled his eyes.

"Why don't you ask Violet or Stephanie?" he asked, referring to their assistants.

"Well, you're in charge of the event, and I want to be sure that you're keeping an eye on those two—no need for the whole thing to get too frou-frou."

"They know what they're doing; it's not their first major event," Gabe pointed out.

"It's the first time I'll be handing my company over to someone else." Mike Richmond would officially hand over the reigns to Gabe at the company's annual Valentine's Day Ball. Gabe knew that the older man felt ambivalent about retiring, even though his eldest son, Edward—who also happened to be his physician—insisted on it.

"Don't worry, I'll make sure Stephanie reminds Violet to keep it elegant."

"No hearts and flowers everywhere," Mike stipulated.

"Not a single one," Gabe assured.

"Okay, I suppose we can't have a party without some flowers," Mike conceded. "But they don't have to overdo it. It's not a funeral. I'm not dying, just retiring." Gabe grinned, happy that the cantankerous old man couldn't see him.

"Understood."

"Right then. Anything else I need to know?" Gabe had a moment of blind panic and cold sweat as he imagined Mike Richmond looking out of his bedroom window last night and seeing Bobbi leading Gabe across the lawn toward the fence. Or *worse*, had he come back down to the den last night? Gabe and Bobbi had been so wrapped up in each other they wouldn't have noticed a herd of stampeding elephants passing through the room. Logic reasserted itself as he figured that this conversation wouldn't be *quite* so amicable if Mike Richmond had seen them last night.

"Gabriel?" the older man prompted, and Gabe cleared his throat.

"Nothing. Everything's fine," he said.

"Okay, well, I have yet *another* meeting with Clyde and his crew of bloodsuckers in a couple of minutes." Clyde was Mike's second son, a corporate attorney whose firm handled all their contracts. "I'll get back to you later." He disconnected the call abruptly.

"Right," Gabe muttered, and replaced the handset carefully. He glanced at his desktop monitor—the spreadsheet was still there, looking even more boring than before. A quick look at the clock told him that it was barely after ten. He wondered what Bobbi was doing. How did she feel after last night?

He might not have wanted things to change, but there had been a fundamental shift in their relationship last night and he should have known it would happen. He had been an idiot to expect things to remain the same. There was an emotional element that he hadn't considered and he was concerned about her. It wasn't something that he had ever felt for any of his former lovers—he had never wondered if they were okay physically, mentally, and emotionally. They had known the stakes and had remained detached, but this was Bobbi, and despite everything he had said last night, separating emotion from sex when it came to someone he knew so well wasn't easy.

He glanced at the clock again: barely two minutes had passed since he'd last checked the time. Was it too early to call her? Or perhaps he should have called earlier? Maybe he looked like an insensitive jerk for not contacting her first thing this morning? He didn't know what to do and that was a weird sensation for him. He was always so sure of what to do. Maybe he should go to the shop and take her out to brunch?

He cracked his knuckles as he considered his options. He had to call her, not knowing what was going on in her head was driving him crazy. He reached for his cell and speed-dialed her number. It rang for ages before going to voice mail. He peered at the phone's screen contemplatively before trying again.

This time it went straight to voice mail.

Was she avoiding his calls? Why would she do that? Was she angry? Sad? Hurt? The possibilities were endless, and he decided to find out for himself. He grabbed his jacket and headed out of the office.

"Postpone my afternoon appointments, Stephanie," he told his assistant on his way out.

"Oh, but . . ."

"And don't call my cell, I'll be busy." He interrupted what he knew would be a protest. "And remind Violet to keep things classy at that damned Valentine's Day Ball. She knows what the Old Man likes." The last was yelled over his shoulder as he exited her office and all but ran to the elevator before she could stop him.

He felt strangely exhilarated as he climbed into his car and headed for Bobbi's shop. He told himself that it was because he was skiving off work, but a larger part of him admitted that he was excited about seeing Bobbi again.

Bobbi felt a tad out of sorts. Her morning had gone from bad to worse. She had slept through her alarm and then rushed into the shop forty minutes late. Pieter was off with *measles* of all things, leaving her shorthanded. The parts that she had ordered for the

Corvette had arrived but they were all wrong and she had been on the phone for half an hour trying to reach the supplier to sort the mess out. Added to all that her entire body was buzzing with sensation after her encounter with Gabe last night. Her nipples were so sensitive that even the brush of cotton against them was uncomfortable, her muscles ached, and her hips and inner thighs were bruised from the friction of his hips and the clutch of his fingers. But none of those things compared to the extreme discomfort she felt . . . down there. She had had one really terrible sexual encounter before Gabe—during her first year of university—and the miserable experience hadn't really prepared her for the full effect of a man as large as Gabe.

All those jokes women made about not being able to "walk right" after great sex? Bobbi totally got it now.

But that was really no big deal in light of how emotionally devastated she felt after Gabe's demeaning stipulations on how they conduct this new aspect of their relationship. Her decision to have sex with him despite that had seemed like a brave step forward last night but now seemed absurdly naïve.

If she felt this awful about herself after just one night, how much worse would it get if they continued to have sex on a regular basis? She didn't know if she had the stomach for this. Gabe had made her feel small and cheap. No that wasn't fair . . . *she* had allowed Gabe to make her feel small and cheap. She bore half of the blame for this dreadful situation and she knew that.

She exhaled impatiently as she listened to the ridiculous "hold" music while she waited for the supplier to come onto the line.

"Are you ignoring my calls, sweetheart?" The dark voice coming from the doorway of her tiny office nearly shocked her into dropping the receiver, and she fumbled frantically to keep it from falling.

"*God*," she gasped. "You nearly scared me half to death."

"Sorry," he said, sounding not at all remorseful. "I didn't mean to sneak up on you."

She watched him warily as he stepped into the tiny glass booth and shut the door behind him. He dominated the tiny space and she immediately felt boxed in and claustrophobic.

"Do you *mind*?" she snarled. "I'm working."

"Why haven't you answered my calls?" he asked, using his pristine white handkerchief to wipe down the chair opposite hers before seating himself and raising his eyes to hers expectantly. She merely stared back at him with a raised eyebrow and he smiled at her. The sincerity on his face nearly undid her, and she had to bite her lip to keep from smiling back at him.

He glanced down at his handkerchief and his nose wrinkled fastidiously when he saw that it was covered in a layer of gray dust and grime from the chair. Nonetheless he folded it meticulously before dropping it into one of his jacket pockets. He was a classic fish out of water in this environment, and it saddened her to realize exactly how far removed his world was from hers.

"Well?" he prompted, and she looked at him blankly, forcing him to elaborate. "My phone calls? You've been ignoring them."

"I haven't, the line's just been busy all morning." She held up the receiver pointedly and he shook his head.

"I've been calling your cell," he told her, and her brow furrowed as she patted herself down with one hand, before glancing around her cluttered desk.

"I must have forgotten it at home," she said. "I've been having a bit of a Monday."

"Have you eaten?" he asked.

"Not hungry." She shrugged. The music in her ear paused and she perked up, only to slump back down when it resumed again.

"Oh my God, maybe they figure if they keep me on hold long enough I'll simply give up?"

"Want to have brunch with me?" he asked, and she glared at him irritably.

"What part of 'I'm working' did you not understand?" she asked sarcastically. "And why aren't *you* at work for that matter? Does my dad know that you're slacking off like this?"

"I *am* one of the bosses you know?" he pointed out levelly. "I can take some personal time."

"Oooh, color me impressed," she rejoined caustically, and he grinned at her sarcasm. One thing about Gabe, he always seemed to enjoy her sense of humor.

"I wanted to see if you were okay," he said, the grin fading. "You know? After last night."

"Really? You want to have this conversation *now*? *Here*?" she asked in disbelief, gesturing expansively toward the glass walls and the phone in her hand.

"No time like the present," he stated, and she sighed long-sufferingly.

Gabe watched her struggle with whatever she wanted to say to him and waited with baited breath for her response. She looked gorgeous this morning, her skin glowed with good health and vitality and her lips were still swollen from his kisses. God, she was so damned exquisite he could spend hours just watching her. He was resentful of every second he had wasted in the past—all those moments when he had simply not *seen* her. Had he been completely blind?

"Look Gabe, I . . . ," she began seriously, only to tilt her head toward the telephone receiver that she held pressed against her ear.

"Hello? This is Roberta Richmond from Richmond's Auto Repair Shop. You sent me the wrong shipment and I . . . no, wait! Don't put me on hold again. Don't put . . . damn it." The last two words emerged in a frustrated whisper and her shoulders slumped in despair. Her eyes darted back up to meet his.

"I'm fine," she assured him. "No need to worry about me. We had some fun and today it's business as usual right?"

"Right," he concurred, feeling nauseated at the thought of returning to "business as usual." It felt dishonest.

"Then why are you here?" she asked angrily, keeping her voice low. "This behavior is *not* the way we usually operate. You've never come to my shop on a Monday morning before to ask me if I'm okay. We don't do *brunch*. Ever. I don't go to your office and you don't come to mine. At least you *didn't* before last week. That's not the way our friendship operates. So what the hell is going on? What do you want from me?" She had a point. Gabe was the one who had insisted that they behave normally, yet here he was, acting completely out of character.

"You're right," he acknowledged. "But if you had answered my calls, there wouldn't have been any need for me to come over here to check if you were okay."

"Come on, Gabe," she derided. "Last week you would have tried to reach me, failed, and thought nothing of it."

"Yeah, well, last week was *before* I'd had you pinned down and writhing beneath me in desire. Last week was before I'd had my tongue in your mouth, your breasts in my hands, and your breathless voice in my ear begging me for more." His voice rose with every word until he was practically shouting and she frantically shushed him.

"Fine, okay." She held up a placating hand. "But after today I'd appreciate it if you stopped contradicting yourself. It's confusing the hell out of me."

"Noted," he murmured, feeling confused himself. He leaned forward, trying to catch her eye again. She was downright cagey this morning and still hadn't told him if she was okay or not. Despite that magnificent glow she had about her, she still looked somewhat strained around the eyes and he wondered if she had managed to get any sleep the night before. *He* certainly hadn't—he had been turned on and miserable because she had left him before he had had his fill of her.

"Will you come over tonight?" he asked softly, but she didn't seem to hear him, keeping her eyes glued to the order form on her desk and her attention focused on the telephone receiver clamped to her ear. Gabe wasn't used to being ignored by women, and he now discovered that he didn't like it at all. But he swallowed down his anger as he reminded himself that Bobbi wasn't just any woman and that she habitually ignored him when it suited her. She was just being . . . *Bobbi*. He had wanted things to remain the same between them but hadn't counted on the status quo being frustrating as hell.

"Bobbi?" he prompted, and she lifted her eyes to his. They were so damned pretty they literally took his breath away and he struggled to form the words for a brief moment. "Will you come over tonight?"

She chewed on her lower lip, plumping it up invitingly, and he coughed to cover up a groan. God, this was torturous—he wanted to kiss her so badly he had to curl his hands into fists to prevent himself from dragging her across the damned desk and into his lap.

"I don't know," she responded at last and he nearly swore in frustration. She was clearly trying to drive him insane. "Maybe."

He had to content himself with that vague response and pushed out of the chair.

"Call me if you change your mind about getting something to eat."

"I won't," she said, with a brief shake of her head. He was about to respond to that when her body language changed and she looked away from him again. Effectively dismissing him. "Yes? I'm Roberta Richmond from Richmond's Auto Repair Shop and I received the wrong goods . . ."

He gave her one last glance but it was as if she had forgotten he was there. Feeling rather despondent, Gabe left.

∾

Bobbi watched as he gracefully made his way back out of the shop, exchanging a few laughing comments with Craig as he left. She listened to the dial tone in her ear—her call had been dropped about three minutes ago but she had clung to the handset like it was a shield, knowing that if she put it down she would have to give him her undivided attention and she hadn't been quite ready for that. She replaced the handset carefully. She would have to call them back but she didn't have the energy just yet.

Suddenly the weight of problems the day had dumped onto her shoulders felt unbearably heavy and she slumped in her chair, wanting to do nothing more than bury her face in her hands and weep.

∾

The day had seemed interminable; after several more frustrating phone calls, Bobbi had finally managed to sort out the shipment error but the setback had cost her valuable time. Pieter's measles would put him out of commission for at least a week and the loss of manpower would result in a forfeiture of revenue that she really couldn't afford.

The only *good* thing about the seemingly insurmountable heap of complications was that it had pushed the situation with Gabe firmly to the back of her mind. But by the time she closed shop after seven that night, thoughts of him came creeping insidiously back into her head.

By the time she made her way home, all she could think of was heading over to his place. God, she was so tempted. So what if she felt awful afterward? She could work around that . . . what he made her feel *during* was pretty damned spectacular. If she rationed her time with him wisely—maybe she could keep her already broken heart shielded from further harm?

She bargained with herself all through the late dinner that Faye had left in the microwave for her. She had had a stressful day and needed something to help her relax . . . just a couple of hours to help her take the edge off. They had already had sex after all; so one more time wouldn't make *that* much difference, would it?

God, she sounded like an addict! She laughed bitterly when she recognized that that was exactly what she *was* and that Gabe was her drug of choice.

She barely tasted her dinner and trudged upstairs afterward to grab a shower. She took extra care with shampooing her hair and shaving her legs and armpits, telling herself that she was just doing it because she needed to pamper herself a bit. She brushed her teeth and used the expensive body lotion that Theresa had given her for Christmas. She hadn't even opened the bottle before now but she applied it generously, relishing how smooth her skin felt afterward. Why hadn't she ever used the stuff before? It felt and smelled amazing.

She dragged on her usual sleepwear of boy shorts and a tank top and went back downstairs to the library for a book. She was surprised to find her father asleep on one of the comfortable leather sofas, an open book lying facedown on his chest. The sound of the door opening startled him out of his light snooze and he smiled at her sleepily.

"I feel like I haven't seen you in days," he said warmly, and she returned his smile, curling up on the sofa next to him.

"You haven't," she replied, dropping a kiss on his cheek. "I've been busy."

"Yes, you've had quite the active social life lately," he said, and she flushed guiltily.

"What do you mean?" He looked surprised by her reaction and question and his gaze sharpened.

"What do you *think* I mean?" he asked pointedly.

"Nothing." She tried not to look too uncomfortable with his line of questioning.

"Roberta, do you have a male friend you're not telling me about? Gabe mentioned something about a guy yesterday? Someone you met at the pub?" The sound of Gabe's name startled her, but her father misinterpreted her reaction and grinned gleefully. "You *do* have a male friend! I'd like to meet him."

"It's uh . . . it's not that serious yet," she whispered, aghast by the awful turn the conversation had taken.

"What's his name?"

"K-Kyle Foster, he's a landscape architect." Oh *God*, what the hell was she doing?

"And you like him? He's a good man?"

"He's very nice." *Stop talking, Bobbi!* her conscience was shrieking at her. *Just shut the hell up!*

"You should consider bringing him to the Valentine's Day Ball," her father said, and her mind went completely blank as she thought about that horrible annual event. She usually managed to avoid it but her father, who so rarely made any demands on his children, had insisted that Bobbi and her brothers attend this year. Since he planned to announce his retirement, Bobbi knew that she had no option other than to show her support. But she had forgotten that she would probably have to bring a date to the event. That thought was followed by an even worse one . . .

Would Gabe be bringing a date? God, she wouldn't be able to stand it. Not with everything that had happened—was still happening—between them.

"I'll consider it," she said absently—her mind on Gabe and the gorgeous woman he would probably bring to the formal event.

"Good," her father said. "And bring him to dinner sometime, I'd like to meet him."

"Sure," she said, still on autopilot. Her father dropped an arm around her shoulder and planted a swift kiss on the top of her head. The show of affection was so rare that it startled Bobbi out of her reverie.

"I'm off to bed," he told her. "Good night, baby."

"Good night, Daddy," she replied, warmed by the endearment. He left the room in his usual brisk manner. Bobbi sat immersed in her chaotic thoughts for a long time. She had lied to her father, dragged poor Kyle into this mess, and now had to find a date to the damned Valentine's Day Ball.

Maybe Gabe would ask her. Once the wistful thought had entered her mind it continued to float around in there like a hopeful sprite. She tried to bat it away, knowing that it was ridiculous to even consider the possibility, but the part of her that liked to wish for impossible things couldn't help but hope.

"Gabe won't ask you," she said out loud, and flinched at the inescapable truth in the words.

Gabe stared blankly at the television screen, not really absorbing what he was seeing as he tried to swallow past the lump of bitter disappointment that had lodged in his throat. She wasn't coming.

It was nearly one in the morning and he had held out hope until about an hour ago when the huge grandfather clock in the foyer had struck twelve. After that he had simply gone numb and continued to sit here unable to summon up the energy to head up to bed. So maybe the night before hadn't had quite the same impact on her as it had on him? The thought was humbling and hard to accept, but there wasn't much else he could take away from this resounding rejection.

He buried his face in his hands. This was probably for the best; he already felt like he was in too deep. They would simply forget that it had ever happened and go back to normal.

He winced at that thought. As if it would be that easy. He could never *unsee* the perfection of her naked body, or *untaste* the honey of her mouth, or *unfeel* her clenching heat around him. He was so screwed . . .

He reached for the remote and switched off the television and the sudden echoing silence unsettled him. He sat there for a moment longer, willing himself to get up and go to bed. He had just pushed himself out of the chair when he heard the quiet knock on the front door. His breath caught in his throat and his heart stuttered to a stop before resuming its rhythm erratically.

The knock came again, louder this time, and he leapt into action running to the front door, skidding on the foyer's polished floor and nearly falling on his butt, in a bid to get there before she changed her mind and left. He was breathless by the time he wrest open the heavy door and barely took in the fact that she was in her night-clothes before dragging her into his arms and planting a hungry kiss on her lips.

She kissed him back, wrapping her arms around his neck and her legs around his waist. He staggered back and kicked the front door shut before pinning her to the heavy wooden door and taking his fill of her mouth.

He lifted his head and cupped her face with his hands.

"I thought you weren't coming," he gasped, fighting for breath. She grinned at him, her legs tightening around his waist.

"Really? I was kind of hoping that I'd be coming." It was a silly play on words that barely made sense but it delighted him.

"I'll work on that for you," he promised, thrusting his hardness against her core and she moaned, burying her face in the hollow of his neck as she pushed herself against him, establishing a quick rhythm that nearly had them both spending in seconds. Luckily reason reasserted itself and Gabe groaned before dropping his hands to her hips to stop her sensual grinding.

"Stop that, damn it! I want to get you to a bed this time," he growled.

"Well, what are you waiting for?" she asked impatiently, and he wrapped one hand around her back and cupped the other beneath her butt to support her as he clumsily made his way upstairs with her still clinging to him tightly.

When he reached his room, he stumbled his way to the bed, dropped her down on the soft mattress and climbed up with her in the same motion. He studied her appreciatively as she lay spread out beneath him and growled ferally before hunching down and unceremoniously dragging down her top and sucking one tight nipple into his mouth with a rough finesse that had her arching her back off the bed.

"Oh *God*," she cried out, clamping her thighs against his hips and curling her fingers into his hair.

"This isn't going to last long," he muttered against her breast.

"I don't care," she sobbed, reaching down between them to fumble with his belt and fly. He hissed when she managed to get everything undone and *finally* wrapped her hands around his length. She stroked him with both hands and he shuddered in response.

He didn't bother removing her shorts; he merely pushed them aside and positioned himself at her entrance before shoving his way in. The contrasting sensations of the cotton of her underwear and the wet silk of her intimate flesh against his responsive shaft nearly made him come before he'd gotten more than the head in and he swore gutturally when he realized that the reason he was feeling so damned much was because he wasn't wearing a condom. He *never* forgot to put on a condom and he was momentarily disconcerted by the lapse.

"Shit, shit, *shit*. No condom. I'm sorry." It nearly killed him to withdraw and Bobbi wailed when he left her but he took care of the protection as quickly as he could under the circumstances and was back with her seconds later.

"Don't do that to me again," she rebuked, and he apologized with a kiss before thrusting his way back in. They *didn't* last long. It was rough and fast and over in less than four minutes.

Gabe watched her come in that erotic way of hers, so quiet with just a gasp and a moan and then a long release of breath. He couldn't imagine ever tiring of that or of feeling her orgasm around his shaft. The way she pulsed around him pulled his own climax from him.

"*Bobbi*," he groaned as he poured himself into her. Just that. Just her name. It was all that needed saying.

~

She had stayed longer this time, Gabe reflected hours later as he watched her slight figure walk across the lawn toward the high fence between their properties. Long enough for them to have a round two—which had been slow, sensual, and utterly devastating—and round three in the shower. She had left immediately after the shower, ignoring Gabe's entreaties for her to stay longer. She hadn't even wanted him to walk her to the gate, insisting that she would be fine.

As he reflected upon the past few hours, he realized that she hadn't spoken much at all. She had told him what she liked and where she liked it. Had expressed her appreciation when he had done something that she enjoyed. Had said his name in so many different ways that he'd lost count of them but she hadn't spoken of anything else. Hadn't told him how work on the Corvette was progressing, hadn't said if she'd solved the delivery mix up of that afternoon.

The animated chatter that he was used to from her had been completely missing and the absence disturbed him.

CHAPTER EIGHT

Gabe groaned and blindly reached for the cell phone on the nightstand. Who in the hell would be calling before six in the morning? He glared at the display but it read "unknown" and he dragged his thumb across the screen to answer.

"Gabriel Braddock," he snapped.

"It's me." *Chase.* Gabe pushed himself up and winced when he felt a burning sensation on the skin of his shoulders. He reached up gingerly with his free hand and investigated. There were three deep scratches scored into the flesh of both shoulders. He remembered Bobbi dragging her fingers down his back during their second bout of lovemaking and grinned at the memory—half aroused as he recalled exactly *why* she had made them. He had taken her to the brink and then eased off, she had been pissed off but he had made it up to her, prolonging the encounter until she had been out of her mind with lust.

"Gabe?" Chase's voice brought him back down to earth with a jolt.

"Yeah, sorry. I'm here . . . When are you arriving?" Despite everything that had happened over the last few days, thoughts of his brother had remained very firmly in his mind. He was happy that Chase was returning home and would be out of immediate danger for the moment at least.

"I'll be landing in Cape Town at eight thirty this morning. Can you pick me up? Or send a car?"

"I'll pick you up," Gabe said.

"Thanks. See you later." His brother still sounded *off.* Gabe couldn't put his finger on it but something was very wrong. Chase disconnected the call before he could respond and Gabe put his phone aside and lay there for a while. He wondered if Bobbi was awake yet. She usually got an early start to the day. He decided to check and sent her an SMS.

Up yet? When she didn't immediately respond, he threw the bed covers off and padded—naked—to the closet to drag out his jogging shorts and T-shirt. When his phone buzzed, he all but dove for it but it was buried somewhere beneath the covers and he swore irritably while he hunted for it. When he found it he was rewarded with a single word.

Yeah.

Well . . . hell.

I'm going for a run. Wanna join me? This time he didn't have to wait too long for the response.

Sure. Meet me at the gate in ten mins.

He grinned, feeling ridiculously happy that she'd agreed and dragged on his running shoes before doing a few perfunctory stretches, keeping an eye on the clock. He didn't want to be late.

He left the house within seven minutes and was at the gate a minute after that. Bobbi wasn't there yet. He did a few more stretches, enjoying the fresh air and early morning birdsong. It was a perfect summer morning and still cool enough for a leisurely jog around the neighborhood. Bobbi didn't enjoy jogging as much as he did and joined him on his morning runs only occasionally. He heard a voice and looked up through the bars of the two-meter high gate. She was waving and shouting out a greeting to one of the security guards on the Richmond property. She made her way toward Gabe with that usual insouciant amble of hers and he looked his fill, appreciating the sensuous roll of her hips. He drank in the skintight running shorts and racerback sports bra that she usually wore for jogging and couldn't quite fathom how he had managed to run with her before without wanting to lick every expanse of silky flesh on display. She was toned and tanned all over and while she didn't have the most generous curves, the shape she *did* have was tight, sexy, and undeniably feminine.

"Morning." She grinned when she reached him.

"Hey."

"It's been a while since we've gone jogging together," she noted, executing a graceful overhead stretch that emphasised the flatness of her belly and pert roundness of her breasts. She then turned and placed her hands on the gate to do a calf stretch and Gabe bit back a groan at the sight of her firm butt in those indecent shorts. God they clung to her like a second skin and just barely covered the lower curve of her behind.

"I haven't been jogging in a while." He was so completely distracted by her sexy, sinuous stretches that he could barely concentrate on what he was saying. "Busy."

"Well, I'm going to kick some serious butt today, Braddock." They were back in friend mode, he realized. It was as if last night hadn't happened at all. She was her usual teasing and playful self and it created a disconnect in Gabe who couldn't transition from lover to friend as easily as she apparently could. This was the *same* woman he had held and kissed and touched and pleasured just hours before and it was crazy not to be able to acknowledge that fact with a caress or a kiss or even an endearment.

But these were *his* rules and if she could play by them, then so should he.

"Don't count on it, Richmond," he countered, trying to inject some humor into his voice. "I have a couple of secret weapons."

"Oh? And what would they be?" She slanted her head curiously and looked damned adorable in the process.

"Longer legs and . . . *stamina*," he responded before taking off at a sprint and laughing when she shouted a protest.

He got a good head start before slowing down and allowing her to catch up with him. He shortened his stride so that she could keep pace with him and they settled into an easy jog. After less than a kilometer she glared up at him.

"I hate running," she groused. "Why do you make me do this?"

"Stop complaining, I didn't *make* you do anything. I just invited you along. You didn't *have* to come."

"Then why do you keep letting me do this to myself?" She puffed and he grinned again.

"You're being pathetic, Richmond, stop whining so much and focus on your breathing." She was a good runner but hated the exertion. She needed coaxing and teasing to keep going. He'd been half coaching, half haranguing her during their jogs for years. It usually worked and she always finished the entire seventeen-kilometer course around the neighborhood in under an hour.

They ended up back at his place about fifty minutes later and did a few cool-down exercises in silence.

"I'm picking Chase up in an hour or so," he told her, after taking a sip of water. The day was going to be a scorcher with the morning temperature already in the mid to upper twenties. He handed her his water bottle and she drank thirstily.

"Did he say anything about his reasons for coming home?" she asked, running a hand through her damp hair. A few tendrils stuck to her forehead and he had to stop himself from reaching out and brushing them back.

"Nothing yet . . . but something's definitely wrong." He frowned as he recalled his brother's uncharacteristically subdued voice on the phone that morning.

"At least he'll be at home, so you'll have plenty of time to figure out what the problem is," she said, and he nodded.

"Right. I've got to get showered, call Stephanie to tell her not to expect me this morning, and hit the road," he said, wiping the dripping sweat from his brow with the back of his hand.

"Me too, we're short-staffed. Pieter has measles and there's a lot to do." She turned away but his voice halted her progress.

"Bobbi?" He waited until she had turned back to face him before hooking a hand around the nape of her neck and dragging her over until she was plastered against his sweaty body. He dropped a hard kiss on her delicate mouth before she could utter a word of protest and before she could even think to push him away, he had already released her. She swayed and he put a hand on one of her shoulders to steady her.

"Easy there," he crooned, amused when she fixed a bemused look on his face. She looked completely dazed and incapable of speech.

"Uh . . . right," she finally said. "Thanks. I mean . . ."

"You're welcome." He grinned.

"Right. I've got to go . . ." She still looked completely discombobulated when she turned away from him again.

"Have a good day," he called to her back and she acknowledged the sentiment with a wave. "See you tonight." So maybe he had presumed too much with that last statement, but aside from straightening her shoulders, she said nothing in response to it.

She had already disappeared through the gate by the time Gabe realized that he was still standing on his front steps with a ridiculously goofy grin on his face and made his way back into the house. The grin didn't fade until after his shower.

He wasn't grinning an hour later when he watched Chase make his way through the domestic arrivals gate at Cape Town International Airport. Chase looked haggard. That was the only word he could think of to describe his twin. He looked like he had lost at least ten kilograms, his hair was a shaggy mess, he obviously hadn't shaved in days, and his cheeks were sunken hollows.

"Jesus," Gabe whispered in shock when he first caught sight of the man. He plastered a smile onto his lips when Chase saw him and heartily embraced the man who was a mere ten minutes older than Gabe. When they had been younger even their own mother had had difficulty telling them apart. Their mother would burst into tears if she were to see Chase right now. Gabe, himself, felt like weeping.

He held onto his brother longer than he usually would and Chase seemed content to let him. They eventually moved apart and Gabe cleared his throat awkwardly, kind of embarrassed to note the sheen of tears in his brother's eyes but then even more self-conscious when he realized that he was doing a lot of blinking to clear his misty vision as well.

"Missed you, bro," he muttered. He grabbed Chase's tog bag, knowing that Chase would prefer to carry his precious camera equipment.

"Yeah, it's been too long between assignments," Chase agreed. He hadn't set foot in the country in more than six months. He had inherited their father's wanderlust and sense of adventure but had channelled it more productively. They chatted about the flight and airline food on the long walk back to the car—keeping things simple and impersonal.

Chase whistled appreciatively when he saw the Lamborghini.

"This is a gorgeous piece of machinery." He grinned boyishly, giving Gabe a glimpse of his old self. He did a slow circle around the car before coming to a halt at the driver's side.

"Keys?" he asked hopefully.

"Yeah right," Gabe scoffed. "If you think I'm letting your travel-weary butt drive this baby, you can think again."

"You suck," his brother groused.

"You sound like Bobbi," Gabe chuckled, his heart doing a bizarre loop-the-loop in his chest at the mere mention of her name. *What the hell?* He busied himself with loading his brother's gear into the car, hastily stifling that weird reaction. Luckily Chase traveled light—an occupational hazard—or they would have run into trouble. The car wasn't exactly designed to carry a lot of luggage.

"You haven't let her drive it yet?" Chase asked, after they had left the airport.

"Yet?" Gabe snorted. "Try *ever*. She's too reckless, she could get herself killed." He went ice cold at the very thought.

"Come on, she's not that bad," Chase dismissed. "She's actually damned good at racing—competent and in control—you're too much of a nervous ninny to see that."

"Do *not* encourage her," Gabe warned, and Chase shrugged.

"Whatever, man."

"So will you be staying at your flat?" he asked Chase, referring to the luxury apartment in Camps Bay. When Chase didn't immediately respond, Gabe glanced over at him in concern and saw that his brother was absently staring out at the passing scenery. He looked lost and haunted.

"Chase?"

"I'd prefer to stay at home this time round, bro. If that's okay with you?"

"Of course it's okay with me," Gabe reassured. "It's your house too."

"I mean I don't wanna cramp your style or anything. I know you always have some brainy blonde on call." Gabe froze as he thought of Bobbi. How the hell were they going to work this with Chase staying under the same roof? The house was huge but . . .

"That's a weighty silence." Chase's voice intruded in his thoughts and Gabe glanced over at him. "I take it things are more serious with this latest one then? What is she? An astronaut? A professor? No, you've already dated a professor . . . an astrophysicist? Neurosurgeon?"

"I'm not seeing anyone right now." Gabe ended the speculation and the look of blatant disbelief on Chase's face was almost comical. Gabe grinned reluctantly.

"I'm not exactly Don Juan, you know. I *do* occasionally find myself between relationships."

"You *lie*," Chase mocked. "No, say it ain't so! My baby brother always has a bevy of beautiful blondes at his beck and call. Don't tell me my hero has feet of clay. Don't *tell* me!"

"Shut up," Gabe laughed, enjoying his brother's banter. He had been watching Chase grow more relaxed with every passing kilometer as if whatever emotional burden he was carrying grew lighter and lighter the closer they got to home.

～

Bobbi got through the morning somehow, but it was hard when she couldn't think of anything other than Gabe and the things they had done to each other the night before. Then there was that morning's kiss, which had been hard and fast and filled with so much promise that all she could think about was going back for more. It was seriously distracting.

Her cell phone rang just before lunch and her heart leapt in excitement as she reached for it, wondering if it was Gabe. She doubted it since he probably wanted to spend time with Chase but she was hopeful. She rolled her eyes when she read the name on screen.

"Billy, hi," she greeted. He was five years her senior, the closest brother to her in age and the one who had given her the most grief growing up. They were pretty close though and often hung out together. Edward and Clyde were closer to each other in age—they had been fifteen and seventeen when their mother had died and had handled the sudden loss a lot better than their younger siblings had.

The younger Richmond siblings, feeling abandoned by the adults and near-adults in their family at such a confusing time in their lives, had instead adopted the Braddock family as their own and had spent many long hours playing with the twins. Lucy Templeton-Braddock had taken them under her wing and had provided the stable maternal influence that they had lost. She had often referred to them as her "lost little lambs" and had treated them like they were her own.

"Hey, Bobbi, I have a huge favor to ask you." Her brother started his conversation without preamble and her eyes widened in surprise. He hardly ever asked her for favors.

"Jase told me that you met Kyle Foster the other day?" That wasn't at all what she had been expecting and she couldn't do more than make a soft sound of confirmation. "I was hoping you could introduce me?"

"What? *No.* Ask Jason, Kyle is his buddy." *Why* were people constantly asking her about Kyle Foster? It was bizarre. "I don't even know him."

"According to Jason, the guy has the hots for you," Billy pointed out and Bobbi went bright red, grateful that her brother couldn't see her face.

"Why do you want to meet him anyway?"

"He's one of the best landscape architects around and in high demand. I've wanted to work with him for years." Billy was an architect. A really *great* architect.

"You're a professional, Billy, your reputation speaks for itself. You don't need *me* to make your contacts for you, just call him up and tell him you want to work with him. I'm sure he'll jump at the opportunity."

"I've already tried that. I need him for a project in April, but he's booked through to November. I figured if I could chat with him in a less formal setting, dinner maybe, and tell him about the project he'll be interested enough to work on it with me."

"Dinner?" she asked in disbelief.

"Yeah, like a double date kind of thing; you bring Foster, I bring one of my female friends and . . ."

"Should I sleep with him to sweeten the deal?" she asked sarcastically.

"Bobbi!" Her brother sounded so scandalized that for a moment she gave in to the impulse to grin. "Of course not, that's not what . . ."

"Billy, my answer is *no*. Do the professional thing and have your secretary call his secretary or whatever. Just leave me out of it."

"Dad tells me you're bringing him to the Valentine's Day thing." Her jaw dropped.

"Oh my God! *What?*" Her voice was so shrill Sean and Craig looked up from the shop floor to peer at her through the glass of her office door. "I met the guy *once*, why the hell is everybody asking me about him?"

"Well, you hardly ever go out with guys, I'm pretty sure Dad was starting to think you batted for the other team," he said, and Bobbi sighed and dropped her head back on the headrest of her chair, staring at the ceiling in frustration. She absently noted a daddy longlegs sitting idly in its web in one of the corners and her eyes automatically tracked across to the other corners to ensure that they were spider-free. "Dad seems to think you're totally in love with the guy."

Her father had completely gotten the wrong end of the stick on that one, Bobbi thought with a sigh. Right emotion, wrong guy.

"Well, I'm not," she denied. "Now leave me alone, I'm busy."

"Aww come on, Bobbi," he reproved. "Throw me a bone, won't you? You used to be a better sister than this."

"And you and Dad need to stop talking about me behind my back," she added. She disconnected the call while he was in mid-plea and glared at the screen irritably.

"Be seen with *one* guy in public," she grumbled. "And they're planning your wedding and naming your first-born child." Their peaceful berg was too small and the Richmond and Braddock families were too well known for any juicy bit of news to slip by unnoticed. She knew that it was one of the main reasons Gabe wanted to keep their affair, if that's what it could be called, secret. They would never be able to get away with just sleeping together, the pressure on him to do the "respectable" thing with the daughter of such a prominent family would be immense. And Gabe being Gabe wouldn't allow himself to be forced into anything and that could have some pretty major repercussions for him—personally and professionally— if her father decided to take offense.

But even while she understood his reasoning, it just really hurt to be nothing more to him than an itch that needed scratching. She ran her hands over her face and groaned.

"Stop thinking about it," she told herself, her voice muffled behind her hands. *Just enjoy it while it lasts.*

She picked up her phone again, wanting to touch base with Gabe and genuinely concerned about Chase.

Hey. Chase ok? She tapped out the message swiftly and then put the phone aside to pick up a couple of requisition forms. She hated the paperwork aspect of her job; it kept her away from what she really loved which was being elbow deep in the innards of an automobile. Unfortunately owning a business meant that she had to deal with the boring stuff too and sadly the boring stuff seemed to completely outweigh the fun stuff. Her phone buzzed.

I don't know. I'm worried. Something wrong. I didn't talk to him about it yet—had to come to work.

Give him time, she responded.

Yeah.

She watched her phone for a while longer but no other message was forthcoming so she put her head down and went back to her paperwork. The phone buzzed a minute later and she grabbed it eagerly.

So . . . are you wearing a bra today? She was equal parts embarrassed and amused by the question and not sure how to respond to it. She was saved from making that decision when the buzzer went again.

Sorry. Out of line but . . . are you?

She laughed out loud at that bit of nerve, bit her lip and tapped out a quick message, and pushed "Send" before she could change her mind.

YEAH you're out of line . . . and no. I'm not. His next reply made her breath catch.

SO hard I hurt right now. Thanks!!!

Wish I was there to kiss it better. Her response was more risqué than she'd intended. It was like her fingers had taken on a life of their own.

OMG!! You're killing me. Can't concentrate on work now cos that's all I'll be thinking about. She grinned. She was still thinking about how to respond when a new message buzzed its way to her screen.

Crap. Gtg—your dad's on his way to my office!

Bobbi choked back a laugh as she pictured him jumping like a guilty schoolboy just because her father had nearly caught him indulging in a bit of PG-13 sexting. Okay, so maybe Mike Richmond wouldn't take it too well if he knew that *Bobbi* was the recipient of the racy messages—but it was still a funny thought. Gabe respected her father so much, Bobbi knew that he would hate to do anything to upset or disappoint the man. She shook her head and put her phone down.

She didn't know what she was doing here. The lines between the role of friend and lover were becoming less distinct. That morning, the jog, it had started off friendly and then he had ended it with that kiss. The SMSs they'd just exchanged—her initial inquiry had been that of a concerned friend and it had turned into a mild sexting session. How was she supposed to keep these two roles straight when Gabe was the one who kept mixing things up? She was going have to talk to him about it and try to reestablish some of the ground rules.

~

Gabe had wanted to eat in and have a talk with his brother, but Chase had insisted they head down to the pub for dinner. Gabe knew his brother well enough to recognize the delaying tactic. Chase was aware that Gabe had questions and he didn't want to answer them. He had even asked Gabe to delay telling their mother that he was back in Cape Town. She knew that he was in the country but thought he was staying in Johannesburg for a couple of days.

When they walked into the pub, the friends they had known all their lives flocked around them to welcome Chase home with back thumps and pints of beer; it took a while before they could make their way to a table and order some food, and even then somebody was always stopping by for a chat.

"God, it's good to be home," Chase said during one of the rare moments they were alone at their table.

"You should come home more often," Gabe told him, trying to keep his tone light.

"I've been thinking about it." Chase's tired response had Gabe leaning forward intently.

"Thinking about *what* exactly?" he prompted.

"Staying home and working on that book." Chase had been thinking of compiling a book of photographs for years. He always tried to capture the beauty hidden beneath the ugliness of the war torn places he found himself in and that was what his book would focus on. A single rose blooming on a battlefield, a glorious sunrise over a minefield. He had once told Gabe that he took those photos to maintain his sanity.

"Won't you get bored at home?" Gabe asked, taking a sip of beer.

"I can't see the beauty anymore, Gabe." His brother's voice sounded completely desolate and Gabe's throat tightened. "I look around me and all I see is ugliness, despair, fear, poverty . . . *violence*. There's no beauty. Not even here."

"Ah, man," Gabe shook his head, blinking away that sting in the back of his eyes again. "I'm glad you're home, brother."

"Yeah, me too . . ."

∾

"Movie?" Chase asked when they got home an hour and a half later and Gabe nodded.

"Yeah, lemme get some chips and beer. You pick the movie." Gabe moved toward the kitchen and then turned back. "Hey!"

Chase paused on his way to the den and looked back at him.

"No chick flicks!" Gabe instructed, and Chase blinked, studied him for a second, and then, for the first time since returning, truly laughed. The sound was deep and spontaneous and just a tad rusty and made Gabe feel rather sentimental.

"Damn," Chase bantered. "I was so looking forward to watching *Pretty Woman* again. Or *Titanic* maybe."

Chase chose a comedy, one they had seen several times before, but Gabe recognized that his brother was seeking the familiar and that a violent action movie wasn't what Chase needed.

The movie had been on for less than half an hour when the doorbell rang. Gabe tensed, knowing instantly who it was. He had forgotten to tell her that Chase would be staying with him.

"It's nearly twelve." Chase sat up with a frown and paused the movie. "Who would be visiting at this time of night?"

"I have an inkling," Gabe replied. "I'll get it."

He left the room before Chase could question him any further and hurried to the front door. The sight of Bobbi standing there in nothing but a pair of skimpy Snoopy pyjama shorts and a matching pink tank top made him groan. She looked good enough to eat and that *had* been his plan for the night before Chase had come to stay. She smiled at him and took his breath away.

"Hi," she whispered, and stepped into his arms. She reached up and entangled her hands in his hair before tugging his head down for a kiss. He wrapped his arms around her slender body and captured her lips in a tender embrace that was filled with longing and desire. Her soft moan as she wound her arms around his neck undid him and he deepened the kiss, stroking his tongue into her mouth for a brief instant before reason reasserted itself and he dragged his head back. She made a disappointed sound and tried to capture his lips again but he brought his hands up to her arms and moved her firmly away, turning his head to avoid her kiss. He winced at the hurt confusion that clouded her eyes.

"Chase is here," he muttered, and the pain deepened for an instant before she stepped back.

"Bobbi," he whispered, uncomfortable with the brief flash of rejection that he had seen in her eyes and despising himself for putting it there. "I'm . . ."

"Oh please *don't* . . ." She held up a hand in entreaty. "Just *don't* say you're sorry. It's okay. It's just part of the agreement."

"But . . ."

"Gabe," she warned, and he sighed deeply.

"This isn't easy for me either, Bobbi."

"Yeah, I'm sure it's not." But she sounded bitter and unconvinced and it was killing Gabe not to reach for her and drag her back into his arms. "Can I say hello to Chase? It would look weird if I didn't. I won't stay too long."

"You can stay as long as you want," he said, ill at ease. He hated how badly he was mishandling the situation and hated the awful certainty that in his quest to keep her from getting hurt, he was not only wounding her but irreparably damaging their friendship in the process.

She brushed past him and padded into the den, the soles of her trainers squeaking on the tiled floor. He absently rubbed at the gnawing ache in his chest as he followed her in. Chase looked up when they entered the room and his face lit up when he saw her.

"Well, look who it is." He sounded delighted and leapt to his feet to envelop Bobbi in a tight hug. She laughed and returned the embrace, squealing when Chase lifted her off her feet and swung her around.

"Put me down, you giant oaf." She giggled and he complied, smacking a big kiss on her mouth.

"I've missed you, sweetie," he told her and she stood on her toes to ruffle his hair.

"I've missed you too, you sexy beast," she said affectionately, cuddling up to his chest again. Gabe could feel his brow settling into a scowl as he watched the excessive kissing and cuddling between the two. Had they always been this *physical?* He found himself wanting to wade between them and push them apart. This was ridiculous. When Chase planted yet *another* kiss on Bobbi's cheek, Gabe felt a growl building in his chest. *Enough*, for God's sake!

"Bobbi's not staying long," he said loudly enough to interrupt the snuggle fest. Chase looked into Bobbi's upturned face with a mock frown.

"Ridiculous, you're watching the movie with us, aren't you?" he asked Bobbi, who darted a tentative glance at Gabe.

"I'm not sure."

Gabe winced at the small waver in her voice, knowing that he had put it there. God, he was being a total dick. He just didn't like seeing Chase's hands all over her. And that thought was shocking in its own right. It was as if he was jealous . . . of *Chase.*

"It's *Talladega Nights*," Gabe informed her, gentling his tone. "Stay, I'll get you a beer."

"If you're sure you don't mind," she said hesitantly.

"Of course we don't mind," Chase scoffed, dragging her to the sofa and planting her next to him. "Why would we mind? You sit with me, I've missed the hell out of you and I'm keeping you close."

Gabe tried to keep another frown from settling on his face and turned away from the cozy pair, heading for the kitchen. When he returned, Bobbi had her shoes off and her feet curled under her butt on the sofa. Chase had an arm around her shoulders while she had her head on his chest and was absently playing with his free hand as she told him about the Corvette she was renovating for Jason. Chase was giving her his full attention and neither of them noticed Gabe's return until he slammed the beer bottle onto the coffee table in front of them. Chase looked up in surprise, and Bobbi eyed him with that awful look of uncertainty on her face again.

"Sorry," Gabe muttered. "It slipped."

Chase seemed to accept that and rested his cheek on Bobbi's head, but she still kept a wary eye on Gabe as he slumped down on the recliner next to the sofa.

~

Bobbi felt incredibly awkward, it was clear that Gabe didn't want her here. Maybe he didn't trust her to keep her mouth shut about their sexual arrangement, maybe he wanted to spend time with his brother and resented Bobbi's presence, or maybe he just plain didn't want to be in her company right now. Whatever it was, it made her feel uncomfortable and for the first time ever, she felt unsure of her welcome in this house. She could sense the waves of disapproval wafting off him even after he'd put the movie back on and she couldn't relax, despite Chase's solid and reassuring presence beside her.

She couldn't concentrate on the movie and was lost in her thoughts when a soft snore in her ear startled her out of her reverie. She twisted her neck to look up at Chase and came to the gradual realization that his arm was heavy across her shoulders and his body was becoming uncomfortably heavy. She tossed a glance over at Gabe, who was staring at the television screen grimly—he seemed as lost in his thoughts as she had been.

"Gabe," she whispered. He didn't seem to hear her and she escalated her voice to an urgent hiss. *"Gabe!"*

He was startled into jerking his head around to where she and Chase were sitting on the sofa. The questioning look on his face was immediately replaced by amusement when he saw her predicament.

"He's getting heavy," she grunted, and Gabe chuckled before coming over to prod his brother.

"Chase, you're crushing Bobbi." There was no response, and he shook Chase more firmly. Chase sat bolt upright and one hand wrapped around Gabe's throat while the other arm drew back to deliver a punch. Bobbi screamed and the sound seemed to snap Chase out of whatever daze he was in, because his grip immediately loosened. His arms fell to his sides and his hands clenched into tight fists.

"Shit," he swore shakily, his entire body trembling. "I'm sorry. I was . . . I was having a dream."

"Some dream." Gabe kept his voice light, even though Bobbi could see the concern in his eyes. "No harm done. You're knackered though. You should get some sleep."

Chase ran a trembling hand through his hair and nodded. He cast an apologetic glance at Bobbi.

"Sorry about that, sweetie," he said. "I didn't mean to scare you."

"It's all good," she said with a wobbly smile. "You just get a decent night's sleep. We can catch up tomorrow." She got up and hugged him again, her concern for him making her grip tighter than usual. He returned the desperate hug with equal fervor before reluctantly releasing her. He spared a brief shamefaced glance for Gabe before saying a hurried good night and leaving the room. There was an odd and uncomfortable silence after Chase's departure and Bobbi darted a quick look at Gabe. There was a troubled expression on his face as he looked at the door through which Chase had exited the room.

"He's too thin," Bobbi said, and Gabe turned his moody regard on her.

"I know," he agreed.

"I can see why you're worried about him. He looks terrible," she observed, and Gabe sighed deeply, thrusting his hands into his trouser pockets and hunching his shoulders. He didn't bother replying.

"I should go," she said after another prolonged silence and watched Gabe's jaw tighten in response. She looked around for her trainers but could find only one. Frustrated, she went down on her knees to have a look beneath the sofa. Of course it wasn't within easy reach and she fumbled around for it—swearing softly beneath her breath when it kept evading her grasp. When—after a long while—she managed to snag a shoelace and drag it out, her cheeks were flushed with both embarrassment and exertion and she tugged her shoes on self-consciously, acutely aware of the fact that Gabe had been staring at her the entire time.

"Anyway . . ." She tucked back a strand of her hair and focused her eyes on the wall above his left shoulder. "I'll see you. Good night."

"Don't go." The words sounded torn from him and his voice was filled with enough urgency to bring her eyes up to meet his. The entreaty she saw there stole her breath.

"I thought you didn't want me here," she said, and hated how needy she sounded. He held out an unsteady hand to her. She hesitated before stepping toward him. He entwined his fingers with hers and gently tugged her closer until he had her loosely clasped in his arms.

"I want you here." His voice was soft and his eyes gleamed with sincerity as they burned into hers. He cupped her face in his hands and just looked at her for the longest time, his gaze running from her hair, down to eyebrows, nose, mouth—it lingered there—and then back up to her eyes. "You're so damned beautiful, Bobbi mine. I'm happy you're here and I'm sorry if I made you feel unwelcome."

Stunned by the intimate endearment—had he really just called her *his*?—it took Bobbi a moment to gather her thoughts enough to answer. "You didn't want Chase to know about us, I get it."

"That's not it."

"You wanted to spend time with him. I didn't mean to intrude."

"Nope." His thumbs were starting a slow, seductive sweep from her jaw, up to the corners of her mouth and back again.

"Then, I don't understand . . ."

"I wanted to spend time with *you*." He totally dumfounded her with those words and she reached up to his wrists, meaning to stop the distracting stroke of his thumbs so that she could concentrate on his words, but not really succeeding. Instead her hands explored the bones in his wrists and then swept up his strong, veiny forearms and further up to his hard biceps.

"You had a funny way of showing it," she murmured, and his face was so close to hers that her lips brushed against his as she said the words.

"I hated seeing Chase's hands all over you," he confessed. "Absolutely hated it." She drew her head back so that she could look into his eyes.

"What are you talking about? Chase and I hugged."

"You didn't hug, you cuddled and caressed and damned near crept into each other's skins." He looked and sounded completely pissed off and Bobbi felt her eyebrows lift into her hairline.

"Gabe, it's *Chase*, he's like a brother to me," she said.

"*I* was like a brother to you," he pointed out grimly. "And there's not a hell of a lot of difference physically between Chase and me."

"You're *jealous*," she breathed, unable to believe it.

"I'm not," he denied. "I just don't like sharing. Especially not with my brother."

"Hmm, but I don't want Chase, I want *you*," she whispered, stroking her hands over his triceps and down to his waist, where they found the bottom edge of his shirt and crept under it to the warm, muscular flesh beneath. She felt the taut muscles in his abdomen jump against her questing fingers.

"Why?" His question astonished her and her hands stopped their exploration.

"Why what?" she asked warily.

"Why do you want *me*? Why not Chase, who happens to look exactly like me?" Bobbi hesitated, terrified of revealing too much. Gabe knowing that she wanted him physically was one thing but him discovering that she was in love with him was something entirely different. It would complicate an already stressful situation and add even more strain on their already overburdened friendship.

"Because Chase isn't you," she said after a thoughtful pause. She could see that her answer didn't satisfy him and went up on to her toes to kiss him, hoping that it would provide a distraction from his searching questions. It worked, Gabe moaned into her mouth and returned the kiss with a sweet intensity that blew her mind. He had never kissed her like this before. It was almost . . . worshipful and quite loving.

CHAPTER NINE

Bobbi's entire body was humming when she floated her way home across the lawn in the early hours of the morning. Gabe had spent hours making gentle, almost reverential, love to her and that—combined with his display of jealousy earlier—had left her feeling cherished. And hopeful.

She quashed that feeling; it would lead to expectations, which would lead to disappointment and eventually heartbreak. She kept leaving her heart wide open and it would be her downfall. When this thing ended, she would be left alone with her broken heart and unable to talk to anybody because nobody would know about it. It was a difficult position to be in. But nevertheless—while her body still buzzed with the aftereffects of Gabe's expert ministrations—it was easy to fool herself into believing that what they had was real.

She snuck into the house, knowing that the entire security staff knew about her nightly visitations to the Braddock house, but she trusted them to be discreet. Unless her actions put her or her family into direct physical danger, they wouldn't utter a word. In fact she didn't see a single one of them on her return walk home but counted on the fact that *they* knew exactly where she was. They were being tactful, and she thought it was kind of sweet.

She fell into bed with Gabe's scent still all over her, his taste in her mouth. She could still feel the hot, hard thrust of him inside her body and the scrape of his stubble in her neck and on her breasts. She fell asleep with a smile on her lips.

～

Gabe was whistling cheerfully when he drifted down to breakfast that morning. He felt amazing, well rested and in a brilliant mood. He had been utterly sated by the time he had reluctantly let Bobbi leave his bed last night. He wished she had stayed longer though, he may have been unable to perform after their *four* bouts last night, but he'd still wanted to have her curl up next to him and fall asleep. He'd wanted to open his eyes and see her face in the morning light, but she had gently extricated herself and planted one last kiss on his mouth before creeping out of the room with her shoes clutched to her chest.

Gabe grinned when he saw the housekeeper, Letty, who smiled in return.

"Mr. Chase requested a buffet breakfast on the patio," she informed him.

"Thanks, Letty." She nodded and went back to doing whatever it was she did to keep his home running smoothly. He appreciated the work she did and paid her handsomely but wasn't one of those people who got too chatty with the household staff. Chase probably knew her entire life story, including how many children and grandchildren she had and their names. That's just the way he was—warm and approachable for the most part, which was why Chase's sudden unapproachability and unwillingness to talk was so disturbing. He was the complete opposite of Gabe—who tended to keep people at a distance until he got to know them. Only his inner circle ever saw Gabe joke and laugh and play.

When Gabe got to the sunny patio, Chase was staring pensively at the gleaming swimming pool.

"Morning." Chase's head jerked in surprise. He looked up, his expression so tormented for a moment that Gabe's breath caught. The look lasted for only an instant before he shook himself and smiled.

"Morning."

"You get a decent night's sleep?" Gabe asked, as he sat down opposite his brother after helping himself to scrambled eggs, bacon, and toast.

"Hmm . . . you know how it is after you've been on a long-haul flight. I was up at some ungodly hour again, feeling refreshed but frustrated." Gabe suspected that it was more than that disturbing Chase's sleep but before he could ask about it, Chase blindsided him with a question of his own.

"Speaking of which, Bobbi left pretty late, didn't she? Did you guys watch another movie after I went up to bed?" Chase was buttering a slice of toast and didn't see Gabe's expression freeze for a panicked instant. He glanced up before Gabe could reply and whatever he saw on Gabe's face made his eyes widen in shock.

"Oh *God*," he breathed. "Oh my God, Gabe, are you out of your ever-loving *mind*?" Gabe swallowed and felt his face flush with heat.

"It's not what you think," he said lamely.

"You're *not* having sex with Bobbi?" his brother asked, his voice absolutely crawling with disbelief. "With *Bobbi*, for Christ's sake! What the hell are you thinking? Who else knows about this?"

"Nobody," Gabe admitted. "It's nobody's damned business."

"And how long has this been going on?"

"Not long." He couldn't believe it had been only three nights and the more he had of her the more he craved. This need he had for her seemed to grow with every touch.

"And what are your . . ." Chase shook his head and then snorted. "I can't believe I'm asking this, but what are your intentions?"

"My intentions?" Gabe asked, meeting his brother's disapproving stare head on. "My *intentions* are to have breakfast and go to work."

"You know that's not what I meant," Chase growled.

"That's the only answer you're getting though," Gabe retorted, shoveling a forkful of eggs into his mouth and glaring at his brother defiantly.

"This won't end well," Chase predicted. "How the hell could you allow this to happen?"

"It's none of your business." Gabe hated how his brother automatically assumed that whatever was going on between Bobbi and Gabe would end, even though he knew it would as well.

"I'm *making* it my business," Chase responded. "You're going to hurt her."

"You don't know what you're talking about," Gabe said heatedly. "You're making assumptions based on *what*? You don't know what the paradigms of my relationship with Bobbi are."

"Yeah? So what are they? You guys are involved in some secret romance that will eventually lead to marriage and kids? Is that it? Because if that's *not* it, then I'm going to have to kick your dumb arse!"

"Look, we're attracted to each other. That's it. We're working it out of our systems. It's between us and nobody else needs to know about it."

"Bobbi isn't the type of woman you work out of your system, Gabe."

"Why not? Because I happen to have known her longer than the women I've dated and slept with before? They were all daughters, sisters, and friends too, you know? It's hypocritical of you to insist I treat Bobbi differently. We have a mutual respect for each other and we're indulging in an adult relationship with clear-cut boundaries that we've both agreed to."

"You're so full of shit," Chase lambasted him. "You never *hid* your relationships with those other women like they were dirty little secrets. If Bobbi is no different than any of them, *why* are you hiding this from everybody? Have you been out with her in public?"

"We're always out in public," Gabe replied, knowing that it wasn't what Chase had meant.

"Oh cut the crap, Gabriel," Chase derided. "You know that's not what I meant. Bobbi doesn't deserve to be treated like some second-class citizen, good enough for warming your bed but nothing else. You're embarrassed to be seen with her, that's what this is about."

"Don't be ridiculous," Gabe said, feeling guilty as hell. Bobbi *wasn't* the type of woman he was usually seen with. She didn't have the dress sense, the gloss, or the elegance he enjoyed in a woman. Where would he take her for Christ's sake? When she didn't seem to own more than that one ugly dress?

"You're going to hurt her," Chase repeated.

"I'm not a cruel man, Chase," Gabe said, annoyed by his brother's self-righteous attitude.

"No, you're not," Chase agreed, leaving Gabe waiting for the "but" to come. "You're not cruel, you're merely indifferent. Your previous lovers knew the score, when you got bored or they got bored, you both walked away. No ill feelings on either side. You were okay and they were okay. Everything was just . . . *okay*. So what happens when you grow bored with this relationship? When the novelty wears off and you feel the need to move on to the next woman? How do you cut *Bobbi* out of your life? Because that's what you do, Gabe. It's almost surgical—once you call it quits, you never mention them again. No pictures, no fond recollections—it's as if they were never a part of your life. You're a good guy, Gabe. The bloody best man I know and you treat women with the utmost respect when you're with them, but you've never been in a relationship that lasted longer than a month or two. And this thing with Bobbi can't really even qualify as a relationship, can it? Not when you're skulking around pretending that it doesn't even exist."

"That's rich, coming from you, Chase! You're not exactly Mr. Reliable when it comes to women," Gabe retorted, feeling his temper bubbling to the surface.

"I'm not the one who's *shagging* my best friend, you idiot!" Chase's own temper was always quicker to rise than Gabe's, and Gabe could see it sparking in his eyes. "You're going to hurt her but you're too blinded by your own lust to see it."

"Bobbi knows the score." He felt driven to make his brother understand that this wasn't as bad as he seemed to think it was. "And one of the main reasons we decided to keep this quiet was because we feared reactions like yours. The less people who know, the less external pressure from family and friends, and when it ends, there'll be no awkwardness from people who would feel compelled to take sides."

"Oh, so you're doing it for all of us?" Chase asked sarcastically. "How big of you! What a relief to hear that you're not just covering your own butt so that you don't look like a complete dick when you dump Bobbi and move on to your next conquest."

"You have no idea what you're talking about." Gabe pushed his plate aside and shook his head in disgust. He was pissed off and hurt by his brother's low opinion of him. "*None.* This thing between Bobbi and me sprang up out of nowhere; it's not something I went looking for. It just happened and I'm trying to deal with it as best I can. So, I'd appreciate it if you'd butt out. This is between Bobbi and me."

Chase looked like he was about to respond but he clamped his lips together and said nothing. His eyes were stormy and he still looked royally pissed off, but he thankfully said nothing further. Gabe knew better than to think that his brother would let it go though and he already dreaded the next confrontation.

∽

Gabe's day didn't improve. Mike was being difficult and insisted on knowing every single detail about the Valentine's Day Ball. Since Gabe didn't know a *single* damned thing about the ball, trusting their assistants to get it done, his replies to the older man's questions hadn't satisfied Mike and had led to a heated debate about what each man believed leadership roles entailed. Accusing Mike of micromanaging hadn't helped the escalating argument and the man had hung up in a huff, leaving Gabe frustrated and bad-tempered. He and Mike often disagreed, but this was a petty argument, which had escalated because of Mike's misgivings about retiring and Gabe's already foul temper after that morning's argument with Chase.

An hour later, while he was instructing Stephanie to set up a meeting with one of the GNT accounting executives about restructuring the company's pricing packages, his cell phone rang. He glanced down and grimaced when he saw his mother's photo on the screen.

"I have to take this," he told his assistant and the woman politely excused herself. Gabe watched her leave before picking up the call.

"Hi, Mum," he greeted.

"Hello, darling," his mother greeted warmly. "How are you?"

"All good here, Mum."

"Wonderful." His mother wasn't one to waste time before getting to the point and that was the case now. "I've been concerned about your brother. When will he be back in town?"

Great. Gabe winced. He didn't want to lie to his mother, but Chase had put him in an impossible situation. If he came clean now, they'd both be in the crapper.

"You might want to talk to Chase about that, Mum," he said carefully and there was a long pause before his mother replied.

"I asked you a straightforward question, Gabriel. Why can't you give me a straightforward answer?" Full name. Fabulous. This wasn't going to end well. Their mother knew that something was up.

"I thought I *did* give you a straightforward answer," he said.

"No, you tried to divert me back to your brother."

"Mum . . ."

"Where's your brother, Gabriel?" she asked bluntly.

"Mum . . ."

"Don't you 'mum' *me*, young man. Just answer the question." Lucy Templeton-Braddock Colbert could be downright terrifying when she wanted to be.

"At home," he confessed miserably.

"And why did neither of you see fit to inform me before now?" She sounded unsurprised, which meant that she had known beforehand but had decided to put him in the hot seat for the sheer hell of it.

"You knew," he accused.

"Roberta told me." Their mother had never called her Bobbi. "I called her earlier to ask her about her new boyfriend and *she* tried to distract me too, by saying that I must be happy to have Chase back in town. This time the distraction worked because I wasn't aware that my *own son* was home."

"Mum, you should talk to Chase about . . ." He paused as his mother's words sank in. "What new boyfriend?"

"Don't change the subject, Gabriel," she said, but he barely heard her.

"Mum, what boyfriend are you talking about?" he asked urgently, wondering if there were any rumors floating around about Bobbi and him.

"The landscape architect she's seeing, Kyle something. I heard about him from Suzie Claiborne," his mother said dismissively before continuing on her original course of chastisement, but Gabe wasn't listening anymore. He was wondering why the hell Jason's mother seemed to think that Bobbi was seeing that Kyle guy.

"Gabe, are you listening to me?" His mother's voice had elevated shrilly and he shook himself and refocused on her tirade.

"Sorry mum, I was distracted by . . . stuff." He grimaced at the lame excuse but his mother wasn't paying attention.

"I said we're coming around for dinner," she said.

"Mum, look . . ." He sighed. "I'm sorry we didn't tell you that Chase is home but you have to prepare yourself. He looks . . . he doesn't look great. He's lost a lot of weight and he just seems exhausted. I think he knew that it would worry you, so try to lay off the guilt tripping, okay? I can take it but I don't think he's in a great place at the moment." He and Chase may be at odds, but that didn't mean that Gabe was going to hang his brother out to dry.

His mother was quiet for a long while after he had spoken and a shuddering sigh on the other end of the line told him that she was crying.

"I'm just happy he's home," she said, punctuating the sentiment with a wet sniff. "I won't say anything about his appearance. Thank you for the warning."

"No problem," he said. "Love you, Mum."

"I know, darling," his mother said softly. "I love you too."

Gabe disconnected the call and then glared off into the middle distance, thinking about Bobbi's *boyfriend*. What was that all about?

~

"I hear you're seeing that Kyle guy." Gabe's deep voice sent a shudder of longing down Bobbi's spine before she registered his words.

"Oh my God . . . ," she groaned. "Not you too."

"No truth to the rumor then?" He asked in a strained voice.

"That's a stupid question," she shot back. "When exactly was I supposed to squeeze in a budding romance with Kyle Foster when I've been spending my free time in dead-end shagfest with *you*?"

There was a long silence at the other end of the line.

"My mother, Frank, and Kim are coming round for dinner tonight," he said after a while. "I think it'll be a late night, so it'll probably be best if you didn't come around."

Wow. That hurt more than it should have. Under normal circumstances, he would have included Bobbi in what was essentially a family gathering. So this was what it would be like after they ended their *thing*. They would remain friends, of a sort, but he would start excluding Bobbi from more and more of the family meals and outings until they would simply have "drifted apart." It wouldn't be intentional but it would be the inexorable result of an impossible situation.

"Okay," she whispered. "I'll chat with you tomorrow then."

"Yeah . . . ," he said, sounding reluctant, and she winced. "Okay, I've got to go. Take care."

"You too," she said, forcing the words out, hating how thick with tears they sounded.

"Bobbi," he said, just before she disconnected, and her heart leapt hopefully. "Chase saw you leave this morning. He knows about us . . . our having sex. I thought you should be aware of that."

"Oh." Chase knew? How did he feel about it? What did he think of her? Of Gabe? She wanted to ask Gabe but he didn't seem open to discussion at the moment.

"Thanks for letting me know."

"Right." God, he sounded so cold that it sent an icy tremor through her body. "See you."

He disconnected before she could reply, and she carefully put her phone down and unseeingly stared at the shop floor through the windows of her office. Sean and Craig were working on the Corvette and she was taking care of the paperwork as always. She bowed her head over another of the endless order forms that was piled in front of her and desperately tried to keep her tears at bay. She never cried. Never. And she refused to cry now. She had gone into this knowing full well how it would end; so crying over it would be stupid.

She picked up her pen and started to write again. She was stronger than this. She knew she was. She wouldn't cry. Not now. Not for this.

Gabe was miserable throughout dinner. He shouldn't have told her not to come around. As the time came for his mother, Frank, and Kim to head home, all he could think about was that he wouldn't be seeing Bobbi later. He thought about calling her and telling her to come by after his mother left, but he wasn't sure if she was even speaking to him at the moment. He knew that he'd been a bit abrupt with her that afternoon. But once he explained the strain he had been under she would surely understand? Hearing that everyone thought that she was dating Kyle Foster hadn't really helped the situation, not when Gabe suddenly and inexplicably found himself wanting to go out and tell everybody who she was *really* involved with.

He ignored the small voice in the back of his mind that told him he was a selfish arsehole and instead tried to figure out how to get her to come around. He was still trying to figure it out when he kissed his mother and hugged his stepfather and sister good-bye. Chase had been quiet throughout the evening and their mother had been extremely tactful around him. All in all it had been a relatively successful evening.

He dragged his phone out of his pocket, hoping to see a message from Bobbi, but there was nothing. His heart sank in disappointment and he knew he'd probably have to apologize for his earlier dickishness.

"Are you going to tell Bobbi to come sneaking over?" The unexpected sound of Chase's voice startled him into nearly dropping the phone.

"That's none of your damned business," he growled over his shoulder and Chase glowered at him.

"Stop telling me it's none of my business!" he retorted, coming around to face Gabe. "I love that girl like a sister and you're my brother. Not only is this extremely weird for me, it is *totally* my business. I don't want to see either of you get hurt."

"Nice of you to show some concern for me too," Gabe said sarcastically.

"You've been around the block a few times more than she has, but that doesn't mean that you don't stand to lose as much as she does," Chase pointed out.

"What do you mean?" Gabe asked, confused.

"If . . . *when* this thing goes south, you're going to lose Bobbi," Chase said.

"No, we have . . ."

"An arrangement," Chase completed. "Yeah, I know. You're still going to lose her and I can't believe you're unable to see that."

"We know what we're doing," Gabe maintained stubbornly, and Chase sighed.

"God," he said tiredly. "I can't decide if you're being willfully blind or deliberately stupid. You know, Gabe, if it was just *your* happiness at stake, I'd leave you to make your own dumb mistakes, but I don't know if I can stand idly by while you hurt Bobbi. "

"You seem to have an extremely low opinion of me, Chase. Why can't you trust me to know what's best for both Bobbi and me?"

"Because I don't think you know what's best, right now, Gabe," Chase said, laying a gentle hand on Gabe's shoulder. "I don't have a low opinion of you. I just think you've lost sight of the bigger picture."

"I'm going to bed," Gabe said, shrugging off his brother's hand. "Don't worry, Bobbi is safe from my nefarious attentions tonight. I'll see you in the morning."

~

Bobbi didn't hear from Gabe the next day, and she tried to keep her mind occupied with work. She was running on empty from lack of sleep and food. She felt like a zombie and was functioning on auto-pilot. She felt alone and desperately needed to talk to someone. So when Chase walked into her shop at five that afternoon, she felt a warm tide of relief and gratitude flood through her entire being.

"Chase," she murmured, and dropped what she was doing to walk straight into his arms.

"Hey, sweetie." He kissed her head and it was all she could do not to melt into a messy puddle of tears. "Want to get a drink somewhere?"

She nodded and his arms tightened for a brief moment before he looked down into her miserable face and dropped a swift kiss on her forehead.

"I'll just tell the guys to close shop early and grab my things," she said, feeling somewhat embarrassed. It was a relief that Chase knew about her and Gabe because it gave her someone to talk to, but it also made her feel incredibly shy and self-conscious. His eyes were filled with gentle understanding though and not in the slightest bit judgmental, which was something she had feared after Gabe had told her that Chase knew.

Sean and Craig had watched the scene unfold and both looked concerned when she told them that she would be leaving early. Craig followed her to her office and watched as she shut down her computer and straightened up her desk.

"You okay, boss?" he asked gruffly. "We noticed that you seemed off today. We were worried about you."

"Thank you for asking, Craig," she said, touched by their concern. "I'm fine, just feeling out of sorts. You know how paperwork depresses me."

He looked unconvinced and shoved his hands into his overall pockets and swayed back and forth on his heels.

"You sure?" he asked, and she felt a surge of affection for the tough, no-nonsense man. He had a rough exterior but he was a huge softie, a family man devoted to his wife and daughters. That paternal instinct sometimes carried over in his dealings with Bobbi.

"I'm sure . . ." She went onto her toes and pressed a quick kiss on his cheek. "Thank you."

He looked embarrassed and cleared his throat before backing away.

"No problem. Anytime you need to talk . . ." He left the statement open-ended and hastened out of the room. Bobbi grinned at his retreating back before unzipping her overalls and hanging them up on the hook beside the door. She rinsed her face and hands before heading back out to meet Chase.

"Ready?" Chase asked, when she joined him again and she nodded.

"You drive," she suggested. "We can come back here later to pick up my car." He nodded and led her toward the Jeep that he always drove when he was home. The Jeep belonged to Gabe, but he was always happy to let Chase use it.

Chase automatically ran ahead to get the passenger door for her and she smiled at him in appreciation as she clambered into the seat. The Jeep was like a comfortable old friend. She always felt a fuzzy sense of homecoming when she slid into its passenger seat.

When Chase climbed into the driver's side, Bobbi turned to speak to him.

"Do you mind if we avoid Manny's tonight?" she asked softly. "I'm not really in the mood to hang out with everybody."

"Yeah, me either." He grimaced at the thought. He drove them to the nearby Hout Bay instead, which had more choices when it came to restaurants and pubs. They agreed on a place that neither had been to before, less chance of running into chatty old friends that way.

Once they were seated and ordered their drinks, they stared at each other for a long while.

"I guess you think I'm an idiot." Bobbi broke the silence between them, toying with the basket of cutlery on the table.

"Not even close." He shook his head. "I think Gabe is the idiot."

"For getting involved with me?" she asked miserably.

"For not telling the world that he snagged you," Chase corrected, and she raised hopeful eyes to his, not sure if he was joking. His eyes were serious and met hers without flinching, and he only broke eye contact when the server brought his beer and her gin and tonic.

"You mean that?" she asked, after the smiling server had left, hating the wavering note in her voice.

"Damned right I mean that," he growled. "He's made a complete mess of things."

"Try not to judge him too harshly, he's doing what he thinks is right," she said softly, fishing the lime out of her drink and dropping it onto a paper napkin. "He didn't know how to handle the attraction between us. It shocked the hell out of him, and he's still not sure how to cope with it."

"*You* seem to be handling it just fine," Chase pointed out, and Bobbi flushed miserably. She focused on swirling the plastic swizzle stick around her glass, making sure her drink was thoroughly mixed, before raising her eyes back to his.

"I've had more time to get used to it. I've been attracted to Gabe for years and I've learned how to deal with my feelings. Gabe . . . hasn't yet."

"Years?" Chase asked in disbelief, and Bobbi nodded.

"Years."

"You never let on, not once," he said, sounding staggered.

"I still haven't. He thinks this is as new to me as it is to him and I feel dishonest because of that. And he would still quite happily be treating me like his little sister if I hadn't gotten drunk at a party last Friday and kissed him, so don't go thinking he seduced me or anything," she warned.

"Still, he finds that he has a previously undiscovered passion for you and his first instinct is to cover it up?"

"Chase, one day I was his best buddy, and the next day he was fighting to keep his hands off me." She was trying to be logical and hated herself for defending Gabe despite knowing that it would be unfair to blame him for every wrong choice. "I should never have kissed him. I didn't know how he would respond and I'm pretty sure I wrecked our friendship because of one reckless and stupid decision."

Chase took a long, thirsty swig of his beer before he replied.

"I don't like the secrecy, Bobbi," he said, and she sighed.

"I knew what I was doing when I agreed to his terms, Chase. I just didn't expect it to be so difficult. One minute I'm floating on cloud nine and the next I feel . . . small and unworthy and just so *stupid*." Chase swore roughly and she flinched.

"I want to kill him for making you feel like that," he growled, and she reached over to stroke his hand, where it rested beside his drink.

"Thank you but . . . *he's* not the one who made me feel that way. I am. I agreed to his terms, I thought I could handle it. A quick affair, that is all he has to offer. At first I thought—" She broke off what she'd been about to say, knowing that it would only infuriate Chase further. Admitting that she'd expected Gabe to want a proper relationship with her after discovering his attraction to her still made her feel ridiculously naïve.

"At first you thought . . . ?" Chase prompted, and she shook her head, sipping her drink to avoid replying.

"It's nothing," she said with a dismissive wave of her hand, and Chase's face was a study in sheer frustration.

"Bobbi, you do know that you deserve more than this shoddy treatment, right?" Chase asked, and she sighed.

"I know. I just spent years mooning over the guy and this seemed like the only way I could get him. I knew that it would be temporary; I knew that it would place an enormous strain on our friendship and I kind of knew that it would probably hurt like hell when it ended. Knowing all of that doesn't make the process any easier though," she admitted.

"This is such a mess," Chase said.

"Hmm, but it's not your mess, Chase. Gabe and I will deal with it. I need you to be my friend though, and Gabe needs his brother. We don't need you to take sides . . . please don't take sides," she said, her voice soft with entreaty.

"Both you and Gabe keep saying that you know what you're doing," Chase observed in a low voice. "But from where I'm sitting you both look totally clueless. It's frustrating the hell out of me because it's like I can see the road ahead of you and it's leading straight off a cliff."

"I see the cliff," she said. "I'm pretty sure Gabe sees it too . . . but sometimes falling is just inevitable."

CHAPTER TEN

Gabe kept checking his phone for messages from Bobbi but of course there were none. He knew that she wouldn't call or SMS—not after the way he had blown her off the night before—but he didn't know what her reaction would be to a call from him.

He missed her.

Not just the sexy woman who had become his lover but the endearing friend who brightened up his days with her endless chatter about cars, her silly pranks in the past, and her quirky—often insightful—observations about life in general. It was after ten and he was sitting in the den, morosely staring at his phone, unsure of his next move.

Chase ambled into the room and Gabe's first instinct was to tuck the phone beneath the sofa cushions. Chase raised an eyebrow at him and Gabe flushed, feeling like a defensive teenager.

"Really?" His brother shook his head and sat down on one of the recliners. "You're hiding your phone from me? Just call her. It's better than having you mope around the house."

"I'm not moping," Gabe responded automatically, and then felt even more adolescent. Sometimes his brother brought out the worst in him.

"Could have fooled me." Chase rolled his eyes, reached for the TV remote, and started to rapidly flick through the channels and every microsecond of noisy color that flashed onto the screen irritated the hell out of Gabe.

"Pick a damned channel," he snapped, but Chase ignored him, continuing to cycle through the channels at the speed of light. Swearing irritably, Gabe vacated the room, seeking solitude.

He settled for the patio and dropped into a lounger beside the lighted pool. For a few minutes he just sat there, listening to the sounds of the night insects and frogs chirping, croaking, and whirring as they went about their business.

Just call her. He repeated Chase's words to himself. What was the worst she could do? Hang up on him? He winced at the thought. God, he hoped she didn't hang up on him. He had no Plan B.

He pushed the "Call" button and listened to the phone ring for a few endless moments. It rang for so long he was almost certain it would switch to voice mail, but when her breathless voice answered, he found himself both relieved and panicked.

"Hello?" His mouth had gone dry and he couldn't quite bring himself to respond to her greeting. He considered hanging up but . . . "Gabe?"

Yeah, Caller ID screwed him over. Of course she knew who it was.

"Hi, Bobbi," he croaked, ridiculously nervous. "How are you?"

"Fine," she said after a long silence. "And you?"

"I'm . . ." The *fine* hovered on his tongue and he opened his mouth to say it. "I'm a jerk. An idiot. A complete dick. And so, *so* sorry, Bobbi mine. I shouldn't have been so abrupt with you last night. But . . . I *was*. And that's no excuse. I have no excuse. I just hope you'll forgive me?"

No response.

"Bobbi? Are you there?" he asked nervously.

"Yes," she whispered.

"I've missed you," he told her softly, wishing he could see her. It frustrated him, not being able to see her face and read her mood.

"I missed you too, Gabe." There was another long silence.

"Are you still angry with me?"

"I wasn't angry with you," she corrected.

"Will you come around tonight?" he asked.

"I-I don't think so, Gabe," she said after another endless pause and Gabe's entire world started crumbling around him at the rejection. "I'll be there for the football tomorrow night."

"Right," he responded numbly. He'd forgotten about the Friday night game. The guys and their significant others would be descending on his house the following evening. "Football. Of course."

"I'll see you then, okay?"

"Okay," he repeated. He held the phone to his ear for a long time after she'd disconnected the call before dropping his arm. He sat on the lounger, hands clasped between his knees, elbows resting on thighs, and head down as he tried to figure out what to do next.

"Gabe." Chase's voice startled him and he looked up to see his brother standing in front of him. Chase sat down on the lounger opposite his. "You okay?"

"Not really," he responded honestly, and Chase sighed. "You'll be happy to know she's not coming around tonight."

"Seeing you like this doesn't make me happy, Gabe." Chase's voice was almost gentle.

"You were right, you know? I don't know what the hell I'm doing, Chase." Gabe hated how his voice cracked. "I should never have touched her . . . but she's just so damned alluring, so completely irresistible with that quirky smile, those lively eyes, and that wicked sense of humor."

"You do realize that you don't sound like a man who's just physically attracted to a woman, right?" Chase pointed out, and Gabe frowned.

"What do you mean?"

"Smile? Eyes? Sense of humor?" Chase repeated. "I was expecting tits, arse, and killer legs."

"*Watch* it," Gabe warned. "And she does have all of those as well, of course."

"Gabe, you need to figure out what you want from her and fast, before you muck things up even more than you already have."

Gabe snorted. Like he didn't know that already.

Twenty-four hours later, Bobbi nervously made her way across the lawn toward the gate. She hadn't heard from Gabe since his phone call the night before and she wasn't quite sure what to expect from him tonight. She had felt awful after that awkward telephone conversation. It had been so tempting to just say yes and rush to his side again—but he couldn't keep blowing hot and cold like that. It was too emotionally draining.

She crossed the threshold of the gate onto Braddock property and followed the echoing sound of masculine laughter coming from the back of the house. Gabe had a standard-sized football field, complete with lines and goalposts in his huge backyard. He'd even had small bleachers built on either side of the pitch. Their friends and family only ever used the stands closest to the house and there were never enough people to actually fill them but Gabe liked symmetry—so of course he had to have two sets of bleachers.

The group of men were standing around, chatting and stretching, a couple of them had pregame beers clutched in their hands. Their original group had grown to include Rick and Bryce Palmer, Pierre De Coursey, and Rick's business partner, Vuyo Mashego. Bryce was more of a rugby player and didn't take the Friday night games as seriously as some of the other men. He was one of the guys with a beer in hand, and so was his brother and Max Kinsley, a joker who didn't seem to take anything seriously.

They usually played five a side: goalkeeper, two defenders, a midfielder, and a striker. Chase saw her first and ran over to meet her halfway.

"Hey." He grinned when he saw her all kitted out in her usual football gear.

"Hi. Are you playing tonight?" she asked. With Chase there they had eleven players.

"I'm thinking of substituting." He shrugged, not seeming particularly concerned about it. "Or refereeing, maybe."

"Is everybody here?" Bobbi casually glanced around the field.

"He's inside," Chase told her, and she rolled her eyes, hating how obvious she was. "He's waiting for Sandro. Everybody else is here. Except Billy, who called to say he'd be a bit late."

"Did he say wh—" She stopped mid-word when she caught sight of Gabe exiting the house with Sandro and Theresa in tow. He had his arm wrapped around Rosalie De Lucci's slender shoulders, and Bobbi felt like she took a blow to her solar plexus. She fought to catch her breath and couldn't take her eyes off the gorgeous couple.

Bobbi hadn't given the other woman any further thought after last Saturday. When the stunning woman hadn't been at the girls' night out, Bobbi had assumed that Rosalie De Lucci had returned to Italy. But no, here she was, showing up again like the proverbial bad penny. Gabe had his head bent toward hers, giving her his full attention as she said something to him.

"What's wrong?" Chase asked, following the direction of her gaze. She was vaguely aware of him tensing beside her. "Who the hell is *that*?"

"Sandro's sister, Rosalie," she supplied, her voice sounding hollow even to her own ears. Theresa and Sandro finally reached the gathering beside the stands and everybody shouted out friendly greetings. Sandro was toting their sleeping toddler on his hip, he had his free arm around his wife's waist, and he drew her in for a hug and a kiss before transferring the baby to her.

"Go on," Theresa prompted her husband with a laugh. "Run. Be free." Sandro grinned and jogged onto the field lazily, doing a series of stretches along the way. Like Gabe, he tended to take football more seriously than Bryce and Max did.

Bobbi couldn't drag her eyes away from Gabe and Rosalie though. They had paused halfway to the field, and he was brushing her hair off her brow with a grin. The wind kept catching the silky strands and blowing it back into her face, so Gabe was fighting a losing battle. They looked like the cover of a romance novel standing there, leaning into each other with the wind in her hair and the backlights from the house delineating their shapes in silver. Bobbi would never look *that* perfect standing next to him. People would constantly wonder what he was doing with her. With Rosalie De Lucci they'd only nod and think, *Of course those two are together.*

She felt Chase's arm creep around her waist and she leaned against his solid frame, needing the support.

"I don't know what the hell that's about," Chase murmured in her ear. "But it's probably not what it looks like. Turn away, before he sees that look on your face. You look like a woman who's just had her heart ripped out of her chest."

How apt. Since that was how she felt. She allowed him to turn her toward the field and watched the men warm up. Some of them, like Sandro, Vuyo, Pierre, and Rafael Dante looked almost professional, while the rest goofed around, kicking the ball to and fro and bantering while they did it.

"Let's go get warmed up," Chase suggested, and she nodded, needing to find some way to distract herself from the fact that Gabe still hadn't joined them on the field. She maintained such total focus on her running and stretching that she barely noticed when someone came up to jog beside her until he spoke.

"I'm glad you're here." His voice made her break stride and stumble. She would have fallen if he hadn't reached out to steady her.

"Gabe, I'm surprised you were able to drag yourself from Rosalie De Lucci's side," she said, and then winced at how bitter she sounded. She had promised herself she wouldn't say anything but there she was putting her foot in her mouth again. She self-consciously wiped her sweaty face on the shoulder of her T-shirt before realizing how completely unsexy that must have looked. Especially in comparison with the ever-fresh, ever-polished Rosalie De Lucci.

"Don't be childish, Bobbi. Rosalie is a friend and a very nice woman on top of that." And he obviously found her attractive.

"You think she's beautiful though."

"Because she *is*," he said impatiently, clearly done with the conversation. "You've been warming up for a while, the guys are ready to play." He nodded toward the group of tall men standing in the middle of the field, and she felt her face flush in embarrassment. "Billy isn't here yet, so Chase is subbing for whichever team picks him."

She nodded brusquely and jogged toward the waiting group, leaving him standing there. When he joined them seconds later, the team captains, Sandro and Gabe, flipped a coin to see who would have first pick of the players. Gabe won and immediately picked Bobbi. She didn't know how she felt about that; he'd *never* picked her first before. Neither of the men ever had. She wasn't the strongest player, but she made up for it with speed and agility. Still the guys usually chose the bigger men first and the last choice always came down to Max and Bobbi, and she generally always got picked before poor Max.

~

They were well into the first half of the game when Billy came jogging out of the house and toward the field. He was followed by Jason, who joined their football game only occasionally and . . . Bobbi stopped so abruptly that she got a ball kicked straight in the face. The impact made her reel for a second, before she actually lost her footing and sank down on her butt. The game came to a halt as everybody gathered around her to check if she was okay. Gabe muscled his way through the huddled men and went down on his haunches in front of her, looking pale and shaken.

"Are you okay?" he asked in an unsteady voice, wincing as he reached out to touch the enflamed skin of her cheek. Bobbi grimaced and shied away from his hand before he could make contact. She didn't want him touching her in front of an audience because—despite the stinging pain—she knew that she would totally embarrass herself by leaning into his touch.

"I'm fine." She dismissed all the concerned queries and instead focused on her brother and Jason and the creative ways she planned to murder them both. They had brought Kyle Foster. Of *course* they had brought Kyle Foster! God, could her life be any more complicated? Last Friday she'd been just another woman mooning over her handsome best friend. A week later and she was involved in a super-secret affair with said best friend and had an *admirer* who all of her friends and family thought was her new boyfriend.

Gabe looked like he was about to help her up, but Chase leapt in and took Bobbi's hand to tug her up. She smiled at him gratefully.

"Are you sure you're okay to play?" Gabe asked. She waved off his concern and trotted off to the sidelines for a quick drink of water. Billy, Kyle, and Jason joined her.

"That was quite a hit," Billy said with brotherly glee. "You're gonna look like hell tomorrow." She glared at him, or she would have if the left side of her face didn't felt so numb and swollen.

"Hi, Bobbi," Kyle greeted, while Jason not so subtly elbowed Billy in the ribs and the two backed off like pubescent teens.

"Hey, Kyle, nice seeing you again." He winced as he looked at her face and reached out to run a gentle finger over the stinging area.

"Looks painful," he observed.

"It hurts like hell," she managed cheerfully. "But you know, it's all part of the game. I lost focus for a second and took my eye off the ball. It's my own fault, really."

He smiled and she returned the smile, but when she happened to look over his shoulder it was to see her brother making kissy faces at her. She diverted her attention to the bleachers, where Bronwyn and Lisa were winking at her suggestively. Bobbi sighed and directed her eyes down at her feet, knowing that she probably appeared coy but was too afraid to meet anybody else's eye. Seriously, what was wrong with everybody?

～

Gabe was furious. When he saw Bobbi go down, his entire body had constricted with fear, and he just couldn't seem to reach her fast enough. He had felt like he was running through a lake of molasses to get to her. When he had eventually fought his way through the seemingly impenetrable wall of men surrounding her, he had nearly howled at the sight of her red and swollen face. He had wanted nothing more than to sweep her up into his arms and transport her to some place where he could protect her, spoil her, and take care of her, but she had flinched away from his touch, and that more than anything else had cut him to the core. He had no claim on her. He would *never* have any claim on her. Some other man would one day have the right to do everything Gabe had wanted to do. But that didn't mean that Gabe had to *like* the thought of that future man.

He watched her walk off the field and frowned when he saw Billy, Jason, and a third man make their way over to her. Billy and Jason backed off and the third man . . .

A growl worked its way up to his throat as he watched the guy *touch* her. Exactly the way Gabe had wanted to touch her earlier. This guy had even less claim on her than Gabe and yet he had the utter gall to touch her? And worse she was allowing it? That well and truly pissed him off, and he stalked over to the sidelines toward them. The closer her got, the more about the stranger he recognized—it *looked* like that Kyle Foster guy from the pub, but why the hell was he here? Who had invited him?

A fulminating glare at Billy and Jason, who were quite merrily watching Bobbi and Kyle exchange awkward pleasantries, confirmed that one—or likely both—of them was the culprit.

"Bobbi," he snapped when he reached them. "Are you ready to join the game again?"

She looked surprised to see Gabe standing right beside her but she nodded, and Kyle took her water bottle from her, with a promise to "guard it" with his "life." Did the idiot think someone would steal her damned water bottle? Gabe glowered at the jerk, who merely looked back at him impassively.

"Braddock." He nodded, a small smile on his lips. Gabe refused to acknowledge the greeting, no matter how damned petty he seemed and trotted onto the field after Bobbi. The game resumed moments later.

∼

Bobbi didn't see the hit coming. One second she was skillfully maneuvering the football through a duo of hapless defenders, and the next she was flat on her back, blinking up at the star-filled night sky and battling to suck in her next breath.

Panic set in when she realized that she was unable to draw in that breath and a distant, detached part of her brain recognized that she'd had the wind knocked out of her. It was a highly unpleasant sensation that she hadn't had the dubious privilege of experiencing since childhood. Man, she was having a really terrible night.

"Bobbi?" A group of concerned faces popped into her field of vision, and she tried to assure them that she was fine, but only a wheeze emerged from her chest.

"What the hell, Kinsley?" Gabe's face was hovering on her left and he fixed a glare on Max, who seemed to be hovering on her right. "What's up with the frikkin body check?"

"I slipped," Max explained defensively. "It was totally unintentional."

"She could have been seriously injured, she's just a tiny thing," Gabe pointed out insultingly. If Bobbi had her breath back she would have taken exception to that, but she was barely getting in a decent gasp of air every few seconds and it took all of her concentration to breathe normally again.

"Oh come, Gabe. She can handle herself." Bobbi lifted a limp hand and gave Max a thumbs-up in agreement.

"See?" Max pointed toward her. Bobbi mentally rolled her eyes and cursed them for worrying about her in theory but not in practice. Neither of them had even bothered to ask her if she was okay. Feeling neglected, she pushed herself up into a sitting position and gingerly prodded her ribs to ensure that they were still intact. She grimaced. They were a bit sore but it was nothing major.

Gabe and Max were so focused on each other they barely noticed when she shakily made her way to her feet. The other players were all too caught up in the unfolding drama of Gabe and Max squaring off to pay much attention to her. She always felt like a little person in the land of giants when she stood amongst all of them like this. It didn't help that she found herself practically sandwiched between Gabe and Max. They were the tallest guys there.

The men were both bristling with outrage and an overabundance of testosterone, and Bobbi hissed impatiently before placing a small, restraining hand on each of their chests. She wrinkled her nose in disgust as her hands settled onto equally sweat-soaked T-shirts and tried not to appreciate the well-defined musculature of the chests beneath the revoltingly wet shirts. Especially not Gabe's; she was trying very hard not to appreciate Gabe's chest too much. It felt like every time she took one step forward she took about eighty-seven steps back.

"I'm fine," she asserted firmly, trying very hard not to sound wheezy, knowing that it would set Gabe off again. He looked down at her and his eyes went flat with fury.

"Damn it," he gritted. "She's bleeding."

"I am?" she asked blankly, hesitantly reaching up to touch her face. She blanched when her fingers came away covered in blood. "Oh my God, I am!" Bobbi was tough and could withstand quite a lot of things, but she couldn't stomach the sight of her own blood. Anybody else's? *Sure!* Her own? Not at all.

She swayed woozily and Gabe reached out a hand to steady her. He ducked his head to peer into her eyes intently.

"Take a deep breath," he advised, and she complied with a shallow gasp.

"*Deep* breath, Bobbi," he repeated authoritatively. Nope. She couldn't get her lungs to work and she swayed again, as black dots swirled in front of her eyes. God, how embarrassing! She felt like she was about to faint. She vaguely wondered how she knew that, when she had never fainted in her life before. Gabe swore beneath his breath and shifted one of his arms to her back and the other to the back of her thighs before hefting her up to his chest like a sack of potatoes. He carried her to the sidelines, where the other women had all anxiously gathered around and lowered her gently to the grass.

"Oh my God, Gabriel, is she okay?" Bobbi blinked up into the worried faces around her, recognizing the voice as Theresa's. Her friend knelt down on the grass beside her and pressed a towel to the profusely bleeding cut on Bobbi's eyebrow.

"She's fine," Gabe reassured. "The sight of her own blood makes her a bit queasy." *Of course* he would know that embarrassing fact about her.

"Take care of her, will you?" Gabe handed her care over with one last grim look down at her before trotting back out onto the field.

Theresa sucked in a shocked breath, and Bobbi looked up at her in alarm. Was the cut worse than it seemed? Was that why her friend seemed so appalled? But Theresa wasn't even looking at her; the other woman's eyes were fixed on something on the field. Bobbi watched as her friend cringed and followed the direction of her stare to whatever was happening out on the field. The guys were all huddled in a tight circle, and Bobbi couldn't quite make sense of what was going on.

"What's happening?" she asked, her injury forgotten.

"Gabe and Max just got into a bit of a shoving match." Theresa, usually so kind and gentle, seemed to find that fact hilarious.

"Oh my God. That idiot," Bobbi moaned, pushing herself up unsteadily before standing up on wobbly legs. Theresa held on to her arm, obviously afraid Bobbi would lose her balance. She shook off the remnants of her dizziness like a dog shaking off water and marched purposefully back onto the field.

The other guys had managed to separate the two men and Gabe was standing off to the side with Sandro. He was still glaring at an unconcerned Max, who was ignoring him and calmly chatting with Chase. It was clear from the handsome Italian's stance that Sandro was trying to keep Gabe calm.

"Sandro, would you excuse us please?" Bobbi planted herself between the two men, and Sandro shrugged.

"I'll get the grill started. I think maybe my Theresa is hungry. I say this match is probably over."

"Yeah, getting the *braai* started is a good idea. I doubt any of us are in the mood to finish this game," Bobbi agreed, and Sandro walked off to where Theresa stood waiting for him.

"What the hell is *wrong* with you?" Bobbi turned on Gabe, who was watching her with a moody expression on his face. His brow lowered at the sight of the blood on her forehead and the rapidly forming bruise on the left side of her face. Bobbi knew she looked awful but wished that fact wasn't so clearly reflected in his disgusted expression.

"Look at you," he muttered. "Just *look* at the state of you! How am I supposed to even consider having a real relationship with a woman who wears overalls to work, hasn't styled her hair in years, never wears makeup, and has *grease* under her fingernails? And then there's this tendency of yours to get into the weirdest bloody situations. You get hurt and bruised and scuffed up. How am I supposed to deal with that, for God's sake? I can't keep you insulated against the entire world. I just can't. How would you fit into my life? Where would I even put you?" The words were despairing and made no sense to Bobbi. She was just so astonished by this meltdown from a man who was used to keeping his cool. "I need someone else, someone who knows how to dress and handle herself in public, someone who won't show up at events with questionable bruises . . ."

"*Stop*," she whispered. "Please just stop, Gabe. Before you say something that we can't come back from."

"Don't you understand?" His voice was edged with panic. "We're already done . . . When we were just friends, your rough and tumble ways didn't bother me half as much. The way things stand between us now? I just can't watch you get hurt anymore."

"Then *stop hurting me*." Her quietly wailed plea seemed to register and the panicked glaze left his eyes to be replaced by a different kind of alarm. She shoved against his chest with both hands with enough strength to send him staggering back a step. The rest of the group was trying to maintain a discreet distance but she could see that they were all hovering close by, probably not sure if they should intervene or not. "Just stop hurting me! Because that's all you've been doing. You don't think I'm good enough for you. Did you think I was ever unaware of that fact? But, I swallowed my pride and allowed you to hatch this insane *arrangement*—God I *hate* that word so much—between us. Any romantic notions I had about you died that night in my father's den. Because I was imagining a real relationship with you, while *you* were trying to fix it so that we could shag regularly without anybody ever finding out.

"I felt small and cheap and stupid but I allowed it because I knew that it was the only way I could have you. I knew it was my *one* chance to be with you." Her eyes were burning with the tears she refused to shed. Gabe looked completely shell-shocked and his own eyes were suspiciously bright. "And that's on me. I should have refused but I was in love with you. I had been for *years* and I knew that it was the best damned offer I would ever get from you. I told myself if that was all I could get of you then I'd take it, but you know what? I deserve more than that. More than *you* and I can't believe it's taken me *this* long to figure that out.

"I deserve a real relationship with a man who loves me for who I am. Grease, calluses, unstyled hair and all. I'll never be good enough for you and I refuse to twist myself up in knots over that anymore—because you know what? You're not good enough for *me* either. If our so-called friendship has to be sacrificed as a result of all this, then so be it because right now I don't know why the hell I ever considered you such a good friend in the first place."

She ignored the look of slack-jawed distress on his handsome face and turned on her heel to stalk off the field. She brushed past the men who still stood around in stunned silence, then toward the women—her friends—none of whom she dared look at for fear of bursting into tears. Billy and Chase both looked like they wanted to say something, but she held them off with a shake of her head. They retreated tactfully and she was grateful for that.

She was so distraught that she was halfway home before she noticed the tall man silently shadowing her.

"I'm not great company at the moment, Kyle," she whispered, trying very hard to keep herself together.

"I'm aware of that," the man said calmly. "I just figured that if you wanted to talk it would be best to do so with someone who won't feel obligated to see 'both sides of the story' so to speak. Someone who's one hundred percent in your corner and has no loyalty whatsoever to the other guy."

"And you're that guy, are you?" she asked softly. If she didn't feel so completely gutted, she would have been charmed by him.

"I'm that guy," he affirmed. "You don't *have* to talk though. I'm just walking you home." They were at the gate and out of sight of the football pitch when she turned to the tall stoic man with a wobbly smile.

"Thank you."

"You're quite welcome." The three words were delivered so gently that Bobbi couldn't hold back anymore. This man didn't know her; he didn't know that she never cried . . . so it was perfectly okay to cry all over him. When her tears came, he made a deep, comforting sound in the back of his throat, folded her in his arms, and simply let her weep.

~

Gabe watched her walk away . . . and felt a staggering sense of loss that nearly sent him to his knees. There had been a chilling finality to her words that terrified him.

She was in love with him? How could she be in love with him? They were friends. They had always been friends. Even after this physical thing between them had popped up out of nowhere, Gabe had never doubted that one truth. So how the hell could she have been in love with him? *For years*? How could his *friend* have hidden something like that from him for so long? Did he even know her at all?

If he had had access to that one important piece of information, he would never have suggested a no-strings sexual arrangement between them. He would have known that it would hurt her too much. He would have backed the hell off . . .

He would have run scared.

And *that* was why she had kept it from him. She knew him better than he knew her. She knew that he wouldn't have handled the whole love thing well at all. Why would she tell him when it would probably have destroyed their friendship? He sighed heavily—the deep inhalation of breath intensifying the ache in his chest—and acknowledged that the friendship was pretty much destroyed now anyway. Neither of them had handled the situation particularly well and Gabe knew that he bore the brunt of responsibility for it. He had just lost it when he'd seen her take that body blow from Max and then the *blood*. He felt vaguely nauseated just recalling it. He had absolutely hated the sight of her blood. It had brought out a primal protective instinct that had made him want to pummel Max into the ground. He didn't understand it, but it had made him irrationally angry with both Max *and* with Bobbi for constantly putting herself in harm's way. How the hell was he supposed to take care of her when she was always doing things that could get her hurt?

He didn't know what was going on with him. He had never felt more lost and confused than he did at this moment. He was still standing in the middle of the football field and staring off in the direction Bobbi had taken. Kyle Foster had gone with her. He felt irrationally angry about that. Who did that guy think he was? He blindly moved to follow them, but Chase moved into his path. His brother's stance was nonconfrontational but immovable, nonetheless, with arms crossed over his chest and legs braced shoulder length apart.

"No."

"I have to . . ."

"No, Gabe. You're not thinking rationally and whatever it is you're planning to do right now will most likely be ill-advised. Let her go for now."

"I hurt her," Gabe confessed helplessly. "I tried so hard *not* to hurt her but I did anyway."

"I know," Chase said, and his body language changed, softened. His hands dropped to his sides and his chest heaved.

"What the hell do I do now?" Gabe asked, and Chase hooked a hand around the back of Gabe's neck and tugged him closer until his mouth was next to his brother's ear.

"You leave her alone until you figure that out," Chase advised—his voice a low growl. "And if you can't figure it out, then you let her go."

CHAPTER ELEVEN

The Corvette looked amazing and she handled like a dream. Bobbi stood back and examined the grand old dame with misty eyes. Jason would be picking her up in half an hour, and Bobbi felt like a parent sending her child off to school for the first time. Her proud sense of accomplishment was accompanied by a bittersweet pang of loss. She had put so much into this project, both financially and emotionally.

It had helped keep her mind off Gabe, who hadn't called, e-mailed, or SMS'd since that awful night nearly two weeks before. Bobbi couldn't believe that she hadn't seen or spoken to him in so long. She felt so empty, like she was missing a piece of her soul. The longest they had gone without speaking before had been a week and that had been because Gabe had been in a part of Africa that had little to no cell-phone reception and dodgy Internet connections.

She saw Chase quite often, but even that was starting to get painful because he was looking healthier by the day, which meant that he and Gabe were starting to look identical again. Even though Bobbi hadn't ever confused one for the other, the physical resemblance was still hard to deal with. She tried her best not to let Chase see how much it hurt her sometimes to look at him.

She wiped away a smudge on the car's gleaming red bonnet, talking to it all the while.

"He has promised to take really good care of you this time. He'll take you out on lovely scenic drives, and he'll have you washed and serviced regularly. I know you're scared that he'll just leave you to gather more rust and dust, but when he sees you he's going to fall in love with you. I promise."

"Boss?" She turned around to see Pieter, fully recovered from his unfortunate case of measles. He was slouching as usual with his hands shoved into his overall pockets.

"Yes?"

"You have a phone call." He jerked his head toward her office, and Bobbi gave the Corvette one last polish before retreating to her office. She had managed to clear some of the paperwork off her desk over the past few weeks—one of the very few perks of having a broken heart.

"Bobbi Richmond," she greeted absently, preoccupied as she remembered that she had wanted to check the radiator hose on the Corvette one final time. She was sure that it was fine but even new hoses could be flawed and Bobbi was a perfectionist when it came to her work.

"Hello, Bobbi." She was so busy hunting for a pen to write down a reminder to check the hose that the voice didn't register at first. When it did, she forgot all else and sank down into her ancient office chair, her legs suddenly losing their ability to support her.

"Gabe," she murmured. She wasn't sure how else to respond.

"How are you?" he asked, his voice revealing absolutely nothing of what he was feeling.

"I'm good. Busy." There was a long pause.

"I wanted to ask you something," he said, only after the silence had stretched past the point of painfully awkward. There was more excruciating silence as he waited for a response from her. She swallowed and refused to make this any easier for him than it had to be.

"Uh . . . anyway. I was wondering if you would do me the honor . . . I mean, if you would grace me . . ." His voice faded away and her eyebrows leapt up into her hairline, she was so stunned by his uncharacteristic lack of eloquence. He cleared his throat. "I was hoping you'd go to the Valentine's Day event . . . with me." The words emerged on one breath and practically merged together he said them so swiftly.

Bobbi's jaw had dropped and she wasn't quite sure she had heard him correctly.

"What?" she asked unsteadily.

"Will you go the Valentine's Day Ball with me?" he repeated, his voice more measured now but still with a slight wobble. Bobbi's fingers tightened around the receiver uncertainly.

"Why are you doing this?" she whispered, her throat tight with tears.

"I . . . miss you. I want you back in my life. I want us to, you know, do it right this time and . . ."

"No." She interrupted whatever he'd been about to say, her voice vehement. "I don't want to hear any more about what *you* want, Gabe. I can't go to the ball with you. I have a date. And even if I didn't have a date . . . I wouldn't have gone with you." She paused for a moment to allow that to sink in. "I have to go. I'm busy right now."

She replaced the receiver back in its cradle with the utmost care and blindly turned away from her desk. She wouldn't allow him to creep into her life only to make her feel inadequate again. She was determined to be stronger than that.

∼

A date? The knowledge filled Gabe with panic. Was he too late? Had somebody else snatched her up while Gabe had sat around feeling sorry for himself? The thought was unbearable.

He studied the surface of his meticulously arranged desk. Just the way he liked it—everything neatly stowed away. Not a paperclip out of place. Bobbi had been the only bit of chaos in his life, but he now found that without her, his well-ordered life was . . . *bland*. He missed his lover and he missed his friend. He had foolishly tried to keep those two facets of her in separate boxes and it had naturally backfired on him. He was damned well going to do this thing right from now onward. Amateur hour was coming to an end.

Bobbi started monitoring her calls after that. After that football night, she hadn't expected him to hear from again for a long time and that phone call to the shop had rattled her immensely. She had Craig on phone duties, knowing that he would be vigilant about not letting any calls from Gabe slip through the cracks. She ignored any calls to her cell phone from him and simply came home too late for him to call the house.

His messages started to pile up over the next few days. Voice mails clogged up her cell-phone inbox and handwritten notes from her father were left outside her bedroom door.

"Please call me."

"I'm sorry I missed you. Please call."

"I missed you again. Please call."

"Call me."

And on and on it went. The voice mails he left on her cell phone were more detailed:

"I know I hurt you. I just want a chance to make it right. I miss you. Please call me."

"Bobbi, I miss you. Call me."

"I wish you'd answer my calls."

"I can't do this (he never elaborated on what "this" meant) *in a message. I need to speak with you. Let me know when it'll be convenient for me to call you or see you."*

It was driving her crazy. At her previous girls' night a few days before, each woman said she'd had at least one message from Gabe. They never urged her to call him though. They merely relayed the messages and then carried on as if nothing out of the ordinary had happened. Nobody had forced her to *talk* about it. They respected her silence on the matter. And she was eternally grateful for that.

∼

"Good. You're home." Her father met Bobbi at the door when she let herself in that evening. He looked flustered and annoyed.

"Dad? What's wrong?" She stepped past her agitated father and tried to drop her messenger bag carelessly onto a side table in the foyer, as she usually did. A huge bouquet of white roses resting on the tiny table thwarted the automatic gesture. She frowned and glanced around, looking for a different table, but they were all covered in gorgeous bouquets of white roses.

"Oh," she said blankly.

"Yes, *oh*," her father groused. "They're everywhere."

"Where did they come from?" she asked, wondering if there had been some kind of planning mishap with the Valentine's Day thing. She knew that their theme was red and white—*so* original—maybe they had miscalculated the number of white roses they needed?

"They're for you," he said pointedly, and her eyes widened.

"But . . ."

"Look, I know you and Gabe have had some kind of tiff and if this is any indication, he feels terrible about it." Her father knew nothing about what had happened between Gabe and Bobbi.

Thankfully Billy had kept his mouth shut about the incident at the football match, even though her brother had futilely tried—on numerous occasions—to open up a dialogue with Bobbi about it.

"They're from Gabe?" She knew her voice sounded flat and if her father's frown was any indication, he didn't understand why she wasn't more enthusiastic about the floral "apology."

"They are . . ." He nodded. "Gabe called after the first delivery and asked me to grab the card out of one of the bouquets and to be sure that you received and read it."

That sneaky rat! He knew that if it had been up to her the card would have been tossed into the bin unread, but by involving her father, Gabe had made it impossible for her *not* to read it. She took the pretty cream card from her father and glanced down at it. Gabe's bold handwriting slashed across the surface of the small square of paper, and it took her a second to decipher the elegant cursive script.

Did you know that white roses signify new beginnings? I was hoping you'd appreciate that sentiment. Please turn over for more . . .

She refused to smile at the polite instruction on the bottom of the tiny card. Anybody else would have been satisfied with an abbreviated *PTO*, but Gabe, of course, had to write a properly structured and well-mannered sentence. She turned over.

These roses are white
Most violets are blue (well they're actually violet but for the purposes of this poem we'll say blue)
Bobbi, my sweet
I really miss you
(I'm sorry. I'm really bad at poetry—G)

She covered her mouth with a hand as she tried to stifle the half laugh, half sob that threatened to bubble up from her throat. This was . . . what *was* this? She didn't even know what he meant to achieve with this.

"I'm going up for a shower, I'll see you at dinner," she said, folding her hand around the card and feeling the expensive bond paper cut into her palm. Her father's face fell when she made no mention of the card's contents. After she reached her room, she put the card onto her dresser and meticulously smoothed the creases out of the stiff paper. She read the words one last time before tearing the card up into four squares and tossing them into her dresser drawer.

After a quick shower, she decided to call Chase. He answered his cell phone almost immediately.

"Tell him to *stop* this," she said, seething, before he'd even had a chance say hello.

"What?" he asked in confusion.

"Chase, tell him to stop! I'm not amused." She hung up and tossed the phone aside.

≈

"So what's going on?" Chase asked Gabe, who was sitting in the den, staring at the muted television.

"What do you mean?" Gabe asked, looking up from the dancing couple on the screen.

"What the hell are you watching?" Chase was momentarily diverted by the garish costumes and blindingly white smiles.

"Some competition about vaguely famous people learning ball-room dancing, I think." Gabe shrugged listlessly.

"Why are you watching it with the sound turned down?"

"The music is *terrible*," Gabe said before going back to Chase's original subject. "What did you mean by that first question?"

Still staring at the screen in horrified fascination, Chase stumbled around the back of the sofa and sat down next to Gabe.

"Bobbi just called me." That snagged Gabe's interest and he sat up—wondering how pissed off she had been by his gesture. He knew her well enough to know that she wouldn't have been happy, but it would have gotten her attention at least.

"She wants you to *stop*. She's not amused." Pretty much what Gabe had expected and he felt a reluctant smile tug at the corners of his mouth. He hadn't felt like smiling in weeks, but one angry message from her and he felt like a drowning man who had been thrown a lifeline.

"What did you do?" Chase asked curiously—his eyes glued to the screen. The whirling couple had stopped dancing and now seemed to be standing in front of a panel of excitable judges.

"I sent her flowers," Gabe said, and Chase choked before turning to stare at Gabe in complete disbelief.

"Uh . . ." His brother seemed at a loss for words.

"Roughly twelve dozen white roses. I imagine she's pretty pissed off right now."

"If you knew she'd be angry why did you send them?" Chase looked baffled.

"Because I knew that it would prompt a reaction from her," Gabe said. "She's been ignoring my calls."

"Sending flowers was a pretty public thing to do," Chase commented.

"I know."

"Do you know what you're doing?"

"God, I hope so," Gabe said fervently. Chase merely studied him for a beat before allowing another gaudily outfitted couple on TV to distract him as they took to the dance floor.

"Hey, I've seen that guy before," he said, grabbing the remote control from the coffee table. "That's the guy from that early nineties archery action movie. Remember? We loved that movie when we were kids. What was the title?"

Gabe squinted at the screen and snorted.

"Yeah, I remember. We begged Mum to enroll us in archery classes after that," Gabe recalled.

"And she stuck us in bloody ballet classes instead." They both winced at the memory. Thankfully the ballet classes had only lasted a couple of months; their mother had been forced to remove them after the instructor complained about the eleven-year-old twins' obstructive behavior. They had spent more time ruffling tutus and switching up everybody's toe shoes than they had paying attention to the lessons.

"What *was* the title of that movie?" Gabe wondered aloud. Bobbi would know—she was awesome at remembering movie trivia and she had loved the movie as much as they had. At six years old she had still been young enough to score a plastic bow and arrow set with sucker cups on the ends of the arrows. She had had a fabulous time pretending to be the lead in her own action movie, constantly ambushing them when they least expected it. Gabe smiled at the memory. God, he missed her so much.

"Damn, how much work has this guy had *done*?" Chase leaned forward to peer more closely at the C-list actor who had once been a hero to them. Gabe grimaced at the plasticky sheen to the man's skin. Chase turned the sound up and they both recoiled at the terrible rendition of "Yesterday" that the live band was offering up as an accompaniment to a halfway-decent waltz.

"He's not too bad." Chase was completely riveted by the dancing on the screen and Gabe left him to it. The music was too distracting and Gabe wasn't in the right frame of mind to sit and watch television.

He went up to change into his swim trunks and spent a couple of hours relentlessly swimming laps in the hopes that it would tire him out enough to sleep through the night. He hadn't had a decent night's sleep since that last night with Bobbi and it was starting to wear him down.

On his way up to bed two hours later he passed the open door of the den and was surprised to see Chase still sitting there watching that same god-awful dancing show. It amused him enough to go into the room.

"Why are you still watching this?" he asked. Chase barely acknowledged him, keeping his eyes glued on the screen.

"It's a marathon. Ssh," he shushed urgently. "They're leading up to a double elimination!" Rolling his eyes, Gabe turned and exited the room. The dramatic music reached a crescendo and the announcer's voice rang out to be instantly followed by both boos and cheers.

"Oh my *God*, that's crap. She was the better dancer out there!" Chase yelled, and followed that diatribe up with a string of colorful curses. Gabe left him to it and made his way upstairs, his mind back on Bobbi and his next plan of action.

～

"Oh dear God." Bobbi watched helplessly as an endless stream of deliverymen carried in basket after basket of fresh flowers. She had tried to send them back, but the guy in charge had shrugged and told her that since the flowers were paid for there was nothing he could do except deliver them. If she wanted to return them or send them elsewhere she would have to take it up with his boss. Craig and Sean flanked her and Pieter stood slightly behind her as they watched every surface of their workshop get covered with pretty purple hyacinth and pink rose bouquets. The only reason the flower-illiterate Bobbi even knew the purple flower was a hyacinth was because of the card one of the deliverymen thrust into her hands. She had glanced down instinctively and had been caught off guard by the distinctive script on the paper:

Did you know that purple hyacinths are the perfect flower for begging forgiveness? And pink roses signify my admiration for you (I'm not making this stuff up. Google and Wikipedia are truly my allies here) —G

His handwriting had gotten increasingly cramped as he ran out of space on the small square of paper and this time only an arrow was there to indicate that she should turn over. She stubbornly refused to do so. And shoved the card into the breast pocket of her overalls instead.

"This is pretty embarrassing, boss," Sean groused. "We're an auto shop, not some flower shop."

"I *know* that!" Bobbi snapped. "Do you think I don't *know* that?" Sean backed off.

"I'm just saying." He shrugged.

"Well you don't have to say everything that pops into your head, Sean! Especially not something so perfectly obvious." She glared at him and he shrugged again, wisely choosing not to respond.

"So what are we supposed to do with this stuff?" Pieter asked in that surly way of his, sending death stares at the pretty flowers cluttering up their workspace.

"Hey, boss, do you suppose I could have one of these bouquets for Ellie?" Craig asked hopefully. "She's a bit angry with me at the moment."

"What did you do this time?" Sean asked, and Craig shook his head, lifting his baseball cap to scratch at his slightly receding hairline.

"Take my advice, son, there is *no* right answer to the question, 'how big is my bum in this skirt?' especially not if she asks you to rate the size from one to ten."

"Not even if you say one?" Sean asked curiously.

"It's best to lie through your teeth. Whatever you think the answer is, subtract at least a hundred from it. I thought three and a half was being generous. I mean the woman had three children, for chrissakes! You'd think she'd have been happy with a three and half."

Bobbi was too distracted by the stupid flowers and Gabe's message to pay any attention to the back-and-forth banter between the two men. She told them to help themselves to bouquets for their girlfriends, mothers, or wives and then retreated to her office. It wasn't quite the escape she'd hoped for, not while she could still see the flowers brightening up the place. Gabe's card was burning a hole in her pocket, and she resisted it for a few more minutes before tugging it out. She reread the message on the front before reluctantly flipping it over to have a look at the back:

Violets are purple
You know that it's true
Without you in my life
I truly am blue

"Damn it," she whispered. The words blurred as she fought back angry tears. She itched to call him, even if just to beg him to stop this, but that was what he wanted. He wanted her to call him, to acknowledge him, and she needed more time to get over him. It was going to take a while before she had hardened her heart enough to be in his proximity again.

She knuckled away the stupid tears and decided to have the flowers delivered to old-age homes and hospitals. Maybe if she just continued to ignore him he would stop whatever it was that he thought he was doing.

~

Two nights later she came home to find the house inundated with the garish combination of iris and orange rose bouquets. Her father glared at her when she trudged in wearily after a tough day.

"I don't know what's going on between you and Gabriel—you're both being so stubbornly close-mouthed about it—but I am getting sick of the both of you languishing around me in despair and this . . . endless procession of flowers has *got* to stop. It's wreaking havoc with my allergies."

"You don't have allergies, Daddy," Bobbi pointed out.

"I damned well *will* by the time the two of you come to your senses. I don't know what this fight was about, but Gabriel is running a multimillion-*dollar* corporation, and he's worse than a damned teenager these days. I want my efficient and cold-as-ice CEO back right now. And I tell you what: I'm getting damned sick of your moping around too. So you and he had better fix this ridiculousness as soon as possible. Watching the two of you carefully avoiding each other is depressing as hell."

She didn't say anything and her father threw up his hands in frustration before thrusting the inevitable card into her hand.

"Here's your card," he growled before stalking off toward his man cave.

I know this combination is a bit loud but did you know that irises represent eternal friendship? And the orange roses embody my desire for you.

I know I'm a terrible poet but I hope you'll read my latest attempt on the other side of this card —G

Friendship and desire? That left them in pretty much the same boat as before. The separation between the two roles was too large and Bobbi was so done with being torn between the role of good friend *and* lover. She sighed, bowed down to the inevitable, and flipped the card over.

Your eyes are pretty
Your lips are too
Bobbi, my darling
I'm miserable without you

She examined the card for a long time before carefully tucking it into one of her jeans pockets. A headache was forming above her brow, and she slunk up to her bedroom, deciding to forego dinner in favor of a good night's sleep.

~

"Bobbi," her name was whispered directly into her ear and Bobbi sighed, before murmuring a protest and turning over in bed. "Bobbi, wake up."

She groaned and batted at the person hovering above her. Her hand made contact with warm flesh.

"Ouch." She frowned at the muffled exclamation and opened her eyes in confusion. The light was still off and she could just make out the dark silhouette of the man in her room outlined against the slightly lighter backdrop of the window.

"What . . ." She sat up and clutched her comforter to her chest, staring at the large figure in fright. "Who . . . ?"

"*Ssh*, don't panic," the *very* familiar voice whispered frantically. "It's me."

"Gabe? What are you doing here? Who let you in?"

"I wanted to come in through the window, like in the old days." He and Chase had often climbed the rose trellis below her second floor window and snuck into the house when they were children, and the three of them would then slink into Billy's room and they would spend the night playing. By the time Faye would come to wake them up in the morning, the four of them would be piled on Billy's bed, fast asleep, which had always resulted in a severe scolding from their parents, but it had never deterred them from doing it again.

"You *didn't*?" She gasped, and could just make him shaking his head in the gloomy light.

"I think your security guys would probably have had me arrested if I'd attempted it. No I came in through the front door and your dad very happily told me where to find you—after ordering me to get rid of the orange and purple 'monstrosities' that were stinking up his house." His voice was warm and engaging, clearly inviting her to join in his amusement, but Bobbi was too appalled by his presence in her room to feel anything other than alarm.

"My dad knows you're up here?" she squeaked. "Oh *God!*"

"Relax," Gabe soothed. "Firstly, you're not exactly a teenager sneaking her boyfriend into her room, and secondly, your dad doesn't know that I have licentious designs on your hot little body, now does he?"

"Of course he doesn't," she agreed bitterly. "Why would he? It's not like it's anything you wanted people to know."

He didn't respond to that and the silence seemed much too oppressive in the dark room. Bobbi reached for the lamp switch and flooded the area directly around the bed in a small pool of warm, yellow light. She still couldn't see him clearly because he sat just outside the tiny circle of light, but she knew that he could see her and she immediately felt at a disadvantage.

"Why are you here?" she asked, keeping her voice cold as she folded her arms self-consciously across her chest.

"To see you." The unspoken *duh* following those three words was so clear that he might as well have said it.

"I don't want to see you. I want you to leave," she said in her most authoritative voice. It lost its impact somewhat when the speaker was wearing a Daisy Duck nightshirt.

"Who are you going to the Valentine's Day Ball with?" he asked unexpectedly, and she lifted her chin defiantly.

"None of your business," she informed haughtily.

"Kyle Foster?"

"So what if I am?" She wasn't going with Kyle; she had politely informed the man that while she liked him, it just wasn't fair of her to keep seeing him when she was in love with another man. It would be like doing to someone else what had been done to her, and she understood the pain of unrequited love and passion too much to inflict it on someone else. He had very graciously conceded her point and had backed off.

"I would rather you went with me," Gabe said.

"Well, I'm not. I'd hate to embarrass you in front of your colleagues with my lack of dress sense and grimy fingernails," she said pointedly.

"I'd be honored to have you by my side," he said, after a pause.

"*Would* you now?" she scoffed. "What if I chose to wear a tank top and jeans?"

"I don't see why you would," he said stiffly. "Your dad wouldn't be happy."

"Oh so you're banking on me looking semi-respectable because I wouldn't want to embarrass my father?"

"Bobbi, I know that what I said the other night hurt you, but you have to admit . . . the way you dress sometimes just wouldn't suit my lifestyle."

She swallowed painfully.

"And that's why it's best if we just aren't together," she said pragmatically, attempting to disguise the pain in her eyes by lowering her gaze to the comforter. "I can't possibly fit into your life and you won't fit into mine. I was never interested in the elegant dinners and the fancy events that my dad hosted when we were growing up. I'm still not. I wouldn't have the faintest idea how to speak to some of the people you deal with. You were right, we were just never meant to be more than friends."

"I never said that," he protested.

"You implied it when you said that the way I am never bothered you when we were just friends. If being with you in a more intimate capacity means changing who I am, then I'm afraid it's too big a sacrifice for me to make."

"So *I* am the one who has to make all the changes? That hardly seems fair," he declared.

"What changes? I haven't asked you to change a single thing about yourself for me!" She was outraged that he'd implied as much.

"Of *course* you have," he dissented. "Expecting me to *not* care about the appearance of the woman by my side goes against everything I believe in. I like order and you know that. I like everything to be neat and in its place. Where would I slot you in, if your role in my life changed? And don't get me wrong, Bobbi, I want your role in my life to change. I want to give us a real chance . . . but we have to come to some sort of compromise here."

"And by compromise you mean I change my hair, my clothes, my way of life just for the honor of what exactly? Being your girlfriend? Your mistress? And you, of course, would compromise by . . . ?" She left him to fill in the blank but he remained silent, and she snorted in bitter amusement. "I suppose your great compromise would be getting to tolerate a less than perfect bit of arm candy for the couple of months it'll take you to work me out of your system. And when it does end, you go trotting on your merry way to pick your next conquest in your search to find a woman perfect enough to be Mrs. Gabriel Andrew Braddock and I go back to my shop feeling publicly humiliated for not being good enough to snag the great Gabriel Braddock."

"That's not how it would be." He didn't sound very convincing at all. "I think we have a real chance at something special, it just took me a while to see it. I want us to be together and I want us to go into a relationship with hope for a future together rather than the expectation of failure."

"Do you love me?" she asked, and despite the gloom, she could see that he was visibly startled by the question.

"Of course I love you," he blurted, sounding offended by the question.

"Okay, allow me to rephrase the question. Are you in love with me?"

"That's hardly a fair question, Bobbi," he retorted. "You know that your confession that night threw me. You can't expect me to return your feelings *just* because you actually happened to verbalize them to me. It's not something that can be switched on just like that. What I'm asking is that you give me the *chance* to fall in love with you."

"And while you're busy deciding if I'm someone you can fall in love with, I'm just supposed to put my feelings on hold? What sort of timeline are you looking at? Will a month or two be enough for you to figure out whether I could be worthy of your love? Six months? A year? And what if—after all that time—you didn't fall in love with me? Do you think it's fair that I risk even more heartbreak?"

"That's a lot of questions that I just don't have the answers to," he confessed. "I don't know how it'll work, I've never found myself in this position before. You're so damned important to me and I'm terrified of losing you."

"Then give me a chance to get over this thing we had and we can go back to being friends," she said after a very long moment. "That way everybody's a winner."

"I don't want that," he snapped, losing patience. "I want more than that."

"I'm not prepared to give you more. I won't change who I am for you, Gabe. I just won't, and if I'm really as important to you as you claim, you wouldn't want me to."

"I don't want you to change . . ." He seemed to be speaking through clenched teeth. "I just want you to wear a damned dress on occasion, go to a bloody hairdresser, have your nails done. You're a woman, for God's sake. These things aren't hardships."

"They *are* to me!"

"You seem to be equating a visit to the salon with selling your soul to the devil." He threw his hands up in despair, and she stared back at him with equal misery. He didn't seem to understand that she was afraid that in the middle of all this makeover crap, he would fall in love with someone who simply didn't exist, a Bobbi of his own invention. The prospect scared the hell out of her. If that happened she would be trapped playing a role for the rest of her life. She couldn't do it, not even for Gabe.

"I think you should leave," she said tiredly. "This isn't achieving anything."

"I'm not giving up," he warned.

"Just stop the Campaign of Crazy with the flowers, please. You're driving everybody nuts. I can't be held responsible if my father or the guys at the shop hunt you down and force feed you roses."

He chuckled in response to that quip.

"I really do miss you," he said. "Not just in my bed . . . I miss you in my life. Please come back to me."

"Please just go, Gabe," she softly commanded, hardening her heart against the quiet plea.

He got up and wavered for so long that she feared he would come over and kiss her. He *did* take one hesitant step forward before abruptly turning on his heel and leaving.

Bobbi fought the impulse to run after him and surrender to his terms. It was the way she had always lived her life. She had gone from girl desperate to please and impress her father and big brothers to a woman futilely focused on trying to please just this one man, and she had to fight against the instinct to give him exactly what he asked for, even if it was detrimental to her own heart and sanity.

It took everything she had and then some, but she managed to fight against her instinct and emerge triumphant.

CHAPTER TWELVE

When the delivery van showed up at the shop two days later, Sean and Pieter groaned and Craig rubbed his hands together at the prospect of more free flowers with which to butter up his wife. Apparently she had been *very* forgiving after that last time. Bobbi, in the meantime, was utterly dismayed that Gabe had so completely ignored her plea that he stop sending her flowers.

She stood waiting with her arms folded defensively over her chest. It was the same delivery guy as the last time but he didn't have a cavalcade of trucks following him or an army of guys to carry in the flowers this time. When he saw Bobbi's stance, he shrugged and grinned.

"If you'd just sign the delivery slip I'll get your stuff and be on my way." Bobbi heaved an exasperated sigh and reached for the clipboard.

Bobbi watched him turn back to his truck and withdraw a cellophane wrapped basket from the back of the van. The thing was huge and looked heavy, but he managed to carry it into the shop and drop it onto one of the closest work surfaces with a heavy *thud*.

"I was told to personally hand this over to you," he said, stopping in front of Bobbi on his way out and holding out a familiar card to her. "You should tell your boyfriend to put these cards into envelopes, ma'am. More *private* that way." Which meant that—she peered at the faded stitching on the breast pocket of his shirt—*Quinton* here had probably read the card. Along with whoever else had handled the order.

She had a feeling that Gabe didn't put them in envelopes because he knew that once she caught even the slightest glimpse of what he had written she wouldn't stop reading. If it were in an envelope it would be too easy for her to toss it thoughtlessly aside.

She ignored Quinton, who shrugged and whistled as he returned to his truck. Pieter, Sean, and Craig had gathered around the cellophane-wrapped basket curiously.

"Do you think it's a fruit basket? Or chocolates maybe?" Sean asked eagerly.

"I'm hoping for perfumes and lotions and stuff. Ellie would *love* that," Craig inserted. Pieter cracked his bubblegum and glared at the basket like it had mortally offended him.

"You gonna open it, boss?" Sean asked when she just stood staring at the gigantic basket with dread. What if it *was* "perfumes and lotions and stuff." How would she cope with something so obvious? She absently looked down at the card in her hand and read it slowly.

> *I fully confess to making the following up but since it's what I want them to mean, I'm hoping you'll grant me some leeway. So, did you know that pliers are symbolic for two people coming together? And (true story) wrench is something my heart does every time I see you? —G*

She was baffled by that message and turned the card over, hoping for some clarity.

> *Drill bits are sharp*
> *Handsaws are too*
> *A grease streak or two*
> *Are beautiful on you*

She rapidly blinked away the tears that suddenly flooded her eyes and glanced up at the large basket at which the guys were still poking and prodding. Tucking the card safely into her pocket, she walked over to where they were trying to discern the contents through the layers of dark-blue cellophane.

She dragged off the ridiculous pink bow, tore off the crisp plastic, and gasped when she saw what he had given her.

"Well, I'll be damned." Craig sounded both awed and disappointed.

"That's so cool," Sean whooped. Pieter snorted and turned away to amble back to the old hatchback VW he was servicing. The other two men also drifted off to their tasks and left Bobbi to stand and gape at the tool bouquet in front of her. Brand-spanking-new hand tools—probably worth thousands—arranged quite prettily in one of those round baskets usually reserved for floral arrangements. A complete set of screwdrivers were fanned out in the back, with pink— *pink* for heaven's sake—rubberized handles facing up and sizes arranged from small to large. There were wrenches, levels, hammers, pliers . . . everything a girl could ever ask for from a set of tools. Everything accentuated in the prettiest pink. Gabe must have gone to great lengths to obtain them, and Bobbi found herself ridiculously touched by the gesture.

And then there was that silly little rhyme. It had hit all the right notes, and it scared Bobbi how quickly a part of her heart had melted. He could so easily sneak past her defenses when she wasn't looking, especially if he kept doing things like this.

⚬

When Gabe drove up to Bobbi's shop later that day, the place was busier than usual. He could barely find space to park amongst all the cars in the lot waiting to be serviced. He had seen the masterful work she had done on Jason's Corvette—the car was unrecognizable from the heap he had seen on her shop floor a month ago and Jason was like a new dad with the damned thing. As Jason promised he told everybody who asked and, even those who didn't, where his car had been restored and had even put a sticker endorsing her shop in the rear window of the car. It looked like the advertising was paying off, judging by the amount of cars in the lot. Gabe was proud of Bobbi and ashamed for doubting her. He had known how much his skepticism had hurt her and that his misgivings had read as a complete lack of faith. It was probably another thing she had added to his list of flaws.

He walked into the bustling shop; Craig, Sean, and Pieter were busy with a different car each and Bobbi was in her office in earnest discussion with a debonair-looking older man. She didn't see him, and not wanting to interrupt the flow of her conversation, he wandered over to Craig, who was peering into the innards of an ancient-looking Jeep.

The man glanced up when Gabe came to stand beside the car.

"Hey," Craig said tersely before tugging at something beneath the bonnet of the sick old beast. A spark plug maybe? Gabe was unashamedly clueless when it came to the inner workings of cars.

"Morning," Gabe returned the greeting, and then stood in silence and watched him work.

"Thanks for the flowers," Craig said after a conversational hiatus that had been filled with nothing but the sound of hammering and grinding machinery and rock and roll coming from the CD player stashed in a corner out of harm's way.

Gabe grinned at the man's temerity.

"You're welcome. I'm glad you liked them."

"My wife, Ellie, did. It got me off the sofa that night."

"Why were you on the sofa?"

"She thinks I said her bum was big," the man glowered and tugged at his ear. "Didn't. I gave her a three and a half on a scale of ten. Ten apparently being gigantic."

Gabe winced.

"You're a brave man, Craig. I would have gone with a zero or less."

"I figured three and a half was a good size, not too big and not invisible. No man likes an invisible bum." Gabe wondered why they were standing here discussing the man's wife's behind, and he had a feeling that if the inimitable Ellie ever heard about it, Craig would be back on the sofa.

"Anyway, the flowers helped. I caught a glimpse of the card too," he unapologetically admitted. "You should put those things in envelopes if you want privacy. I liked the forgiveness and admiration stuff. Used that on the missus. She was *very* impressed. Figured I owed you a thank-you."

"Glad I could be of some help," Gabe said with a complete lack of sarcasm. He had known that Bobbi would find some way to disperse of all those flowers; it naturally followed that she would have offered some to every person she knew. He had hoped that she would keep at least one bouquet of each for herself though, but a quick glance around the shop told him that he had hoped in vain.

"She's not into the flowery stuff," Craig said, accurately reading Gabe's glance around.

"I know that," Gabe admitted, irritated that Craig seemed to think he knew Bobbi better than Gabe did. "But the messages that came with the flowers were what I really hoped to get across."

"Now the stuff you sent her this morning," Craig muttered, leaning into gaping maw of the Jeep again and twisting at something. He grunted with effort as he continued to twist for what felt like hours, leaving Gabe hanging in suspense. Craig finally stood upright again and nodded down at the car in satisfaction.

"*What* about the stuff I sent this morning?" Gabe prompted impatiently and Craig looked at him with narrowed eyes.

"That was a stroke of genius." He nodded in approval. "She loved it, even though she tried to pretend that she didn't." He gave Gabe a perusing glance before sighing and removing his filthy baseball cap. He rubbed a hand briskly back and forth over his short, messy hair before sticking the cap back onto his head.

"Can't say I ever liked you," he admitted, his voice gruff. "With your fancy suits, always waiting outside on the rare occasions that you picked our girl up from work. Figured you were scared of getting your posh shoes and pretty clothes dirty. I can't trust a man who's afraid of a bit of grease . . ." Gabe strove to remain unoffended by the less than sterling character assessment, hoping that there was a "but" in there somewhere. "But I reckon you're not so bad."

Gabe waited for the rest, but Craig seemed to be done talking. Well, faint praise was better than no praise he supposed as he watched Craig turn back to the car. It seemed that the man was done talking to him and, feeling comprehensively dismissed, Gabe walked over to the where the youngest guy, Sean, was working.

"He-ey," the young man said with the exuberance of a puppy. "It's the boss's boyfriend. What's up, bru?"

He unselfconsciously held out a grease-covered hand and Gabe took it with barely a flinch. He reminded himself that he had hand-sanitizer in the car and if he was going to be squeamish about this stuff he'd lose major points with Bobbi and just prove her point about them being unsuited.

"Listen." Sean was leaning in conspiratorially. "I was thinking: Miz R loves chocolates and dried fruit and stuff. You should totally consider sending her stuff like that." Gabe bit back a laugh at the transparency of young Sean's ploy. He was just hoping for the bounty to spill over onto him, as it no doubt had with the flowers.

"Did you give the flowers to your girlfriend as well?" Gabe asked, smiling, and Sean grinned before nudging Gabe with a friendly elbow.

"I have three girlfriends, and they all loved the flowers." *Three.* Gabe could barely cope with (or *keep,* for that matter) one. Ah, the vitality of youth. He stifled a laugh and glanced up to see that surly Pieter guy staring daggers at him. Wondering what that was all about, he excused himself and walked over to Pieter's workstation.

"Have I offended you in some way?" he asked directly.

"Yeah, the boss is a nice lady; she don't need some player playing her!" The words were delivered with a bit of heat and a *lot* of ice.

"I assure you, I'm not playing her," he told the skinny man, who had a three-inch height advantage on him.

"You can use your fancy words and all, but she's too good for you."

Gabe reflected on his previous sentence, wondering which of the seven words had been too "fancy" for Pieter.

"I agree," Gabe said. "She *is* too good for me, but I'm trying to become someone worthy of her."

Pieter's pale-blue eyes narrowed assessingly, and Gabe kept his stance open and his eyes level. Gabe watched the fight go out of the other man's bearing.

"You should stop sending her flowers. It's not her thing," Pieter said. Yet another guy who thought he knew Bobbi better than Gabe did. If Gabe weren't so heartened by the fact that her employees obviously liked and respected her enough to fight for her, he would have been beyond annoyed. Besides, Bobbi had never received flowers from anybody precisely because they thought that she wasn't someone who would appreciate them. But she was a woman underneath the overalls, he knew that better than anybody else, and despite everything, he suspected that deep down inside she had loved the flowers—maybe not the excess of them, but definitely the sentiment behind the gesture.

"It's been mentioned before," he said. He heard her voice and leaned to the side to see her past Pieter's lanky bulk. She was leading the customer out of her office, her voice brimming with excitement. He wasn't close enough to hear her words above the noise of the shop but whatever she was saying, she was damned enthusiastic about it.

She shook the man's hand and waved him off as he climbed into his car and drove off. After the car had turned the corner that would take him out of sight of the shop, she pumped her fist in the air and did a happy shimmy.

He could tell exactly when she first caught sight of his car, because her body language tensed immediately. She turned slowly and even with the light behind her he could see her flinch.

"Gabe," she said, her voice wobbling a bit.

"Can we talk?" he asked without preamble, and she nodded warily, indicating that he should follow her into her office. He dusted off the same chair he'd occupied the last time and saw that his handkerchief came away slightly less grimy this time. He noticed, as he sat down, that she had put the tool bouquet on a low filing cabinet next to her desk. She saw his attention drift to the basket and cleared her throat awkwardly.

"Thanks for the tools," she said. "But I can't keep them. They must have cost a fortune."

He laughed. "I *have* a fortune."

"Yes, but I don't want you to spend it on me. That's not your place."

"I don't want to get into this right now," he dismissed. "I'm not taking the tools back; I wouldn't know what to do with them. Use them or don't. Give them away to your employees like you did the flowers, although I don't imagine they'd be happy using pink tools."

"There were way too many flowers," she said, blushing guiltily. "I had to do *something* with them."

214

"Well, the men certainly appreciated them. Did you know that kid has *three* girlfriends?" He shook his head in disbelief, and she grinned in spite of herself.

"He's going to get caught at some point and it won't be pretty." She laughed, sounding so much like her old self that his heart constricted with longing. She caught herself and the laughter faded in her throat. "So what can I do for you?"

"My car needs a tune-up," he lied, and her eyes flew to the Lamborghini. She had been itching to get her hands on—or rather *inside*—it for months now. He could see that she was torn. He had never used her shop in the year that it had been in business and even before that, when she had been tinkering with cars just for fun, he had never allowed her to lay a finger on any of his vehicles.

"And it's making this weird knocking noise every time I change gears." Another lie. The car handled like a dream, but he was willing to let her take it apart from top to bottom if it would make her happy and score him more brownie points with her.

"Is it like a hollow clunking sound?" she asked with a thoughtful frown.

"Yeah?"

"Hmm, it *could* be worn gear linkage, but that seems like an unlikely problem for a car under a year old," she speculated. "And it's not like you've ever tested her capabilities much on the road, so it can't be from wear and tear."

"So you'll take a look?" he asked, trying not to sound too eager. Her eyes were watchful but she nodded.

"I'll get Craig to have a look," she told him.

"But I'd rather *you* did," he said, because he knew how much she was itching to.

"I have other things to take care of," she maintained, her eyes filled with longing as they tracked back to the car. But it was clear that she

215

wouldn't give him the satisfaction of accepting this latest gift—because that's what it was. He was giving her something that she had dying to have for months and . . . she was throwing it back in his face.

"What if I told you that I trusted only you to take care of my car?" he asked softly.

"I'd tell you that it's too late . . . you should have placed your trust in me long before now."

"Why are you being this way?" he asked in frustration. "What the hell did I do to you that was so damned awful? Okay so I wanted to keep our relationship a secret at first, I handled the situation badly, but punishing me for having human failings is petty as hell!"

"Do you really think *I'm* being petty? When you were *ashamed* to admit that you found me attractive and that I was your lover?"

"Let's just be completely honest here, Bobbi! You're punishing me because I'm not in love with you. I have the audacity to *want* you without craving all that romantic and sentimental bullshit as a side dish to the incredibly hot sex. I respect you and I care about you, but that's not enough for you. I don't love you the way you want me to so to hell with me, right?"

"You're right. You're absolutely right. I expected too much from you. But, what do you want from me, Gabe?" she asked gently. "Why have you been sending me flowers and poems and presents?"

"I wanted to . . . romance you, I guess," he admitted.

"To what end?" she asked logically, and he watched her mutely. He wasn't sure how to answer that question. "To get me back into bed? To get me to forgive you for hurting me? To apologize for what you said at the football match?"

"All of that."

"And let's say you succeeded in romancing me, what would the next step be? We go to the ball together, right? And then start a relationship that we both know would be doomed from the start."

"Stop this," he suddenly hissed. "Stop talking to me like I'm a preschooler. Yes, I wanted to romance you, I wanted to apologize, and I wanted to have a proper relationship with you. One that involves spending time together, enjoying each other's company, and *sex*. Because I believe that we can be good together. And if it doesn't last, it's because that's the way relationships go sometimes. Grow up, Bobbi. Sometimes all a couple has going for them is the sex, which can grow into mutual fondness, which can then become that damned Grand Passion that all women seem to aspire to. We're lucky, we *used* to have a pretty good friendship to build a solid foundation on, in addition to better sex than most people have in a lifetime. Everything else will either fall into place or it won't. But you want that happily ever after *right* now. And if you don't get it, like a petulant child, you're hell-bent on spoiling the chance we have to explore something that could actually be quite good between us."

He had a valid point, Bobbi realized. So he wasn't in love with her, but he *did* love her and that really was more than most couples had going for them. He looked hurt and disgusted with her and she could understand how he felt, but all the concerns that she had voiced that night in her room were still there. There was the fear that he would expect her to change too much in order to conform to his idea of the feminine ideal. The fear of more heartbreak—but she acknowledged that the chance of heartbreak was a risk in every relationship—it was part of life. But while most other relationships had a chance of ending well, this one was almost doomed to failure, despite Gabe's grand talk about it possibly growing into something more. But balancing out the fear was the hope that even when it didn't work out, the relationship would die a natural and relatively painless death and leave them both still with a mutual respect and love for each other. Gabe wanted to try and despite all her misgivings—Bobbi now knew that she wanted to try as well.

"I *have* been punishing you," she admitted, and his eyes jerked up to hers. "You mean the world to me, Gabe, and I hated that *I* didn't mean the same to you. I just . . ." She choked up and bit her lip as she tried to get herself under control again. "Let's go to the ball together and see where that takes us, but I'm not promising anything beyond that." He nodded, his face remarkably grim for a man who had just received what he wanted.

"The *other* thing I can't promise you is some major change in appearance," she warned. "If we're going to do this, you're going to have to accept me the way I am."

"Bobbi, you're beautiful the way you are," he assured her. "You always have been. I apologize if I ever made you feel less than that. But I hope you'll deign to wear a bra at the very least—there will be a lot of stodgy old men in attendance, and we wouldn't want any coronary incidents."

That startled a laugh out of her and he looked pleased. Which sparked an epiphany in her: all these years of trying to make Gabe laugh or smile and she only now realized that he had put an equal amount of effort into surprising laughter and smiles out of her as well. And, she acknowledged to herself, he enjoyed doing so.

"So do you really want your car checked? Or was that just an excuse to come here?" She asked, and he smiled. One of those full-on, genuine smiles that she loved so much.

"Well, I wanted to see how you liked the tool bouquet and the car was my foot in the door. Besides, I know you've been itching to get your hands on it."

"So you don't want her checked?" She couldn't quite hide her disappointment and Gabe's smile gentled.

"Of course I do. I hear you have quite the reputation for restoring and fixing vintage and exotic cars," he teased, and she felt a surge of pleasure at his words.

"Did you *see* her?" she asked him.

"If you're referring to that former clunker of Jase's, then yes, I saw it. You did an amazing job. Congratulations." She could see the unmistakable gleam of pride in his eyes and it warmed her from top to toes.

"That man who was in my office earlier?" She had to share the news with someone and she was suddenly excited to tell Gabe. "He has a 1969 Mustang convertible. She's in decent condition but he wants me to service her, and even better? He belongs to an owner's club! If I treat his baby well, he'll recommend the shop to some of the other owners in the area. Isn't that *wonderful?*"

"That is bloody brilliant, sweetheart." He grinned, taking a step toward her and unexpectedly capturing her chin between his thumb and forefinger. He kissed her then, in full view of her employees and anybody else who might walk into the shop. It was a gentle kiss but filled with a longing and desire that matched hers—just his lips on hers and the tip of his tongue tracing along the parted seam of her mouth. He lifted his head with a soft sigh and dragged his eyes open.

"I needed that," he said, and she smiled at him.

"I did too. Thank you."

"You, Roberta Richmond, are so very welcome." He spontaneously wrapped his arms around her and gathered her up in a tight hug. She returned the hug fiercely, so happy to have him back in her arms and in her life. They still had a list of problems a mile long, but she refused to worry about them right now. She just wanted to enjoy the perfection of this moment.

"Have dinner with me tonight?" he asked, and she lifted her head from his chest to meet his hopeful eyes.

"Okay." He smiled, looking relieved, and dropped another sweet kiss on her lips.

"I'll pick you up at five thirty," he informed before reluctantly releasing her. He turned to leave and Bobbi studied his broad back dreamily for a moment before remembering something.

"Wait!"

His wide shoulders tensed, and he slowly turned back to face her. His expression was filled with anxiety, and she wondered if he expected her to change her mind. "You need a replacement car."

"Oh, of course." The naked relief on his face was telling and Bobbi felt a pang in her chest at his uncertainty. They were each going to feel unsure around the other for a while yet. She hoped it was something they could overcome soon.

"You can drive mine until yours is ready to be picked up. Sean can drop me off at home tonight." She tugged the keys from her baggy overall pockets and tossed them at him. He caught them with a grimace of distaste. "Oh come on, she's not that bad."

"Bobbi, you've had that thing since you were eighteen," he protested.

"And she still runs like a dream," Bobbi lifted a challenging eyebrow and Gabe sighed. "I've kept her in perfect condition."

"Fine."

"Stop being such a snob." She grinned. "She may not be as pretty as your Lamborghini but she's got quirk and character."

"I admit to finding quirk and character a lot more interesting that mere good looks these days," he said with a warmth that left no doubt as to his sincerity.

~

Gabe's heart melted when Bobbi's entire face lit up like a beacon in response to his last comment. He hadn't meant the words to be a metaphor for his changing attitude toward superficial good looks but that was certainly how she had taken it, and he found himself thinking of ways to keep that radiant smile on her face forever if he could.

∾

After Gabe rang the doorbell at the Richmond house later that evening, he nervously smoothed down his hair, adjusted his tie, and did a breath check while waiting for someone to open the door. It wasn't long before the door was yanked open by Billy. Gabe tried not to look too dismayed to see his friend; he hadn't expected Billy to be visiting his family. He usually only visited Constantia on weekends. For him to be there on a Thursday night was unusual.

Billy stared at Gabe for an arrested moment before stepping aside to let him in. Gabe hadn't seen him since that football night nearly a month ago, and he soon discovered why. Billy slammed the door shut and turned to face Gabe with a furious expression on his handsome face.

"I don't exactly know what the hell went on between you and Bobbi that night, Gabe," he hissed without any preliminaries. "But you hurt her and it was only because Chase asked me to back off and give you both space that I haven't pushed the issue or kicked your arse before now! I'm warning you . . . hurt her again and, years of friendship aside, I *will* rearrange your face in the most painful way possible." Billy had always had such a colorful way with words.

"I know I hurt her . . . It was never my intention to do so. You know how much she means to me," Gabe murmured. "But I'm trying to figure this out, we both are, and I'd like to ask you to give us the opportunity to do so without any interference from you."

"Figure what out? What exactly is going on between you?" Billy asked, and Gabe inhaled unsteadily, acknowledging that this was it—the point of no return.

"Bobbi and I are . . . um." He coughed. "We're dating." Billy's jaw dropped and he shook his head as if to clear it before gaping at Gabe in disbelief.

"You're *what*?"

"Dating."

"What the . . . Gabe, she's like a sister to you, man!" Billy looked horrified, repulsed, and frankly disbelieving.

"No, she's not," Gabe responded succinctly. "She's not like a sister to me. At all. I don't feel anything remotely brotherly toward her, and you'd better resign yourself to that fact before she comes down those stairs. I won't have you making her feel uncomfortable about our relationship."

"But *I* am uncomfortable with it," Billy admitted. "It's weird as hell. Where did this come from?"

"Damned if I know," Gabe confessed. "But that's how it is, so get over it and don't even *think* about showing that appalled face to Bobbi."

"Does my dad know about this?"

"Not yet."

"How do you think *he'll* feel about it?" Billy asked pointedly, and Gabe fixed a grim look on him.

"I don't really give a damn how he feels about it or how you feel about it. This is between Bobbi and me."

"I don't like it," Billy growled.

"I don't care," Gabe responded. "But Bobbi does . . . so try not to put unfair pressure on her, will you?"

"I'll keep my own counsel, for Bobbi's sake," Billy said after a pause. "But what I said before? About rearranging your face? Forget that. You break my sister's heart and I'll destroy you, Gabe."

Gabe nodded curtly.

"Noted."

~

Bobbi had heard the doorbell five minutes ago but she couldn't bring herself to go downstairs. She checked her appearance for the umpteenth time and morosely concluded that it was still the same. She was wearing her navy-blue, all-purpose dress combined with her favorite tribal jewelry and a pair of flat sandals, which were the only pair of shoes she owned that looked even remotely feminine.

"This is a mistake," she whispered, feeling sick. "Oh God, what are you *doing*, Roberta?"

There was a soft knock on her door, and her stomach sank into her ugly sandals.

"Come in," she called faintly. When the door opened to reveal Billy instead of Gabe, she slumped in relief.

"Gabe's here for you," her brother said, his voice strangely gentle.

"I know," she said.

"Are you coming down?"

"Soon," she whispered. He turned as if to leave but changed his mind and came to stand beside her, staring at her reflection in the full-length mirror.

"This must seem odd to you," she said, and he smiled.

"A bit."

"I'm in love with him, you know," she confessed. "I have been for a long time. He doesn't feel the same way about me and that's okay."

"*Is* it okay?" Billy asked softly and her lips trembled.

"He loves me and he . . ." She blushed, this was her brother after all. "He uh . . . likes me in *that* way, but he's not in love with me. For now, that's enough."

"When will it stop being enough?" Her brother, usually such an obnoxious joker, was being remarkably sweet and understanding and his concern brought a sting to her eyes and warmed her heart.

"Who knows? Maybe it will always be enough."

"Are you content with merely enough?"

"For now," she repeated with a decisive nod.

"Just be happy, Runt." Her brother smiled and gently leaned his shoulder against her until she lost her balance and nudged back with a laugh. "Now are you coming downstairs or not? Your *date* seems rather nervous."

"He does?" That thought was so far beyond the realms of possibility that it boggled her mind for a moment.

"Yep. I left him in the den with Dad. Last I saw, he was trying to explain that he was here to take you out."

"Oh my God, what did Dad say?"

"I don't think he got it. He asked Gabe *where* he was taking you; I left Gabe to sweat it out and came up here to get you."

∾

"A date?" Gabe was getting the full, formidable Mike Richmond death stare and he finally knew what all the man's business competitors had felt like *just* before their downfall. The man was certainly a force to be reckoned with, but Gabe had never had that force turned on him before.

"That's why you sent her all those flowers? You were courting her?" An old-fashioned word that made Gabe wince guiltily when he thought about what those flowers had really been about. Courting? That would have been like shutting the gate after the horse had already bolted.

"Not exactly," Gabe admitted, keeping his hands folded respectfully in front of him and his eyes level. *Don't show any sign of weakness*, he reminded himself. Mike Richmond pounced on weakness.

"So what was that if not a courtship?"

"An apology," Gabe confessed. "We'd had an argument about something."

"Like a lover's spat?" he asked genially, and Gabe swallowed, sensing a trap.

"Just an argument," he maintained.

"How long has this thing been going on between you and Bobbi?" The older man came right out and asked the question Gabe had been dreading.

"Nearly a month."

"And this is the *first* time you see fit to come to my door like a gentleman and take her out? What have you been doing before now?" The man's voice had turned to ice, and Gabe cleared his throat uncomfortably.

"What happened before now is in the past, Mike. I see no reason to revisit it."

"You treat my little girl with *respect*, Gabriel." Mike looked absolutely furious with him and Gabe knew that the man's anger was completely justifiable. "You've both been carrying on doing God knows what for weeks now and she's clearly been miserable! So you show her the respect she deserves from now on."

"Yes, sir." Gabe nodded. "You have my word on that."

They heard the murmur of Bobbi's and Billy's voices outside the door, and after giving him one last warning look, Mike turned to face the door as it swung inward to reveal his two youngest children.

Gabe looked up too and was helpless to prevent the smile that curled his lips when he caught sight of Bobbi. He kept his eyes on her pretty face, not wanting to acknowledge that familiar, ugly dress of hers until he absolutely had to. She looked nervous and when she met his eyes; he winked at her to put her at ease. He made his way to her side and put his arm around her waist, laying an unmistakable claim before he looked up to meet first her father's and then her brother's eyes, arranging his expression to show them nothing but absolute possessiveness. His message was unmistakable: *Mine.*

CHAPTER THIRTEEN

He took her to a four-star restaurant at the Hidden Valley wineries in Stellenbosch. Bobbi had heard about the place, of course. It was one of the top ten restaurants in the country, with excellent food, wine, and absolutely incomparable scenery. It was nearly an hour-long drive to the place, but they managed to get there in time to be seated, just before sunset, at a table that overlooked the entire valley.

"It's so pretty here," she said reverently, and he reached across the table to cover her hand with his. They sat in silence and watched the sky catch fire and go from gold to scarlet to deep crimson and then fade into shades of pink, purple, and violet. The clouds were daubed in lighter pinks and lavenders and looked like a painter's palette above the spectacular Helderberg Mountains.

The waitstaff remained at a discreet distance, allowing them to enjoy the sunset and only after twilight had fallen over the valley, did they come and take their order.

Gabe kept staring at her, throughout their starter course of delicious chilled asparagus velouté, and Bobbi self-consciously fiddled with the stem of her wineglass. She took a sip of the refreshing Semillon to calm her nerves and was aware of the fact that her hands were shaky.

"Stop staring," she whispered, and he grinned.

"I was waiting for you to call me out on that," he admitted with that irresistible charm that she found so lovable about him.

"Well, why do you keep doing it?" she demanded, keeping her voice low.

"Because you're so damned gorgeous and I'm still trying to figure out how I never saw it before." He shook his head in disbelief. She smiled shyly and rolled her eyes at him.

"Maybe because you were always too busy staring at all the *beautiful* women in the room," she said pointedly, and he thought about it for a moment before nodding.

"You're probably right," he acknowledged, before quite deliberately looking around the room at all the elegant, lovely women seated at the other tables. "Well, none of those present here tonight, so I guess I'm stuck staring at you."

"You're such a liar," she groaned, and his eyes went deadly serious.

"I mean it," he emphasized. "There's really no other woman here tonight that I'd rather be looking at."

"You don't have to lay it on so thick," she said, trying to keep the cynicism out of her voice. "I know you're trying, Gabe. But there's no need to pretend I'm something that I'm not."

Gabe bit back a frustrated groan and smiled at her. It was going to take work to convince her of his sincerity, he knew that—but it was worth the effort. He wanted this to succeed. He had honestly thought that her dress and the ugly jewelry and the truly horrific sandals, all of which he had seen on so many other occasions, would bother him. But after that first glance, he had barely given them any other consideration—all he saw was her radiant skin, her luminous amber eyes, and her pink mouth with that plump lower lip. And, of course, that short and messy cap of hair that he always longed to run his fingers through. He wondered how out of line it would be to drag her home with him tonight—mere hours after her father had warned him to treat her with respect. He respected her all right: her mind, her heart, her sexy body, and her ability to drive him crazy in bed.

They finished their starter and for her second course Bobbi had ordered the mushroom vol-au-vent with a pinot noir, and Gabe, who absolutely despised mushrooms, went for the gnocchi, sweetbread, and sage sauté, accompanied by a delicious chenin blanc.

"Chase has become weirdly obsessed with some reality TV show about B- and C-list celebs learning how to ballroom dance." He remembered what he'd been dying to tell her before. She choked on her wine before looking up at him with wide eyes.

"Seriously?"

"He's even rooting for some of the contestants. He's been watching marathons and back seasons." Bobbi did a slow, disbelieving blink that he found inordinately adorable before she dissolved into unladylike snorts of laughter. Gabe loved watching her laugh, she always put her whole body into it—he used to tickle her when they were kids just to hear it. He especially enjoyed the cute snorts that went with the convulsive giggling. As he watched her erupt, he realized that he hadn't heard her laugh like this in too long and that it had been wholly his fault.

"I *know* that show," she said between gasps. Her giggles were starting to attract glances from the other tables. Some people seemed entertained by her amusement; others looked haughty, and Gabe found that he didn't give even the slightest damn about what any of them thought. She was a bloody delight to behold, and people could bask in her radiance or go to hell.

"He's totally hooked," Gabe said dryly. "I'm pretty sure I'll come home one of these days to find him practicing the cha-cha-cha with

Letty." That set her off again and this time her laughter was so infectious that Gabe joined in with a few wry chuckles.

"Truth be told, I'm happy he's found a diversion," Gabe said after the laughter had faded to just the occasional snicker from Bobbi. "I think he has lacked focus since he's been home and I've been concerned about him going into some kind of depression, but weirdly enough this TV show seems to be the distraction he requires."

"He needs a break, Gabe, and maybe this is his way of switching off his brain for a bit," she offered and he nodded.

"That's exactly what I thought," Gabe said.

"Still, it's hard to imagine him watching something so fluffy." Chase had always been into the hard-hitting news programs and documentaries.

"I prefer it to him watching anything remotely connected to the Middle East right now."

"You're terrified he'll leave again, aren't you?" she observed, and Gabe sighed. She knew him so well she could almost always read what was on his mind. It was something that he had taken for granted before—just one of the many things about Bobbi he'd never truly appreciated.

"Yeah," he confirmed. "He's been telling me a little about what had happened on this last assignment and it's not pretty. He had lost his objectivity and had gotten too closely involved with a woman and her young daughter. He tried to help them get out and from what I can gather—he finds it difficult to go into too much detail—it ended badly. He's in such a truly dark place right now, that I don't think he'd come back alive if he left again in his current frame of mind. So if all he does all day is watch terrible reality TV for the next few weeks or months until he's figured out what his next step will be, then I'm all for it."

"Maybe he'll start taking ballroom dancing lessons," she said, striving to lighten the mood, despite her own concern for Chase. She forced a laugh that soon became genuine, as she recalled something from their childhood. "Remember that time your mum forced you guys to go to ballet classes?"

"Funny you should mention that," he chuckled, before telling her the related story about their former hero participating in the same show Chase was hooked on. The rest of the evening passed swiftly and was filled with good food, banter, and ever-increasing sexual tension as their delightful dinner dawdled to an end. By the time Gabe escorted her to the Jeep, which he preferred driving to her old clunker, she was tipsy and just *aglow* with happiness. He held out a hand to help her climb into the passenger seat and felt a dart of ever-present awareness when her fingers closed around his. He couldn't resist tugging her close to plant a quick kiss on her luscious lips before handing her into the car and shutting the door behind her. He took a moment to draw in a calming breath before darting around the front of the car and climbing into the driver's seat.

The long drive home was conducted mostly in silence, the Jeep's radio was broken and neither of them seemed inclined to fill the quiet with inane chatter. It was a companionable silence that was both familiar and welcome.

"I've never asked you this before," Bobbi said twenty minutes into that comfortable silence, when they were still quite a distance from home. He spared her a quick glance and noted that she was curled up on her side and facing him.

"What?"

"Why do you rearrange the condiments everywhere we go?" she asked. "I've been wondering for years and I can't believe I never got around to asking you before now." Gabe watched the road as he considered her question.

"I don't know . . . I just like to have the bottles lined up according to size, it just looks neater and feels less cluttered. You don't know this about me, but I have the pens and pencils in my desk organizer at work arranged according to size as well. My shoes and ties according to color . . ."

"You used to alphabetize the toys on your room shelves," she recalled, and he grinned self-consciously, feeling like a freak. "You went crazy once when Billy put your GI Joe doll next to your Spider-man doll."

"Firstly they weren't dolls, they were action figures," he corrected, and she snorted.

"Whatever floats your boat." She shrugged.

"And secondly GI Joe was sandwiched between my Frankenstein jigsaw puzzle and my Houdini magic set . . . there were at least eight toys separating GI Joe from Spiderman. There was a clear system and he deliberately messed it up. And thirdly, I didn't freak out . . . I merely kicked him out of my room and told him to play in Chase's room if he wanted to mess stuff up."

"You wouldn't let him back in for a month!"

"How do you even remember this?" he asked in disbelief. "Weren't you like five or something?"

"I was six." The boys had been eleven and had drifted onto more mature interests just a year after that spat.

"Anyway, I like to have everything in its place."

Bobbi reflected on those words for a moment, remembering what he had said that terrible night at the football game.

How would you fit into my life? he had asked. *Where would I even put you?*

He needed to have everything in its place and that night he had had the equivalent of a panic attack not knowing where she slotted into his life anymore. And with her standing in front of him, bruised and bleeding, his panic had ratcheted up several notches. It was odd how clearly she could see that now.

"I always figured it had something to do with my father leaving," he volunteered. Surprised by the additional information, she sat up straight. Gabe, *never* spoke about his father. Neither did Chase for that matter. Bobbi had known that he had left, of course, but she had never asked for the details. She didn't press him now, merely sat and waited. "He didn't say good-bye, you know? Just snuck out like a thief in the night. One day he was there and the next he wasn't, and Mum spent day after day closeted away in her room crying.

"Chase and I were only eight." It was the year before the Richmonds had moved in next to the Braddocks. "And our world just fell apart. One day everything made sense and the next it didn't. Nothing felt permanent or safe and according to my mum, I started rearranging things in the closets and kitchen cupboards a couple of months after that. When it proved too hard to control the communal areas in the house, I focused only on my room. The habit stuck with me. If I don't maintain complete governance over every minute detail of my surroundings, I feel like things are spiraling out of control."

"Did you ever hear from him again?" she asked softly, and he flicked her a sideways glance.

"Who? My father?"

"Yes."

"We get a Christmas card and a birthday card—one between the two of us—from him every year." Bobbi couldn't help the surprised sound that emerged from her throat.

"You never mentioned that before," she said, and he shrugged.

"It's not important. He's a narcissist. He *never* makes any kind of polite inquiry as to how we are, but always assumes that we must be dying to know what his latest adventure is. The reality is that both

Chase and I lost interest years ago, but it would never occur to Leighton Braddock that maybe his sons don't *want* to know about his awesome trips to far-flung places. I'm sure he imagines we think he's the coolest dad in the world." A reluctant laugh huffed from him. "He's such an arse. I don't even think he realizes that Mum has divorced him and remarried. I'm pretty sure if he ever swans back here someday he expects to reconcile with his lovely wife and have amazing relationships with his adoring sons."

"*Ooh,*" Bobbi said, wincing, keeping her tone light. "It would almost be worth it just to see him get a huge dose of reality smacked in his face."

They lapsed back into silence for the remainder of the drive as Bobbi reflected upon what she had just learned. She knew Gabe better than most people but had never known how badly his father's abandonment had affected him. Learning that she didn't know everything there was to know about him was kind of exciting. It was like listening to a much-loved CD for the hundredth time only to unexpectedly discover a beautiful, hidden track at the end.

She glanced out of the window when the car took a turn and saw that they were on their street. Her heart sank when Gabe bypassed his gate and drove to hers. Security let them in and he didn't say anything as he maneuvered the Jeep up the long drive toward the house and drew it to a stop in front of the steps leading up to the front door.

"Should I come over later?" she asked in an unsteady voice, and his hands tightened perceptibly on the steering wheel, while he kept his face forward.

"I would *love* that," he muttered before turning to face her. "But . . . I don't want us to rush this."

"Gabe . . . that cat's been out of the bag for a while now," she teased, and his teeth gleamed in the dark as he grinned.

"And what a pretty cat it is. One that I would love to pet and stroke and play with."

She choked and blushed furiously. "Uh . . ." She was at a complete loss for words.

"*But* we're doing it right this time, Bobbi. So you stuff that gorgeous little pussy . . . cat right back in the bag."

"Enough with the cat analogies," she groaned.

"*You* started it," he pointed out. "I merely ran with it."

She shook her head and slammed a palm to her face.

"You going to give me a good-night kiss?" he asked huskily, and she dipped her head coyly.

"Only if you walk me to the door," she retorted.

"It'll be my pleasure." He leapt out of the Jeep and hurried around to help her down like she was one of his elegant blondes and Bobbi thrilled at the gentlemanly treatment. He took her hand and placed it in the crook of his elbow before walking her up the short flight of stairs and onto the well-lit porch.

He stopped right in front of the door and turned to face her, maintaining a frustratingly polite distance between their bodies.

"I had a great evening," he said.

"Me too."

"Does that mean you'll be willing to go out with me again?" he asked, and she rolled her eyes.

"Of course."

"Good." His eyes dropped to her mouth and his tongue wet his lips. Her eyes followed the movement hungrily. He stepped closer to her and inhaled deeply, then exhaled on a shuddery breath before cupping her neck with his palms. He used his thumbs to tilt her jaw and she barely had time to reflect upon how much the masterful gesture turned her on before his lips dropped onto hers for a drugging, sucking, gentle kiss that obliterated her thought processes until all she could do was enjoy the sensuality of his expert mouth.

The kiss demanded nothing and left her wanting so much more. When he lifted his mouth, hers followed his blindly until he stood upright and removed the temptation from her reach.

"I'll pick up my car at lunchtime," he said, and she was in too much of a daze to do anything other than nod. "And we can have lunch together?"

"Lunch. Yes." She nodded again.

"Good night, Bobbi mine," he said, and the endearment had her smiling radiantly and truly feeling like *his* after the wonderful evening they had just enjoyed together.

"Yes, good night," she repeated. He stood there unmoving and she gazed up at him dreamily.

"Aren't you going in?" he asked, and she snapped out of her haze and flushed.

"Uh, *yes*. Of course!" She fumbled with the lock and opened the door . . . eventually.

"See you tomorrow." She stepped inside and he nodded. "Good night." She closed the door before he could respond, quickly reset the alarm, and then stood on tiptoe to peer out of the peephole, wanting to see what he did next. He was smiling as he turned away and when he went down the stairs, he did so with a bounce in his step that she recognized as happiness.

She hugged that knowledge to her chest as she floated up to her room. He was happy. She had done that. Even if this relationship of theirs *was* doomed, she would not have exchanged tonight for anything else in the world.

"Good morning." Gabe was slightly embarrassed by the singsong quality in his voice when he joined his brother for breakfast the following morning. Chase, who had been staring broodingly into his coffee, looked up and smiled when he saw Gabe's grin.

"You're in a good mood," he observed.

"Why *wouldn't* I be?" Gabe said after sitting down opposite him. "It's a gorgeous summer morning. The sky's blue, the birds are out, everything smells fresh and awesome."

"You didn't join me for our jog this morning," Chase said.

"Slept in," Gabe informed before crunching into a slice of whole-wheat toast.

"Good evening last night?" Chase asked.

"The best."

"When will you see her again?"

"Lunch." He couldn't wait. He had enjoyed her company so much the night before that he had disclosed more about himself than he ever had to anybody else. It had been revelatory—he felt like he could tell her anything because she already knew him so well and wouldn't judge him.

Their conversation had been interesting, easygoing, and had flowed as readily as the wine, and it hadn't been filled with only the fluff and banter that had characterized their previous discussions. It had felt more significant, like he was really getting to know her for the first time, and the more he learned the more he liked and respected her.

"Jeez, look at you," Chase groused good-naturedly. "You're beaming so damned brightly, you're practically blinding me."

Gabe's grin merely widened and he winked at his brother before diving into his breakfast.

∽

"Hey, boss, your boyfriend's here for his car." Sean's embarrassingly loud voice rang out across the shop floor where Bobbi was consulting with one of her few new female clients about fixing the brake line on the woman's Mini Cooper.

Bobbi winced and smiled apologetically at the woman, who returned the smile politely. Her client was one of those young twenty-somethings who had the sleek and pampered appearance of a woman who had money and enjoyed spending it on herself. The kind of woman Bobbi should probably have been when one took her background into consideration.

She ignored Sean, knowing that Gabe wouldn't interrupt her while she was in consultation with a client, but a quick peek over the woman's shoulder told her that he had a clear view of them both. He waved at her and she waved back self-consciously. The woman glanced over her shoulder to see who Bobbi was looking at, and her entire body went on alert—shoulders up, chest out, chin up, and a sexy hair flick. She stopped listening to Bobbi and spent her energy projecting "I'm available" vibes toward the other end of the large workroom. Didn't she hear Sean call Gabe Bobbi's boyfriend for God's sake? Or did she think Sean had meant someone else?

Bobbi grimaced as she gathered that that was probably exactly what the woman thought. She wouldn't for a second think Gabe was the "boyfriend" in question.

Bobbi kept talking and explaining what would be done to her car, but the woman was a lost cause, and in the end, Bobbi just told her how much the service would cost and offered her a replacement car while they fixed her Mini.

"All good." The woman dismissed her as her eyes hungrily followed Gabe, who was inspecting his Lamborghini and chatting amiably with Sean.

"I'll get the keys," Bobbi mumbled.

"Thank you. I'll just . . . have a look around while you do that." Bobbi watched as the woman made a beeline for Gabe.

"This is some car," she said when she joined the two men. Sean looked immediately lovestruck, but she ignored him and focused her laser-like attention on Gabe. Bobbi had to admit that he looked even more gorgeous today. In that charcoal pinstriped suit, with a pale blue shirt and dark-blue-and-gray-striped tie, he oozed that conservative elegance Bobbi found so irresistible.

"I noticed it from across the room," the woman was saying, and Bobbi rolled her eyes. *Yeah, right.* She hadn't noticed the car until Gabe had been standing right beside it. Some more hair flicking followed combined with a ridiculous amount of eyelash fluttering. Bobbi snorted and tried not to feel insecure. Smelling of engines and looking grubby, when Bobbi stood beside a woman like that, it would be hard not to find her lacking.

Bobbi made quick work of getting the keys to the woman's replacement car and joined them a moment later. The woman was asking Gabe all these breathless and *interested* questions about his car, ignoring poor Sean, who looked crestfallen.

"Here you are, Ms. Simms," Bobbi announced, holding up the keys. "She's just a Fiat but she's quite reliable."

The woman looked irritated by the interruption, and when she took the keys, she wrinkled her nose when her fingers brushed against Bobbi's hand.

"I don't know about you but I always find the whole garage experience to be such a chore," she told Gabe in a confiding voice. "Everything and everybody's just so . . . *dirty.* No offense of course." The last was directed to Bobbi and absolutely devastated Sean. Gabe's eyes narrowed as he took in Sean's face before they shifted to Bobbi, who maintained a carefully and politely blank expression on her face.

"Well," he said, reaching out and grabbing Bobbi's hand before yanking her over until she was plastered against his side. She had had a bit of an oil spill that morning and her overalls were somewhat the worse for wear, but he didn't hesitate and kept her firmly tucked beneath his arm. "Sometimes a bit of dirt isn't so bad, is it sweetheart?" he asked Bobbi before dropping a long and very hot kiss on her surprised mouth.

"Hey there," he whispered when he lifted his lips and she blinked, completely flustered.

"Uh, hey yourself," she replied.

"You ready for lunch? I'm starving. My good friend here, the mechanical genius Sean, tells me that my car is all fixed and ready to go." He completely ignored the flabbergasted Ms. Simms, whose jaw was gaping unbecomingly.

"Nearly ready, I just need to finish up with my client," she said, and he grinned before releasing her reluctantly.

"I apologize for the lack of professionalism, Ms. Simms," Bobbi told the woman smoothly. "I assure you, we at Richmond's Auto Repair Shop *usually* maintain the highest standards of professionalism. My . . ."

"Boyfriend," Gabe supplied helpfully, and Bobbi blushed, trying not to smile.

"He doesn't work here." Jeez, like that wasn't obvious. "So please allow me to show you to your replacement vehicle."

~

After Bobbi had waved the woman off, she turned to Gabe and put her hands on her hips.

"That was completely . . . ," she began sternly but sighed when he kept smiling sweetly at her. "Just forget it. But don't do it again."

"Don't do what again? Kiss you? I'm afraid I can't make that promise, sweetheart," he teased, and the other guys chuckled.

"What are you three laughing at? Get back to work."

"Yes, boss." Sean, the smart arse, snapped to attention and actually saluted. Pieter and Craig just grinned and went back to their respective tasks.

Gabe followed Bobbi into her office, where she peeled off her overalls and cleaned her face, arms, and hands. When she looked back at Gabe, it was to find him staring at her with some pretty intense heat in his eyes.

"I love watching you strip off those overalls," he groaned. "It's always so damned sexy seeing you reveal more and more skin—it's like witnessing a butterfly emerge from a cocoon." It was such an absurdly flattering thing for him to say that Bobbi was completely taken aback for a moment.

"One day," he continued huskily. "You're gonna do a private striptease just for me. You're going to peel away that outer layer to ever-so-slowly reveal your soft, naked skin beneath it."

"Naked skin?" she repeated, her voice embarrassingly husky as she fought to control her arousal.

"Naked, or maybe in some hot lingerie—God even those plain cotton boy shorts you fancy will do. I'm not picky. It's the execution and what I plan to do to you afterward that count." His breath was coming just a bit faster and he shifted his stance in a way that told her he was as physically affected by his words as she was. His eyes dropped to her chest and she resisted the urge to cross her arms over her hard nipples. A smug smile flirted with his lips.

"*Told* you to start wearing bras," he murmured, and she scowled at him before shaking her head and tossing his car keys at him.

"Let's go," she said bossily, and led the way out. She could feel his eyes on her butt all the way to his car and put a deliberate wiggle in her walk. She grinned when she heard him groan. Two could play this game.

～

Just before they walked into Manny's, Gabe deliberately took Bobbi's hand in his.

"I want them to know that you're with me," he said in response to her questioning look. He couldn't quite decipher her expression, but she squeezed his hand, took a deep breath, and walked into the pub with him close behind.

Because it was a weekday, most of the usual crowd wasn't there—which disappointed Gabe slightly. Still, there were enough recognizable faces around to ensure that word about him and Bobbi would get out. At first nobody seemed to pay any attention to the hand-holding, and figuring that a more drastic course of action was required, he looped an arm around her shoulders as they made their way to an empty table and dropped a kiss onto the curve of her neck. That caused a few speculative glances to be cast their way, but nobody seemed to think too much about it.

"Unless you plan to throw me down on the floor and ravish me in full view of everybody here, nobody's really going to figure it out for a while yet," Bobbi said dryly, her tone alive with amusement. Gabe heaved a frustrated sigh and acknowledged the truth in her words with a nod.

They sat down and he unconsciously started rearranging the condiments. He caught himself in the middle of moving the pepper to the spot he preferred and stopped, after their conversation the night before he was suddenly self-conscious about the habit.

Bobbi's smile was gentle and filled with understanding. She reached over and pushed the pepper grinder toward its spot next to the salt grinder with her finger.

"That's where it goes, right?" she asked softly after she had inched it into place, and he nodded jerkily in reply. He slowly lined up the sugar and toothpicks as well before sitting back and watching her. She had her elbows on the table and her chin resting in her palms and was staring down at the menu like it was the first time she'd ever seen it.

When their server came over, she ordered a beer and pork chops with mashed potatoes.

"I'll have the fish and chips," Gabe said, and Bobbi's head snapped up.

"*What* did you just order?" she asked after the server had left.

"Fish and chips," he muttered, feeling embarrassed again. Even the server had given him a shocked look before leaving their table.

"But . . . *why*?"

"I *can* change, you know?" he said defensively. "I do like trying new things that are out of my comfort zone."

"Oh, Gabe," she breathed. "I know that. You don't have to prove anything to me."

"Really?" he asked with just an edge of sarcasm in his voice. "Because sometimes I feel as if I do. Do you think I don't know you were expecting me to find you somehow lacking in comparison to that woman in the shop earlier?"

"She was really pretty." Her words made Gabe feel like taking her by the shoulders and shaking some sense into her.

"She was also a total *bitch*. Why the hell would I find her more attractive than you just because she happened to be wearing makeup and a dress?"

"*Because* she was wearing makeup and a dress," Bobbi seethed furiously. "Maybe if you hadn't made a such big deal about my crappy dress sense before, I wouldn't think you were comparing me unfavorably to every pretty girl in a dress."

"Yeah, well sometimes I'm an idiot who doesn't always know what the hell he's talking about," he snapped, and her mouth slammed shut as she absorbed his words. He could tell the moment they sank in because her eyes went suspiciously bright with suppressed laughter.

"Yes, you are," she agreed. "I'm so not going to let you forget you said that."

He grinned sheepishly before lifting her hand from the table to toy with her fingers.

"Yeah, sometimes I need to be reminded of the zero point seven percent of the time that I'm wrong. It keeps me grounded." The words startled a laugh out of her and he looked pleased with himself for eliciting the response from her.

～

"I don't believe it," Gabe said, laughing, and Bobbi shook her head, enjoying his astonishment.

"I *love* knitting. It's my secret hobby." Nobody else knew about that but they had been discussing embarrassing hidden talents. Gabe had confessed to being able to wriggle his big toe independently from his other toes, only the left big toe mind you—which Bobbi actually thought was kind of awesome.

"That's not exactly an embarrassing talent, you know," he pointed out.

"It *is* when you can't really knit more than scarves—and *ugly* ones at that. Worse, the wool keeps snagging on my hands." She held them up for Gabe to inspect. "Because of the hideous calluses."

He took her hands in his and placed a sweet kiss in each palm.

"I love your hands," he admitted. "The combination of rough and smooth on my skin sends me out of my mind."

Wow. Okay . . . *blush.* Bobbi was outrageously flattered and quite turned on.

They lingered over lunch for much too long, but in the end they reluctantly got the bill.

"Are you coming to the game tonight?" he asked after paying for lunch. "I've missed you."

"I'll come if you promise not to get into any fights or freak out when I get scraped or bumped or bruised. It's embarrassing."

"Well, then don't get scraped or bumped or bruised," he retorted.

"Gabe . . . ," she said.

"Bobbi, I can't make that promise. I don't like seeing you in pain and I will probably overreact if you get hurt. That's just the way it is when you have a . . ." He paused before shrugging. "A *boyfriend* who would like to see you remain unscathed."

A boyfriend. The word was so damned juvenile, and yet Bobbi felt like she was floating on air for the rest of the afternoon.

CHAPTER FOURTEEN

"So you guys are an item now?" Bronwyn asked after the game that night. The women sat on the bleachers, watching the men, who stood around the grill, staring intently down at the smoldering coals as if they held the answer to all of life's problems.

"I suppose we are," Bobbi admitted shyly.

"That's *wonderful*, Bobbi," Theresa said warmly and hugged her. "You two are such a perfect couple."

"You're such a polite liar, Theresa," Bobbi laughed, and Theresa frowned.

"Why do you say that?"

"We're not exactly the perfect couple. We're totally mismatched. I mean it's all good now, but the very first time he has to take me out to some business thing, I'll be an embarrassment to him. And I refuse to change who I am just for the sake of a few superficial business events."

"That was quite the outburst," Lisa observed, scooting closer. "Why do you think you'll be an embarrassment?"

"Dresses and those things don't matter to me, but they *do* to him."

"If they don't matter to you, then what's wrong with wearing the occasional dress to the occasional party?" Theresa asked, and the other women nodded. "I mean, it's not like you hate them or are morally opposed to them, is it? You just can't be bothered with them."

Bobbi thought about that for a second, feeling a bit confused.

"Bobbi, you're in love with a man whose career sometimes requires him to attend formal events. It's not something he can change; it's a fact of his life. Would it really be such a sacrifice to wear a dress for a few hours every so often?"

"I'm just worried that he'll expect me to be this woman I can never be, someone elegant and always perfectly dressed and made up," she whispered. "I love him so much that it would be easy for me to lose sight of who I really am in an effort to keep him happy."

"What were you wearing to your dinner last night?" Alice asked.

"My navy-blue dress, you know the one?" They all nodded. Of course they knew it, it was all she ever wore when there was any kind of formal or semiformal event.

"And?" Lisa asked. Bobbi stared at her blankly, confused by the question.

"And what?"

"Did he chuck his jacket over your shoulders in an attempt to hide what you were wearing from everybody else?" Lisa elaborated, and Bobbi laughed.

"Of course not."

"Did he look at all embarrassed to be seen with you?" Bobbi thought about Bronwyn's question for a while before shaking her head slowly.

"So what more do you want from him? He's clearly not ashamed of you," Theresa said. "He wants to be seen with you." Bobbi thought back to that afternoon when he had taken her hand before entering the pub, she'd been wearing frayed shorts and a tank top combined with a baseball cap and ankle-high biker boots. They had been the quintessential odd couple, but he hadn't seemed to care.

"He has to present a certain image to the world," Theresa continued. "And when it's just the two of you, or you're going out to the pub or hanging out with us, nobody cares about the way you're dressed. That's just packaging. But there will be times when your usual getup of jeans and T-shirts, or even that navy-blue dress, just won't cut it. You'd humiliate both yourself and Gabe. Who would take him seriously in the business world if you appeared on his arm dressed like that?"

"Why should the way *I* dress reflect badly on him?" Bobbi asked defensively, even though she could see the sense in what Theresa was saying.

"Don't be obtuse, Bobbi," Bronwyn said grimly. "And stop being so damned stubborn. Obviously it would reflect badly on him; how could anybody trust a businessman with bad judgment? And that's what it would look like to everybody else. Bad judgment if he showed up with you on his arm and you were dressed as if you were still back in your workshop."

"I wouldn't feel comfortable. I wouldn't feel like myself," Bobbi whispered.

"That's probably because you haven't found anything that you like yet." Theresa reached over to give Bobbi's hand a supportive squeeze. "You don't go shopping; you get the easiest things off the rack and you're done. Wearing a dress won't change who you are, Bobbi. It couldn't possibly do that, it'll merely add a bit of embellishment."

"Why don't we turn our girls' night into a girls' day tomorrow and do some shopping?" Lisa suggested, and the other women hummed their approval.

"I don't want some Cinderella makeover," Bobbi said in a panic and they all laughed.

"Don't be silly," Theresa said dismissively. "You don't need a makeover. Don't you know that you're gorgeous? You just need some guidance, that's all."

"I'm not sure," Bobbi said. "I have work and other stuff."

She was nervous at the thought of a shopping trip. Shopping wasn't her strong suit, and she had never really had another woman's guidance when going out to buy clothing. It meant the world to her that these four women, who had become such close friends in so short a time, wanted to guide her through the process, but Bobbi really couldn't imagine shopping being anything other than an ordeal. Still, the idea was tempting, and if anybody could turn a day of tedious shopping into something fun, it would be these four.

"Bobbi," Theresa said. "I promise you we will make it as painless and fun as possible. All we're doing is finding some clothes that suit your awesome personality. I mean, what do denim shorts and T-shirts say about you, really?"

"I like comfort?" Bobbi ventured.

"Yes, but how about the fact that you have a sense of fun and an adventurous spirit too?" Theresa responded. "Clothes don't have to be just practical, you know, and evening dresses don't *have* to be intimidating, sexy sheaths. They can be fun and flirty and edgy and cool."

"You need to stop watching *Project Runway*," Bronwyn said with an eye roll.

"I just watch it for the accessories." Theresa went to her stock-in-trade answer.

"*Sure* you do," Lisa said.

"Anyway . . . we're going shopping," Theresa repeated

"Yes, we are," Bronwyn confirmed, as did Alice and Lisa.

Comprehensively outvoted, Bobbi shrugged and bowed to the inevitable.

"I guess we're going shopping."

~

Sandro was the first man, as always, to break free of the hypnotic effect of the grill, and he climbed up the bleachers to slide in behind Theresa and drag her back between his spread thighs.

"You ladies look so serious," he observed, nuzzling Theresa's neck in between words. "What are you talking about?"

"Girls' stuff," Lisa said enigmatically, smiling at her husband, who had come to join them. Bryce and Pierre soon followed Rick and all three men sat down close to their wives. That was the way it usually went. The men huddled by the grill for a while, and then the married guys would drift over to join their wives in the stands. The single men usually remained trapped by the fire's enthralling spell. That's why Bobbi was heartened when Gabe glanced up them, smiled when he caught her eye, and, without a backward glance to the siren song of the flames, made his way over to her. He sat down beside her and wrapped an arm around her waist until she was practically melded against him.

She leaned against him with a contented sigh and rested her hand on his thigh and her head on his shoulder. One of his hands was resting on her leg, just above her knee, and when it went down to cup her kneecap, she twisted her head to meet his eyes.

"What happened here?" he asked gruffly, gently brushing a finger across the grass burn on her knee. She had taken a tumble during the game, which he—fortunately—hadn't seen, but she had scraped her knee pretty badly.

"It's just a grass burn," she explained. "I tripped over my own feet."

"Good game tonight," he said. "Although having both Chase and Kinsley on my team wasn't exactly ideal." Chase wasn't great at football. Cricket was more his sport.

"Did you like my goal?" She smirked, and he glowered at the brightly lit field.

"I would have liked it a hell of a lot better if you were on my team."

"Stop being such a sore loser," she chastised. Gabe's team had lost 3–0 and he was clearly still moody about it—despite the therapeutic fire-heals-all-wounds postgame session at the grill.

"Meat's done," Chase called from the grill, and Bobbi moved to get her food, but Gabe's hand tightened on her leg.

"I'll get it. I don't want you straining that leg too much."

She gaped at him.

"Gabe, it's a *grass burn*," she pointed out.

"It'll still sting," he said. He kissed her quickly before lithely jumping off the stands and heading toward the grill.

"You guys are really sweet together," Bron pointed out after the others had drifted down for food as well. Most of the children were asleep on picnic loungers and covered with blankets just next to the bleachers, but Bronwyn had her sleeping two-and-a-half-year-old daughter, Kayla, tucked against her chest, which meant Bryce had gone for their food. "It's interesting because you were such good friends that I expected a bit of awkwardness, but it's like you've been a couple forever and he clearly adores you."

"What makes you say that?" Bobbi asked curiously.

"The guy was watching you like a hawk throughout the entire game, every time it looked like you would fall we could see him tensing up, ready to fly to your side."

"He didn't see *this* happen," Bobbi pointed to her knee, and Bronwyn laughed.

"Oh, he saw it all right, and if not for Chase grabbing the back of his collar and yanking him nearly off his feet, he'd have come dashing over to rescue you. Whatever Chase said managed to calm Gabe down enough to stop him from carrying you off the field."

"God, that would have been embarrassing," Bobbi groaned. "I warned him not to overreact to every tiny scrape, but he wouldn't give me his word."

She watched him climb back up the bleachers, carefully carrying two loaded plates. He stuck one on her knees before sitting down beside her again.

"Thank you," she said.

"Happy to do it." And he really seemed to be happy. Bobbi studied him for a long moment, reflecting on how eager he was to please her, and thought about her own reluctance to do the one thing guaranteed to please *him*. It left her feeling petty and selfish.

～

After everybody had left that night and Chase had made his way back to the house, Gabe took her hand and led her to the gate.

"I could stay," she whispered, after a long and deeply satisfying kiss.

"Hmmm," he murmured, his hands busily drifting up under her loose shirt, stroking up and down the skin of her back. When they moved around to cup her breasts through the thick cotton of her sports bra, she moaned and pushed herself more fully into his hands.

"Do you want me to stay?" she asked, more urgently, her arms winding around his neck. He didn't answer, sucking and licking at the sensitive skin on her collarbone instead. Bobbi sighed and planted urgent kisses all over his strong jaw, the tip of her tongue tasting the salt on his skin with every caress.

"Gabe," she said softly, rapidly losing her ability to think beyond the next drugging kiss. "Gabe, I'm staying."

He lifted his head and looked down at her with hot eyes.

"Are you sure?" he asked, his voice rough. "Because if you stay it's through the night. There's no negotiating on that. Are you ready for everyone to be aware of the fact that we're sleeping together?"

"Chase knows," she pointed out.

"But you've never had to face him over the breakfast table the next day," Gabe said. "If you stay, there'll be no sneaking out in the middle of the night like we've done something to be ashamed of, and no rushing off in the morning either. Are we clear on that?"

"As crystal," she said, and he smiled.

"Then let's go to bed." He held out his hand and she took it without any hesitation, happy to follow him home.

Gabe gathered her into his arms the moment they set foot in his room and his lips immediately descended over hers. His rapacious mouth swallowed up a small sigh of pleasure, and after that she was just *lost*. His strong hands moved, one down to the small of her back and the other to the back of her head, where his fingers wove themselves into her short, silky hair. Her mouth opened helplessly beneath his and his hungry, searching tongue eagerly responded to the invitation. The kiss was better than anything else that had ever come before it, and it consumed her completely.

She was burning from the inside out and reveling in it. She pushed herself closer and closer, wanting to crawl into his skin, wanting to fuse herself to him and become a part of him. Bobbi could not remember ever surrendering so completely to anyone before. Not even that first time they had made love. This time felt different, it felt more significant, more loving. In that moment Gabriel Braddock was her reason for living and the sum total of her existence.

Bobbi protested when Gabe dragged his lips from hers and tried to pull him back down toward her. He laughed and said something beneath his breath before bringing his hands to the hem of her T-shirt and dragging it up over her head. He tossed it aside and focused on her sports bra. He pushed the straps down the slender slopes of her shoulders, his eyes intently focused on the golden flesh his large hands were revealing. Bobbi sucked in a shocked breath when she felt nothing but air on her breasts, and she groaned painfully at the first tentative touch of his finger on the sensitive peak of one mound. Her nipple surged to swollen life and he smiled in satisfaction before lowering his mouth to the aching bud and suckling it deeply into his hot, velvety mouth.

Bobbi squeaked in shock, overwhelmed by the sudden influx of sensation that raced through her body like an addictive narcotic. She was flat on her back in the middle of his bed by this time and had no clear idea of how she had gotten there. Her baggy football shorts were gone and she was wearing just white cotton panties—their only concession to her femininity being the tiny pink lace borders that were hemmed around the edges.

Gabe was balanced above her with one of his muscular, naked thighs thrust between hers. He continued to do amazing things to her with his clever mouth and his industrious hands. His mouth moved back and forth between one painfully distended, raspberry-red nipple and the other before finding her lips again, plundering ruthlessly, taking as much as he was giving.

"Bobbi." He lifted his head, his voice was thick, slurred, and almost unrecognizable. "My darling Bobbi . . ." He flipped over onto his back and dragged her with him so that she was straddling his thigh.

◠

Gabe knew that Bobbi was unaware of the sexy picture she made, with her breasts spilling over the top of her bra, her nipples and lips swollen and red. Her eyes looked drugged with pleasure and she smiled widely, delighting in her new position.

His hands framed her face and tugged it closer to his own, he lifted his head to claim her lips but she pulled back at the last second and instead struggled to tug his T-shirt off. He sat up and helped her drag it up over his muscular, tanned chest, impatient to feel her hands on him.

"Oh," she sighed contentedly, when she finally managed to stroke his skin. Her small hands found his hard nipples and her fingers tugged a bit too enthusiastically. Gabe yelped in pain and her eyes filled with remorse. She lowered her head and kissed away the sting, licking and sucking almost delicately, until Gabe thought that he would go out of his mind with pleasure.

"Oh yes, sweetheart," he groaned, his hands framing her face again. "Yes . . ."

~

Bobbi moved over to the other nugget and paid it homage as well, savoring the salty taste and warm, musky scent of him.

"You're so gorgeous," she whispered against his flesh.

"God, I want you so much, Bobbi mine." She lifted her head to meet his tormented regard and nodded slowly, her eyes alive with warmth.

"I want you too."

"I've missed you," he confided, sitting up, so that she was wantonly cradled in his lap, her legs wrapped around his waist and her bottom snugly tucked against the swollen flesh pushing against the confines of his shorts. Her eyes filled with tears as the emotion of the moment overwhelmed her.

"I've missed you too."

"Don't cry," he whispered, kissing away the errant tears that had slipped down her cheeks.

"I can't seem to stop," she confessed, a sob catching in her throat.

"Ssh, sweetheart," he said, kissing her again. The caress so gentle it just prompted more tears from her. He lifted his head. "What's this now, sweetheart? Why the tears?"

She shook her head, unable to verbalize what she was feeling and buried her face against his chest, leaving moisture on his skin. She planted hungry kisses all over his chest before inching her hands down to the hard column sawing up against her cleft. Her lips followed her hands down until she was bent over his shorts, her breath washing against his flat abdomen as she tugged at the drawstring.

Gabe groaned when she managed to undo the knot and he lifted his hips to make it easier for her to tug his shorts and briefs down past his thighs. He lifted his head from the bed to watch what she was doing and Bobbi enjoyed the ripple of muscles on his abdomen and torso at the movement.

"Bobbi, what are you doing?" he asked, his voice a tormented whisper. She didn't bother to reply, allowing her actions to speak for her when she took hold of his length in both of her hands and stroked it slowly from top to bottom.

"Oh, sweet *Jesus*," he grated, his hips coming off the bed at her touch. She smiled at him from where she was crouched at his center before dropping an experimental kiss on the sensitive tip of his shaft. "Stop! Bobbi . . . don't."

But she *did*, her mouth enveloped him, and what she couldn't fit, her hands took care of. Gabe felt like the top of his head was about to blow off, and he knew he wouldn't be able to last long if she continued this. It nearly killed him, but he dragged her off and back under him. They were both completely naked in no time at all and he placed his hands on her inner thighs and opened her up to his ravenous gaze. His throat went dry at how perfect she was and he was soon repaying the favor that she had so surprisingly bestowed on him moments before.

~

Bobbi squealed, tears long forgotten, as Gabe used his very talented tongue on her to maximum effect. It wasn't long before her entire body *clenched* and she came with a moan and quiet gasp. He gave her no time to recover; he dragged a condom from his nightstand drawer and put it on, while Bobbi drank in the sight of his splendid nakedness. She was intoxicated by him and aware of nothing more than Gabe and what he could to her with his hands, mouth, and body.

She joyfully welcomed him back into her body, loving how absolutely perfect it felt to have him inside of her again. He moved slowly, gently, and allowed them both to fully savor the physical and emotional closeness of the moment.

"You're amazing," he whispered, and she wrapped her arms around him in response and held him even closer. She could feel his thrusts in every part of her body and it drove her wild. She softly moaned every time he withdrew, lamenting his departure, but gasped happily with every return stroke. Her orgasm snuck up on her and sent her spinning madly out of control before she was fully prepared for it. Her breath caught and held. She didn't think she could physically *stand* the oh-so-exquisite torture! How could *anybody* stand it? But suddenly he was there, calming her down, whispering endearments in her ear and setting her crazily tilted world to rights again.

As she found herself lazily drifting back to earth, she felt it happening to him too: the madness. He was sobbing into her neck as he impaled her wildly, without any rhythm or control. He harshly called out to her, seeking an anchor to hold him steady, the way he had for her and she kissed him gently, whispering reassuringly when he convulsed for what seemed an eternity before collapsing limply on top of her. She soothed him with her words, the same three words over and over again, while her tears overflowed into his already damp hair beneath her cheek.

"I love you, Gabe," she whispered as she clung to him, the words barely audible. "I love you."

~

Gabe heard the emotional words and they meant a hell of a lot in that moment but as much as he wished he could respond in kind, he just didn't want to deceive her or raise her hopes unfairly. So he said nothing, merely removed the condom and was grateful for the moment's respite as he left to discard it. He took an extra minute in the bathroom to compose himself but even so, when he returned to that bed and took her into his arms again, he was still trembling almost uncontrollably.

She was a sweet, warm weight in his arms, and he relished tucking her close to his heart, enjoyed entangling his longer legs with her shapely ones and absolutely straight out *loved* the feeling of her growing heavier against him as sleep claimed her. He forced himself to stay awake for a while, just to watch her sleep and hear her occasional delicate snores. His heart felt full and when he eventually fell asleep, it was with a contented smile on his lips.

~

"Morning." The soft voice was spoken directly into her ear and Bobbi sighed before turning over onto her stomach in an effort to ignore it.

"Come on, Bobbi, it's time for breakfast."

"Don' wan'," she groaned into the pillow, batting at the annoying presence beside her.

"I've forgotten how adorably grumpy you are in the mornings." The voice, which she now recognized as Gabe's, was laden with laughter, but Bobbi didn't see what was so damned amusing about being awoken at the crack of dawn. "I suppose it's not something you outgrow."

"Neither, apparently, is obnoxious cheerfulness at some god-awful hour in the morning," she groused, lifting her head to glare into his handsome, grinning face.

"It's eight a.m. Not quite as god-awful as you seem to think it is. Aren't you working today? I didn't think you'd appreciate being late." He was sitting on the bed wearing sweatpants but nothing else. She blushed as she recalled the nasty, sexy things they had done to each other the night before. She still couldn't believe that she had allowed that first time to happen before a shower. At the time they had both been so carried away that cleaning up after their football match been the last thing on either of their minds. Still . . . *ew*. If it hadn't been such a transcendent experience, she would have been just a bit more squicked out by it.

They had had a shower . . . of sorts, after waking from the initial best-sex-of-their-lives coma. They had managed to clean themselves up, but Bobbi had emerged from that shower feeling like the dirtiest woman in the world. Right now, Gabe was sweeping a soothing hand up and down her naked back, from between her shoulder blades, down to just above the swell of her butt, and then up again. Bobbi arched her back and he applied some more pressure until it was a full on, if one-handed, massage.

"I take it you have to go home and get changed before going to work?" he asked, and she yawned.

"Not going to work," she remembered. "Meeting the ladies instead."

"What are you all going to be doing today?" he asked, curious.

"Stuff," she said cryptically, hiding a wince as she remembered their mission for the day.

"Hmm, intriguing," he responded, bending over to kiss her back lingeringly. "I don't suppose you're in an immediate rush to leave then, are you?"

She stretched and turned over onto her back, deliberately allowing the covers to drop away from her breasts. Gabe's eyes were riveted on the pretty sight before him and she smiled, feeling powerful.

"No rush," she confirmed, reaching her arms up toward him. He smiled happily and responded to the sweet invitation with a hungry kiss.

"Good, because something's come up that I need to discuss with you."

She groaned good-naturedly.

"God, we need to work on your terrible innuendos," she teased, and he laughed, kissing her again until all thought of laughter fled.

~

An hour, a shower, and a change of clothes later, Bobbi made her way downstairs to see if there was any breakfast left. The house seemed empty and Bobbi remembered that Gabe tended to give his household staff the weekends off. She wandered onto the patio and found Chase sitting on a garden chair with his long legs stretched out in front of him and a newspaper folded in his hands. He seemed to be reading the sports page. He glanced up when she moved uncertainly in the doorway, and she blushed a fiery red when he took in the miles-too-big T-shirt she was wearing with a pair of Gabe's old board shorts, which fortunately had a drawstring that she could cinch at the waist to prevent them from falling down around her ankles.

"Morning," she mumbled, and sat down opposite him.

"Hey," he greeted, fumbling with the newspaper. She noticed that he was also flushed with embarrassment, and she lowered her eyes to the table and helped herself to some fruit juice and cereal.

"So . . . did you have a good night?" she asked.

"Yeah, it was okay. Did you?" The question was automatic and her hand halted in the act of reaching for the jug of milk. Her eyes flew up and she saw that his face had gone an even brighter shade of red, and when their eyes met, they both froze for a horrified instant before a hysterical sound burbled up from Bobbi's throat and spilled out in the form of a giggle. Chase's face relaxed into a grin and a soft chuckle burst from his lips. Before they knew it they were both convulsed in laughter, and when Gabe walked out onto the patio he frowned at the sight of them bent over in amusement.

"What's so funny?" he asked, and that just set them off again. In the end Gabe gave up on getting a straight answer from them and just sat down and watched them with a bemused smile. By the time their laughing fit had faded into nothing but intermittent chuckles, they had both overcome their initial embarrassment and had rediscovered their camaraderie.

"So, I'm guessing the answer to that question was yes?" Chase smirked, and Bobbi tossed a grape at him, unable to prevent the slight flush that crept back into her face.

"Shut up before I decide to share details," she threatened, and he winced.

"You wouldn't?" He looked horrified, and she smiled smugly.

"Don't test me."

Gabe rolled his eyes at the banter and sighed.

"I don't think I want to know," he admitted, and Bobbi turned a beatific smile on him before blowing him a kiss.

The rest of breakfast passed pleasantly and before she knew it, Bobbi was waving good-bye to Chase and Gabe was walking her home.

When they reached the gate, she told him she could manage the rest of the way herself, but he insisted on walking her to the door, and she cringed at the thought of her father being at home and seeing her in the state she was in. She wasn't only obviously wearing Gabe's clothes; she had whisker burns on her face and neck and a couple of bruises on her arms that the shirt didn't cover. To his credit, Gabe had been horrified when he'd seen the bruises all over her body that morning.

He held her hand all the way home and when she let herself into the house, it was so quiet she immediately knew that her father wasn't around. She heaved a small sigh and gifted Gabe with a gorgeous smile of relief.

"He's going to find out eventually, Bobbi," he said.

"I know that, but at least it's not today." She hugged Gabe happily. "I mean we *just* told him that we were dating and then two nights later we're sleeping together? Better to get him used the whole dating thing first."

Gabe kissed her cheek before reluctantly letting her go.

"I'm going to miss you today. Stay safe okay?"

"Theresa, Alice, and Bron all have security details. I'll be perfectly fine while I'm with them," she reassured brightly, and while he didn't look completely happy, he looked somewhat mollified.

"Don't speed," he warned as he turned to leave.

"Won't."

"I mean it," he stressed, obviously not convinced.

"So did I." He sighed and gave up, leaving with a frustrated wave.

Bobbi watched him go, keeping that bright smile plastered to her face until he had turned toward the back of the house as he headed for the gate. The smile fell from her lips to be replaced by devastation the moment he was out of sight.

She had told him that she loved him so many times last night and he hadn't come close to responding. It was terrifying to feel so much for someone and have them feel nowhere near to the same emotion in return. At least he couldn't bring himself to lie to her, which was somewhat comforting, she supposed.

She shook her head and went upstairs to get changed for her outing with the Mommy Club ladies. If nothing else, they always cheered her up.

CHAPTER FIFTEEN

A s the Valentine's Day Ball grew closer, Bobbi became more and more of a nervous wreck. She had a dress all picked out for the occasion, one of the many she had bought the week before when she had gone shopping with her friends. She had been astonished to find that after she had been dragged from one boutique to the next that she had a clear fashion point of view that was uniquely hers. The dresses she had chosen made her feel like *Bobbi*. In a dress.

They weren't conventional or conservative or anything remotely similar to what any of Gabe's former lady friends had worn, and Bobbi was anxious about what he would say. As a couple, they were growing closer by the day, and they spent as much time together as possible. Bobbi had slept at his place every night, and while her father obviously knew about it, he never mentioned it to Gabe *or* to Bobbi.

Bobbi told Gabe that she loved him often and while he accepted the words and even seemed happy to hear them, he never reciprocated. And every time it felt like a barb through Bobbi's heart. Still, she was unable to stop and often said it while carried away in the moment.

In the meantime the flowers had started coming again, one a day, every day when she was at work. At least there weren't heaps of bouquets anymore, which Quinton, the sarcastic delivery guy, was grateful for and Craig and Sean were grumpy about.

The cards, which were now in envelopes since he knew she would read them, contained information on what the flower meant along with a really bad "poem," which always brightened up her day.

On Monday she received a single aster—which apparently meant contentment.

Tuesday (after a particularly raunchy night) it was a snapdragon—desire.

Wednesday's white iris had meant that she inspired him.

On Thursday a pretty gardenia had told her that she brought him joy (that had made her choke up a little).

And Friday's flower was hand delivered by the man himself, who had decided to take her to lunch. She was sitting flat on her butt next to the left front tire of a car and working on replacing a broken CV axle joint when he walked in.

"Hey, sweetheart," he greeted as he crouched down next to her. He brought his hand out from behind his back. "I brought you a hibiscus. It commends your delicate beauty." She laughed helplessly at that one, knowing she looked far from delicately beautiful at the moment.

"Thanks. Hold on to it for a while, will you? I'm rather busy right now."

He nodded.

"You wanna grab some lunch once you're done wrestling with that beast?" he asked.

"Hmmm, maybe. This might take a while," she grunted.

"I can wait. I'm going to have a chat with Sean," he informed, and she watched him turn and leave, admiring his butt as he walked away.

She went back to the task at hand and was halfway done when the drift chisel slipped as she was trying to hit the end of the CV joint and angled sharply downward toward her leg. The sharp end sliced through her overalls and scored into her thigh just above the knee. She sucked in a breath as the pain hit her, and the chisel and hammer clanged to the floor as she clutched at her thigh and bit back a scream. She clamped a hand over the wound as she tried to stem the flow of blood and immediately began to feel a bit woozy at the sight of all that red.

~

Sean was busy telling Gabe about girlfriend number two dumping him when they heard Bobbi cry out, followed by the sharp sound of metal hitting the floor. Craig and Pieter looked up too, and they all took an instinctive step toward her that broke into a full-out scramble to reach her when they saw her listing to the side.

Gabe's heart stopped and he dashed over to where Craig and Pieter were already crouched next to her. Craig was swearing profusely and Pieter confirmed Gabe's worst fears by yelling at Sean to call an ambulance.

Gabe slid to his knees beside her and all he could see was red . . . so much damned blood.

"What happened?" he asked, but everybody was bustling and panicking and Bobbi was unconscious and nobody would tell him. "*What the hell happened?*"

~

Craig looked up grimly; he had a hand clamped over her thigh and an arm supporting her back.

"Chisel slipped, I think," he said succinctly. "I'm not sure, there's a lot of blood. It may have nicked an artery."

And in that instant Gabe's own life flashed before his eyes—a future life . . . the one he should have with his Bobbi by his side. A future filled with laughter, joy, love, and children. One that he might lose before he even properly recognized that it was what he desperately wanted.

"No," he ground out between clenched teeth. He would *not* lose her like this. It just wasn't acceptable. He yanked off his tie and leaned in beside Craig, feeling sick at the sight of all that blood. It was actually starting to pool beneath her, and he tried not to think about how much she was losing and how dangerous it was. "Move your hand a bit but don't let up on the pressure." He instructed Craig, who did as he was told without question. Gabe used his tie to fasten a tourniquet around her thigh, just above the wound.

"Come on, sweetheart," he urged. "You stay with me. Don't you *dare* leave me."

He kept talking to her while Craig kept his hand clamped over the wound and Pieter and Sean both stood by helplessly clutching their hats in their hands. The ambulance took *forever* to arrive, and Gabe was in a state of complete terror by the time the paramedics took over. He watched her closely for signs that she wasn't breathing, and he said a grateful prayer with every shallow movement of her chest.

When the paramedics loaded her into the ambulance, he climbed into the back with her. The female paramedic tending to Bobbi said something about the bleeding slowing down and commended him on his tourniquet. Gabe kept his focus on Bobbi, willing her to live as he held tightly onto her hand.

When they got to the hospital, Mike and Billy were already waiting; Sean had called them after calling the ambulance. Mike looked pale and old and Billy looked furious and terrified all rolled into one.

"What happened?" Billy asked, his eyes trained on his sister as they wheeled her past him and straight into the emergency room. Gabe ignored him and moved to follow the gurney but they were all strong-armed out by doctors and nurses, who directed them to a waiting room. Gabe hated not being with her and couldn't stop prowling up and down the confines of the room.

Mike sank into a chair and sat there looking more feeble than Gabe wanted to think about right now. Billy was still demanding answers, and Gabe filled him in as succinctly as possible. Edward and Clyde came in a few minutes later, and Edward, the doctor, immediately went to see if he could get additional information.

Chase strode into the room soon afterward, and when Gabe looked surprised to see him, he said that Billy had SMS'd him. Edward returned and everybody looked at him expectantly.

"The good news is that she's out of danger," he informed, and everybody breathed a sigh of relief. Gabe's legs gave out and he sank down next to Mike. "She's very lucky, it didn't hit her femoral artery, thank God . . . but it was literally millimeters away from doing serious damage." Edward's face went gray at the thought. "One of her veins was nicked though which is why there was so much blood. The tourniquet and applied pressure kept the blood loss under control." He glanced at Gabe as he said this, and Gabe ran a shaky hand through his hair as he tried very hard not to fall apart. "She's in surgery to have the vein stitched up—but she'll recover quickly and there'll be no lasting damage. They also . . ."

Gabe didn't hear the rest, his head was throbbing and he felt nauseous. He needed fresh air, he needed to get out . . . things were too chaotic in this place. Too much noise and craziness, it made him feel boxed in—there was no order here. He shoved to his feet and was vaguely aware of the astonished looks he was getting before he slammed out of the room and walked away.

~

He got as far as the parking lot and then stood there, feeling lost when he realized that he had no car. He looked around at the sea of cars gleaming in the parking lot and caught a glimpse of his reflection in one of the windows. He was covered in blood. His face, his chest, his hands . . . Oh *God*! He leaned over, bracing his hand on one of the cars, and brought up his breakfast, and even after he had emptied his stomach completely, he just couldn't stop heaving.

"Gabe?" It was Chase.

"I'm covered in blood," he said, hearing a faint edge of panic in his voice. "Th-there was *so* much blood, Chase. I thought she would die right there in front of me. And do you know the only thing I could think about? Do you?"

"What was it?" Chase asked quietly.

"Me," Gabe said, his voice rife with self-disgust. "All I could think of was how empty my life would be without her. How much I'd miss her. How I hadn't even told her . . ." A despairing sob escaped from his lips and he fought for control. "I hadn't even told her I *loved* her for God's sake! What kind of man am I?"

"You're a man in love," Chase said simply, and another sob hitched from Gabe's throat. "Don't be so hard on yourself. And Bobbi is going to be *fine*. You still have the opportunity to tell her how you feel."

"Do you think she'll marry me?" Gabe asked uncertainly, and Chase studied him intently before dragging him into a warm hug.

"I'm not the one you should be asking that question, baby brother," Chase told him.

~

Bobbi opened her eyes and blinked for a confused instant, not sure where she was. She had gotten used to waking up in Gabe's bed and this certainly wasn't his room. It was bright and clinical and smelled vaguely antiseptic. There were balloons everywhere and flowers. If she didn't know better, she'd think she was in a hospital. But why would she be in a hospital?

"Hey, you're awake." She turned her head to see Billy sitting in an uncomfortable-looking chair beside the bed. He got up and shocked the heck out of her by dropping a kiss on her forehead.

"What's going on?"

He frowned. "You don't remember?"

She shook her head.

"You had an accident in your shop and stabbed yourself . . . dumbo." His words were teasing but his eyes were serious.

"Oh yes, I remember the blood. I felt so dizzy at the sight of it, there was just so much of it and you know how I feel about my own blood. Surely they didn't rush me to hospital because I fainted? Was this Gabe's doing? He tends to overreact when I get hurt."

"You nearly died, Runt," Billy said somberly, and then stunned her by bursting into tears. It was that macho crying of a strong man, where every sob capitulated looked like an epic internal struggle of good versus evil and every tear shed was *very* reluctantly surrendered. It was all the more powerful because of how short-lived it was—the macho always won out in the end.

"I don't understand," she confessed. "What do you mean I nearly died?"

"The damned chisel thing nicked a vein and nearly sliced your femoral artery. If that had happened you would have bled out on your shop floor. As it was you merely bled like a stuck pig on your shop floor," he elaborated.

Bobbi was stunned. "Oh my God," she whispered. *"Gabe?"* He hated it so much when she got minor scrapes and bruises that he must have lost it completely to have her nearly die right in front of him.

"He was a wreck." Billy confirmed her worst fears. "Fast thinking enough to tie a tourniquet around your leg though. He and Craig probably saved, if not your life, then a large quantity of your blood for sure."

"How long have I been here?" she asked.

"About eight hours. Now I can't hog all your time. Dad will want to see you, and Ed and Clyde have been waiting their turns as well."

What about Gabe? Surely he wanted to see her too?

In the end just about everybody she knew had come to visit her, but by the time she was released the following day, Gabe still hadn't been to see her. Chase had told her to give his brother some time to get over the horrifying experience, but that had pissed her off, since *she* had been the victim of the so-called "horrifying experience."

She was none the worse for wear after her short stint in the hospital, and Clyde, who was really her nicest brother, carried her up to her room. Edward was so self-righteous sometimes and Billy could often be intolerable, but Clyde, despite the terrible things often said about lawyers, was sweet and rarely got on her nerves. He stayed with her for a while after depositing her on her bed and then left her to her moody thoughts.

Why hadn't Gabe come to see her? Was he angry with her after what had happened? He could be so weird about stuff like this sometimes, like when he'd been furious with *her* for being injured during that football game.

She sighed and picked up her cell phone to check for messages. Nothing.

She missed him, the idiot. She just hoped that he didn't let this incident scare him off again.

~

She was staring broodingly at her wall a couple of hours later. She was sick of TV, which had nothing much to offer in the form of entertainment and had already called the shop a half dozen times to make sure the guys weren't slacking off. Of course they weren't. She trusted her guys to do their jobs and knew that Craig would keep an eye on things. So that left her with nothing to do but brood about Gabe and all the possible reasons he could have not to call.

She couldn't come up with a single plausible one and she thought about calling him herself to give him what for. She was about to do that when her door creaked open and he stepped into her room.

She folded her arms over her chest and glared at him, not willing to reveal how happy and relieved she was to see him. Not until she had given him a piece of her mind first.

"Hello, sweetheart," he said softly, stepping farther into her room and approaching her bed cautiously. She noticed for the first time that he was clutching a large bouquet of flowers in his hands, and pursed her lips. If he thought his flowers were going to cut it this time, he had another think coming.

"Where have you been?" she asked bad-temperedly, and he flinched before sitting down on the chair beside her bed. His eyes drifted down to her elevated leg and the clean dressing wrapped around her thigh.

"How do you feel?" He answered her question with a question, and that just pissed her off even more.

"How do you think I feel?" she snapped. "I was careless at work. I'm *never* careless at work. I feel like an idiot. I also feel bored and my leg hurts and I wish I could walk around but everybody keeps telling me I should take it easy. And I feel *angry*. With you."

"I understand," he said, leaning forward, the flowers still clasped in his hands.

"Do you? Because *I* don't understand. Chase told me to give you time to get over the horrific experience, but *you're* not the moron who stabbed herself in the leg with a chisel!"

"Yeah, well," he said, still without heat. "I *am* the one who had to stand there and watch you bleed half to death. I'm the one who was terrified you would die right there in front of me while I was helpless to do anything and afterward . . . I was absolutely covered in your blood, so I had a few things to work out, okay?"

She hadn't considered how extremely traumatic the experience must have been for him or the guys in the shop and felt immediately contrite.

"I'm sorry," she whispered, and he sighed.

"I am too. I should have come sooner, but . . . it was hard." He looked down at the flowers in his hands and held them up for her to see. "I also had to find these. It took a bit of research finding the perfect ones."

"Oh? Is there some flower out there that says, 'sorry you sliced yourself open with a drifting chisel. Hope you feel better soon'?" His lips twitched and he shook his head.

"Not that I've found. I'll keep searching for that one."

"So what do these mean then?" She nodded toward the exquisitely wrapped bouquet in his hands. He swallowed audibly and pointed each flower out to her.

"These are tulips," he said, and she rolled her eyes. He had started with one even she recognized, but she nodded and smiled at the friendly red color of the blooms. "These blue ones are forget-me-nots. These are azaleas; over here we have ambrosia—that was hard to find—and of course, these are daffodils."

"They're very pretty," she said, and he cleared his throat nervously. "Are you going to tell me what they mean?"

He tugged a card out of his jacket breast pocket and handed it over to her with a trembling hand. She gave him a searching look, wondering about this extreme display of nervousness and pulled the card from its envelope.

This time there was writing on only one side. Another poem. She read the words and looked up at him with a confused look on her face before reading them again:

Roses are red
Tulips are too
Every tower in this bouquet
Means, "I love you"

"Gabe?" She asked uncertainly, her own hand starting to shake.

"The red tulips are a declaration of love," he said, his trembling voice gaining strength with every word. "Ambrosia means that I love only you. The forget-me-nots are absolutely *screaming* that you're my true love. The daffodils are saying 'I love you too' in reply to all the times you've said those words to me . . . and just in case you have any doubts about what kind of love we're talking about here, the azaleas are telling you that it's romantic love."

"Oh my God," she whispered, her hands coming up to cover her mouth as she tried to hold back her sobs.

"I'm the only idiot in this room, Bobbi," he told her. "It took the sight of you bleeding and unconscious to make me realize what I'd be missing if I lost you. All I could think of was that we would never get married and have babies and that my life would be utterly miserable without you."

"Married? Babies?" she asked in disbelief, not quite sure if she was awake or not, and he grinned before pointing to a perfect red rose nestled amongst the tulips—she hadn't even noticed it.

"You probably know what a red rose means, right?"

She nodded. True love, of course.

He tugged the rose from the bouquet and she noticed that the long stem was wrapped in cellophane to protect the leaves from breakage. He unwrapped the cellophane and handed the rose to her.

"Watch out for the thorns," he warned. She glanced down instinctively and that's when she saw the ring—dangling prettily from one of the leaves. She looked back at him, her eyes huge in her face, and he smiled lovingly at her before reaching over to tug the ring from the leaf.

He held the ring, an exquisite square-cut canary diamond surrounded by small white diamonds, up in front of her before unexpectedly going down onto one knee beside her bed. It was such a romantic, if somewhat clichéd, gesture that Bobbi was absolutely staggered by it.

"Roberta Rebecca Richmond, I am *so* utterly in love with you, I worship you, and I cherish you. You've always been the finest thing in my life, and I would consider myself the luckiest man in the world if you would consent to be my wife."

"Oh Gabe . . ." She was complete a mess. For someone who never cried, Bobbi had been doing a lot of if over the last few weeks, and she no longer cared who saw her.

"Will you marry me?" he asked, and she grabbed his hand and tried to tug him up onto the bed with her. He got up and sat down next to her.

"Of course I'll marry you, and I'll try to be a good wife, even if I don't conform to some people's idea of the perfect corporate wife," she said, and a growl worked its way up from his chest.

"Who the hell told you that?" he asked with a glower, and she grinned wetly.

"Gabe, I'm a mechanic, remember? More at home in overalls than ball gowns."

"You know what?" he asked thoughtfully. "I once thought I wanted some perfectly bland blonde on my arm for all eternity. But I would have been bored out of my mind in no time flat. I'm so damned happy you kissed me that night at Sandro's party—my life has been a crazy roller coaster ride since then, but with you the chaos always makes sense. I don't *want* you to be a 'good' wife . . . I want you to be my Bobbi, exciting, fun, and adorable. Just be the woman I fell in love with. That's who I want to marry."

He kissed the circlet of gold and diamonds he still held in his hand before lifting her left hand and lovingly sliding the ring onto her finger. Still choked up from his last words, Bobbi couldn't speak, but the kiss she gave him said so much more than words ever could.

⌒

Bobbi experimentally tested her weight on her leg and barely felt a twinge. It had been nearly a week since her accident and she was recovering quite nicely. She and Gabe had argued about when she could go back to work, and in the end she had taken a full week off. Her guys had been managing admirably in her absence.

Bobbi had been bound and determined to be on her feet for this stupid Valentine's Day event. She would be unveiling her new look to Gabe tonight, and while she was no longer anxious about whether he would like it or not—he liked her in everything—she was excited

276

about dressing up for him. Which was something she had never expected to feel in a million years.

She checked her appearance in the mirror for the hundredth time and waited for the doorbell to ring. When it *finally* did, she had to prevent herself from running down the stairs to let him in.

Billy, in a repeat of the first time Gabe had come calling on her, came up to get her and he stopped dead in the doorway when he first caught sight of her. She could see the surprise and pride in his eyes, but he merely lifted an eyebrow at her.

"Skirt's a bit short, isn't it?" He was teasing, but Bobbi immediately gasped and checked herself in the mirror again.

"Oh my God, is it?"

He chuckled and came over to give her a one-armed hug. "You look gorgeous. If Gabe wasn't already completely smitten with you, he'd be a goner tonight."

"Oh . . . well, that's okay then," she said with a blush.

"Come on, let's not keep your fiancé waiting."

Her fiancé! She couldn't get used to the sound of that.

～

Gabe was pouring Mike another drink to settle the older man's nerves when he heard Bobbi's voice just beyond the door. He couldn't keep the smile off his face at the thought of seeing her. The change-over at work had kept both Gabe and Mike busy over the past week, and he had barely seen her over the last couple of days. He had called often but calls didn't cut it.

He turned expectantly to face the door. He couldn't wait for this stupid ball to end so that he could take her home with him and drag that ugly navy dress off until he had her splendidly naked and pinned beneath him. Because of her injury and her resulting weakness due to the amount of blood she had lost, they'd had to forego sex completely, but Bobbi had called him that afternoon to tell him she'd gotten the "all-clear" from her doctor, and Gabe had been a walking hard-on practically from that moment on.

The door swung open and Billy stood aside to let Bobbi precede him into the room and . . .

Wow.

That was the only word that came to mind when he saw her. There were glorious amounts of golden skin on display everywhere he looked—her shoulders, her arms, and her *legs*. She was wearing one of those bustier-type dresses; it was *pale pink,* of all colors. The pretty pink was covered in a dark, gothic print that suited her to a tee. The bell-shaped mini skirt had the silhouette of a chapel printed on it, while the sweetheart bodice had bare black branches crisscrossing dramatically across the front. The short skirt ended at mid-thigh, just below the medical dressing that he knew was still there and revealed a shapely length of leg that made him want to just cover her up before other men saw her.

She wore short biker boots, and Gabe could *just* see the frilly top of her ankle socks above the boot. The only jewelry she wore were the pair of gold hoop earrings that he had given her for Valentine's Day and her engagement ring. Her eyes were dark and smoky and her lips just tinted with a sexy red shade that made him ache to kiss it off.

She was an enchanting combination of hard and soft and was absolutely perfect.

"Well?" she asked impatiently. "What do you think?"

"You look quite . . . lovely." Her father sounded a bit taken aback. "Quite the transformation."

"She always looks lovely, Mike," Gabe corrected. "And I don't see a transformation, I see my Bobbi, and she looks—if you'll excuse the phrase—absolutely smoking *hot*."

Her smile was glorious, and after Gabe had her safely buckled into his car and they were headed for the expensive venue that Richcorp had hired for the event, she turned to him.

"I know it's not super elegant or fancy like the dresses other women will be wearing tonight," she said, smoothing her hand nervously over the satin twill skirt.

"Bobbi, I told you before, those other women are boring. I don't need super elegant or fancy. I just need you, and tonight you look like a badass little fairy and I love it!"

She laughed at that.

"A 'badass fairy'?" she repeated softly. "I *like* that."

"Hmm," he threw her a sideways glance. "You know, as hot as you look in that dress, all I can think of is getting you out of it."

"Behave!"

"Yes, boss," he said in such a perfect imitation of Sean that it startled a snort of laughter from her. He didn't know how he was going to get through the evening without dragging her into a closet somewhere and having his wicked way with her.

After they had reached their destination, he halted at the bottom of the staircase leading up to the hotel's ballroom.

"Right now, while it's just us," he whispered, wrapping his arms around her slender waist and dragging her to his chest. "I wanted to give you your Valentine's Day present."

"You already gave me these." She shook her head to set the earrings dancing, and he smiled.

"Hmm, they make you look like a gypsy, especially with your hair." She had finally had it styled. Nothing too drastic, just a few layers to give it more body. "No, my gift is a promise."

She tilted her head questioningly.

"A vow to forever love you just the way you are. You don't need to change for me, Bobbi mine. You're perfect and I love you so damned much. Never, ever doubt that."

As Bobbi looked into his eyes, she saw nothing but love and sincerity shining in them and had no doubt that he meant every word. He was her best friend, her lover, and her heart's desire.

EPILOGUE

Gabe came jogging over to Bobbi after the game, a triumphant grin on his face as he swooped her into his arms and planted a kiss on her lips.

"Ugh, you're all sweaty, get off me." She pushed at his chest and his grin widened.

"To the victor goes the spoils," he proclaimed, wrapping his arms even tighter around her when she tried to wriggle away. "You're my spoils."

"God, you're insufferable when you win. I don't know how the other guys can stand you."

"We can't," Sandro called from close by. He took a thirsty drink from the water bottle Theresa had handed to him.

"I personally only come here for the *braai*," Rick added, already making his way to the grill.

"Well since you can't play, it's probably time better spent," Sandro retorted, clearly still annoyed with his teammate for missing a last-minute penalty that would have evened the scores.

"Oooh," the other guys jeered, and Rick merely waved the comment aside.

"It's all good," he said with a sanguine grin. "My man San is clearly jealous of my skills with a ball."

"What skills?" Sandro growled. "You look like a headless chicken flapping about whenever you take to the field."

"He's a passable rugby player," Bryce said in defense of his brother.

"And that would be wonderful if we were actually playing rugby," Pierre said irritably.

"Sandro, you don't have to be so rude," Theresa's voice piped up. "Rick was trying his best, you know."

"You always take his side," Sandro complained, looking and sounding like a recalcitrant little boy in that moment. Theresa grinned and stepped up to hug him, before whispering something in his ear. The glower faded from Sandro's face and his head snapped back as he laughed at whatever it was his wife had whispered in his ear.

"Aah, look at their team falling apart at the seams. A tragic loss like the one they suffered today will do that." Gabe tut-tutted as he watched the losing team squabble amongst themselves. He turned back to Bobbi, who had given up her struggles to get away from his big, sweaty body. "And how are my wife and two kids this evening?"

"Annoyed that we couldn't play," she answered, and he grinned before patting her hugely swollen belly. He bent down to talk to the mound, something he did often and sometimes publicly. It would be embarrassing if it weren't so darned sweet.

"Hear that Seamus and Sian, your mummy's annoyed with you."

"No. Just no," she said, pinching the bridge of her nose.

"Uh-oh, Bert and Betty, I think she's annoyed with me too now." He smiled slyly at her, and she felt a reluctant grin tugging at her lips.

"We're naming them Elizabeth and Jonathan," she proclaimed, and he dropped a kiss onto her tummy.

"Daddy loves you too much to call you Lizzy and Johnny. I promise you, I will stop mean old Mummy from naming you that."

They had been having different versions of the same argument since they'd discovered that she was carrying a girl and a boy. They just couldn't come to an agreement on the names, and she was due in just over a month. She couldn't work anymore, which frustrated her, but the shop was doing well enough for them to hire two more employees, and Bobbi had promoted Craig to manager, so she could take maternity leave without worrying too much about how things were going.

Bobbi was blissfully happy with Gabe, and he had kept his promise over the last year of marriage. It didn't matter where they went, how formal the occasion, or how out of place her "badass fairy" dresses were, he always looked at her like she was the most beautiful woman in the room. She looked around at her friends, who were all laughing and squabbling happily, and her brothers—Billy and Chase—who were lightheartedly mediating a fight that had broken out amongst the small children on the sidelines, and felt remarkably blessed. This place, these people, and this moment right now—it was home.

"How did we get so lucky?" she asked Gabe, who stood behind her and wrapped his arms around her front until his hands rested on her belly. He rested his chin on her shoulder as he watched their happy group of family and friends too.

"I don't know . . . but I know *my* luck started improving one night long ago, when a sexy, drunken fairy wiped me out with an unexpected kiss. It was the best damned thing that ever happened to me."

"I love you so much," she said, craning her head to look back at him, and she just managed to see the corner of his lip kick up in a smile.

"Can't possibly be as much as I love you," he teased. She turned within his hold and wrapped her arms around his neck.

"Wanna bet?" she challenged.

"You'll lose," he retorted. Before she could say another word he kissed her, and the caress was sweet, hot, loving, and perfect.

"I think," she whispered when he lifted his head, "that we're both winners."

He smiled and released her briefly before taking hold of her hand and leading her home.

ACKNOWLEDGMENTS

I'd like to express my gratitude to the following amazing people who helped me achieve my publishing dream:

My awesome agent, Kimberly Whalen—thank you so much for everything.

Helen, Jessica, Kelli, and the rest of the wonderful Montlake Romance team—you guys are fabulous.

Melody Guy—the best editor ever. I truly enjoy working with you.

ABOUT THE AUTHOR

Natasha Anders was born in Cape Town, South Africa. She spent the last nine years working as an assistant English teacher in Niigata, Japan, where she became a legendary karaoke diva. Natasha is currently living in Cape Town with her temperamental and opinionated budgie, Sir Oliver Spencer, who has kindly deigned to share his apartment with her. Please feel free to contact her (or Oliver) on Twitter at @satyne1.